TALES OF ALEXANDER THE MACEDONIAN

ספר אלכסנדרוס מוקדון

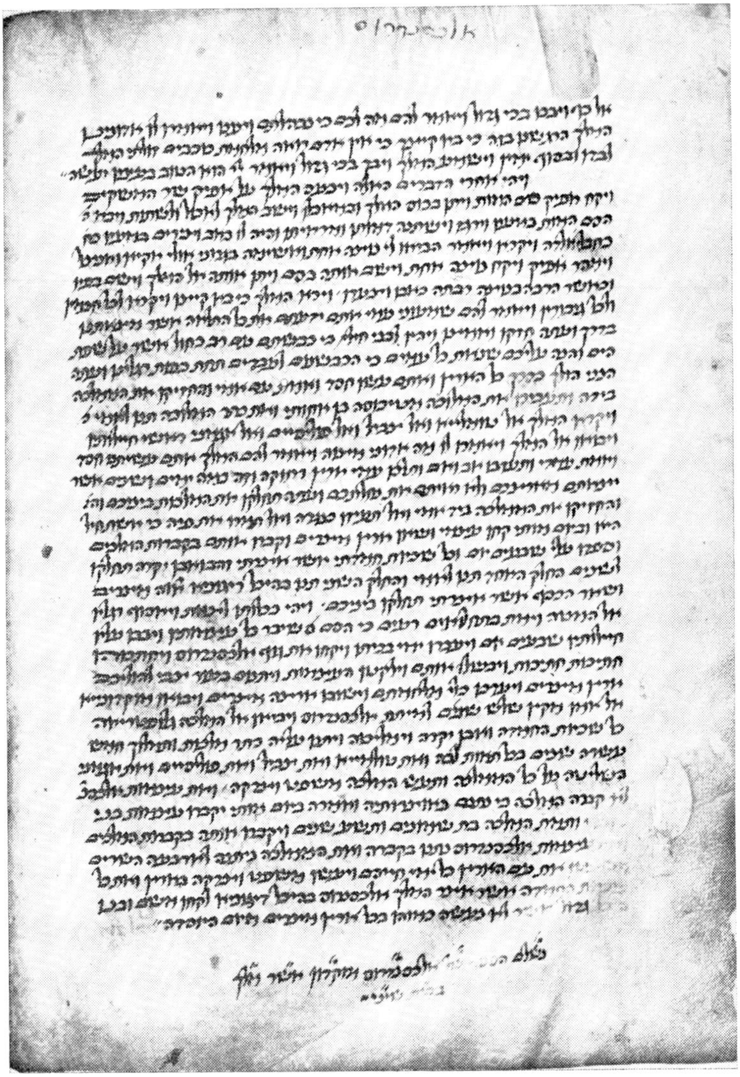

Bodleian Library, Oxford. MS. Heb. d. 11 *folio* 277, *verso.*

TALES OF ALEXANDER
THE MACEDONIAN

ספר אלכסנדרוס מוקדון

A MEDIEVAL HEBREW MANUSCRIPT
TEXT AND TRANSLATION WITH A
LITERARY AND HISTORICAL COMMENTARY

BY

ROSALIE REICH

KTAV PUBLISHING HOUSE, INC.
NEW YORK
1972

Library of Congress Catalogue Card No. LCC 75–176375

Printed and Bound in Israel

Jerusalem Academic Press

To
my beloved husband

"לאשר אהבה נפשי"

and
Yaron, Ilan, and Leora

CONTENTS

ACKNOWLEDGEMENT

I wish to acknowledge my profound gratitude to Professor Lillian Herlands Hornstein of New York University, who guided me in the evolution of this study. Her standards of excellence became my goal and I hope that in some small measure I have accomplished what we envisioned. I was fortunate to have found in her the perfect combination of true scholar, inspiring mentor, and warm personality.

I would also like to thank the following for their varied assistance: Professor Robert R. Raymo of New York University; Rabbi Meir Gruzman of Tel Aviv, Israel; Dr. David Birnbaum, Librarian; the Jewish Division of the New York Public Library; the Bodleian and Estense Libraries for permission to study these manuscripts in photostatic copy. To my mother, for her encouragement throughout the years, my deepest love and gratitude.

I should like to acknowledge a twofold debt of appreciation to my husband, Dr. Leon A. Reich: first, for his example as a scholar, and for his assistance in verifying my transcription and translation; and second, as a devoted and understanding husband, for bolstering me whenever the path seemed too rocky and the goal too difficult.

Certainly words of love and thanks go to our three children who grew up understanding the pressures on a busy mother-teacher-scholar. To them and to their beloved father, this work is fondly dedicated, for all of us are a part of it — in spirit.

FOREWORD

Twenty-three hundred years ago a personality of dynamic dimensions emerged in Pella, one that gripped the minds and imaginations of men for generations thereafter. Alexander the Great, King of Macedonia, left his impress on the civilized world as a military leader and consolidator of an empire, and his image grew from fact into legend. This young, vibrant king seemed to personify, in his image, a god; thus he was acclaimed in legend by the many nations who came in contact with his forces or personality.

Historical accounts of Alexander abound in many languages. They relate the now familiar, daring exploits of the king, and the intrigues surrounding his reign. However, of all the materials that have come down to us, none are as enchanting as the legends that accumulated about his person and feats.

While it is not exactly understood how legend and historical fact mesh to portray heroes, the scholar is ultimately forced to draw his portrait of the heroic figure from the available cultural materials. How infinitely more fascinating it is, therefore, when the literary historian, finding patterns in legends which transcend national and geographical boundaries, recognizes the unique lines of transmission of such legendary material. From the far corners of the world, across continents and oceans, the tales of Alexander have found their way over the centuries, emerging in only slightly different forms in the literature of the East and West.

When fertile minds transformed the figure of Alexander, their hero-king, their imagination knew no bounds. His portrait became an exemplar of diverse qualities, the legends reflecting both the prejudice and open-mindedness of their creators.

Historical accounts first took note of Alexander as he emerged upon the world scene at the age of eighteen, courageously fighting his country's enemies when his father, King Philip, placed him in command. Crowned king of Macedon at twenty, following his father's assassination, Alexander displayed deep wisdom and a personal magnetism which endeared him even to those whom he had conquered. Plutarch relates that as a young man Alexander was tutored by Aristotle, learning moral philosophy, humanity, physics, and the secret doctrines scholars call Acroamata, dealing with things speculative.

He attempted to treat subdued communities as partners, not as subjects, for his great objective was not in mere conquest, but rather in a fusion of Asiatics and Greeks, and in bringing Greek culture to East and West. Many conquests and few retreats marked his amazing career, and it is recorded that Alexander proved merciful in victory as he was valiant in battle. He left no son to succeed him; his commanders administered the lands following his early death at 33.

All Western Alexander romances find their source in the quasi-historical account of Alexander's life,[1] the *Pseudo Callisthenes*, written in Greek by an unknown Alexandrian sometime between 200 B. C. and 300 A. D. The tenth-century Latin translation, *Historia de Preliis*, as well as the numerous recensions stemming from these two sources, deal with similar historical events and legends. However, one group of extant Alexander-romance manuscripts, written in Hebrew and referred to as the Modena, Damascus, and Bodleian manuscripts,[2] and believed to date anywhere from the seventh to the thirteenth centuries, deviate radically from the Greek and Latin versions and their derivatives. Whereas the Greek and Latin romances deal primarily with the historical and pseudo-historical events of Alexander's life and adventures, relating only incidentally some legendary tales, the group of Hebrew manuscripts which are our concern is composed almost entirely of fantastic, fabulous stories.

---

[1] King of Macedon; born in Pella, 365 B.C. and died in Babylon, 323 B.C. Son of Philip and Olympias. For biographies see: Plutarch, *Parallel Lives*, trans., B. Perrin, 11 vols. (London: Loeb ed., 1914–1926), VII; Curtius, *History of Alexander*, trans., J.C. Rolfe, 2 vols. (Cambridge, Mass.:1946); W.W. Tarn, *Alexander the Great*, 2 vols. (Cambridge, Eng.:1948).

[2] MS. Bodl. Heb.d.11 is similar in most of the details of the narrative to MS. Modena Liii, Estense Library, Modena, Italy and to one seen in Damascus in 1888 by Dr. Albert Harkavy of St. Petersburg, Russia. These three medieval Hebrew Alexander romances differ from the Greek and Latin versions of the Alexander romance and from the several other medieval Hebrew Alexander romances derived primarily from the Latin version in that it is a farrago of fabulous adventures, far removed from any historical accuracy.

One group of some eleven tales is common to *Pseudo-Callisthenes*, *Historia de Preliis*, and these three Hebrew Alexander romances; and it is also found in the ancient Hebraic literature of the Talmud and the Midrash. The remainder are unique to the manuscript under study and include — to name but a few, such tales as the story of the king who places a dog on his throne to rule in his stead while he lies in bed for six months after his wife has borne a child; talking trees that predict Alexander's future; the faithless servant whose beheaded body roams the seas, overturning ships. In the opinion of Dr. Moses Gaster,[3] noted nineteenth-century Hebrew scholar, these unique, fantastic episodes may also be part of the very old oral tradition from which *Pseudo-Callisthenes*, as well as other Eastern, Christian, and Hebrew Alexander and non-Alexander romances grew.

The present study, *MS. Bodleian Heb. d.* 11, contains a Hebrew transcription of the medieval script with an English translation on facing pages. I have compared a parallel manuscript, known as the Modena version, to the Bodleian text and used it to clarify missing, corrupt, or unclear words and phrases of the latter manuscript. A third Hebrew version of these parallel manuscripts was seen in Damascus and described by Dr. Albert Harkavy of Russia in 1892, but its present whereabouts are unknown.

Significant to the scholar are these medieval English Alexander romances and non-romance writings which also contain legends similar to those in the Hebrew manuscript. Analogues of these tales are found in Talmudic, Midrashic, and other medieval Hebrew writings — particularly in stories told of King Solomon. These latter are discussed in the introductory section which follows.

No patently direct or immediate influence of these Hebrew manuscripts on any Middle English document can be affirmed. Yet this study has a special value in its presentation of the legendary tradition of Alexander — a tradition which was apparently inspired by the same backgrounds that influenced the vast corpus of Middle English literature dealing with Alexander and literary and folk tales associated with him.

---

[3] Dr. Moses Gaster published a loose paraphrase of MS. Bodl. Heb. d. 11 incorporating parts of MS. Modena Liii: "An Old Hebrew Romance of Alexander," *JRAS* (1897), 485–549 and also printed in *Studies and Texts*, 11 (London: 1925), 814–878.

INTRODUCTION

1. *Manuscript, Style, Author*

The manuscript is one item in a varied collection (some 388 vellum leaves) of materials, the whole titled *Sefer Hazichronot*[1] compiled by one Eleazer, son of Asher ha-Levi living in the Rhine provinces in the Worms district (environs of Cologne) about 1325 A. D. The items are most disparate; among them for example, is a manuscript recording the history of the world from the creation to the death of Judas Maccabaeus, as well as manuscripts containing works on grammar, astronomy, and collections of fables. The author of folios 265–278 is nowhere identified. Its heading *Sefer Alexandrus Mokdon* I have translated as *Tales of Alexander the Macedonian*. The thirteen folio pages [2] containing approximately thirty-five lines to each side are written in Northern Italian Rabbinic characters, apparently the calligraphy of a professional scribe (probably not the compiler). The use of spaces similar to those in Torah scrolls to indicate new paragraphs can be attributed only, in this form of manuscript writing, to an experienced copyist. He wrote with fine strokes, doubtless using a quill (the European writing instrument), and not a reed (the Oriental one). The lines are filled out (justified) by extending or condensing individual letters. The characters are neat and legible, made to appear somewhat cursive by the joining of adjacent

---

[1] Dr. Moses Gaster published a study of this compilation and a translation of a portion of the history of the world. He titled the compilation *The Chronicles of Jerahmeel* after a writer of the eleventh century of southern Italy or Spain whose work comprises most of the collection. See: *The Chronicles of Jerahmeel*, trans. M. Gaster, *Oriental Translation Fund, New Series* IV (1899), Introduction on pp. vii–cvii; text on pp. 1–292.

The Bodleian Library purchased this manuscript in 1887 from R.N. Rabinowitz of Munich who had acquired it in Italy. At the end of the description of the manuscript's contents in *The Catalogue of Manuscripts in the Bodleian Library*, the editor, A. Cowley, lists the owners of this manuscript, all of whom were from Italian cities.

[2] The recto and verso of each folio page I call *a* and *b*.

letters.[3] The size of the folios 265–278 is approximately 6½" wide and 8" long. The writing (both recto and verso) covers an area of approximately 4½" by 6½".

Opinions may well differ as to whether or not the author of this manuscript knew the Bible well. Whereas the manuscript contains segments that are obvious quotations and paraphrases from the Bible, they reveal that the author knew well only a limited area of the Biblical corpus, for he quotes only from those books which were regularly read or chanted in the synagogue on the Sabbath and holidays. During the Sabbath morning service, a portion of the Torah (the Five Books of Moses) and of the Haftorah (the Prophets) are chanted.[4] The author's quotations come primarily from the Torah, the Earlier Prophets, and the Megillot (particularly the Book of Esther). All these are read at prescribed times in the synagogue. References in the manuscript to the Later Prophets or to the Writings (Hagiographa) are infrequent, and when they appear they, too, are the very ones which also occur in the familiar daily or Sabbath prayers.

The writer often made changes in the original Biblical quotations to suit the need of his story, but more often, I would infer, because he was not deeply versed in the Bible. Furthermore, the author of the manuscript was apparently well versed in the narrative sections of the books of the Earlier Prophets, and not the prophetic sections. Many phrases come from the popular Book of Esther — a book which is read once each year in the synagogues and which presumably the author heard read yearly throughout his life, and because it is a popular tale that had captured the imagination of the people and story-tellers alike. Quotations from the Bible, particularly references to Jacob, David, and Solomon, are often exact and are used to describe a similar situation relating to King Alexander.

The area from which the author of the manuscript came may be more positively ascertained by noting which quotations from the Prophets (read on Sabbaths as the Haftarot) the writer knew. Recognizing these quotations from the Haftarot gives us some help in determining to which

[3] I express my deep appreciation to Professor M. Lutzki (Yeshiva University Library), who examined this manuscript and my transcription, and also advised me about its form, copyist, and provenance.

[4] For information on Haftarot see *Ha-Encyclopedia Ha-Ivrit* (Hebrew Encyclopedia), (Jerusalem: 1949–1965), XV (1962), 78.

2

of the five different communities the author belonged: Ashkenazim, Sephardim, Babylonians, Yemenites, Italians. Each group differs in the verses of the Haftarot which is read in its synagogue on the Sabbath. For example, on the Sabbath on which the portion from the Torah called *Ki Tissa* (Exodus 30:11–34:35) is read, the Haftorah which is read comes from I Kings 18. The Ashkenazim read verses 30–39; the Sephardim and Italians read verses 30–39; the Italians also read verses 1–26. On the Sabbath when the Torah portion *Matot* (Numbers 30:2–32:42) is read, the Ashkenazim, Sephardim, and Yemenites read Jeremiah I and the Italians read Joshua 13. My study of some one hundred and seventy Biblical references in this manuscript indicates that the author primarily knew the Haftarot of the Italians and Sephardim, making him a member probably of the Italian or Spanish Jewish community.[5]

On the other hand, it is also possible that the author of the manuscript did not use exact quotations from the Bible if he was abiding by the Talmudic injunction[6] that no more than three words from the Bible may be written together unless they are written on lines (drawn across the parchment), in order to preserve the wholeness and holiness of the text. To circumvent this injunction, one of two things was done; either the verses were changed slightly or dots were made over the words written in the manuscript. Thus, it would seem that our author, knowing that he was writing a secular, rather than a religious work, was reluctant to use exact Biblical quotations. Yet, if this were the case, we would require some other explanation to account for his use in some fifty instances of exact quotations from the Bible.

It should also be pointed out[7] that this manuscript is composed in the

---

[5] A. Neubauer, "Jerahmeel Ben Shlomoh," *JQR*, XI (1897), 366ff. notes that Jerahmeel was a resident of southern Italy and knew Greek. It is possible that travelers carried a manuscript of the tale with them or that Jerahmeel paid a visit to his brethren in the Rhine provinces and had a copy in his possession. Either possibility could account for its presence there several centuries later, when it was finally included in a compilation by Eleazer ben Asher ha-Levi.

[6] For these laws see the Jerusalem Talmud (Vilna: 1911–1917), *Megillah*, chap. 3 and the Babylonian Talmud (Vilna: 1883–1892), *Menachot*, p. 32b, *Megillah*, p. 18b, *Gittin*, p. 6b. The English translation of the Babylonian Talmud is available in the Soncino Press edition (London: 1935–1952). Bibliographical data relevant to this study are found in the Addendum.

[7] Dr. M. Gaster, *Chronicles of Jerahmeel*, op cit., xviii, points out that authors used

3

style popular from the ninth to the fourteenth centuries, a pseudo-Biblical style known as *Melitza*. In this style the writer adapted or paraphrased Biblical language and idioms to suit his narrative needs, while still retaining the Biblical flavor.

2. *Method of Present Transcription and Translation*

This study presents the Hebrew transcription and English translation on facing pages. I have added all marks of punctuation since almost no punctuation appears in the manuscript. Paragraphing conforms to the copyist's indications in the manuscript, i. e., wherever he left large spaces I have taken the liberty of inserting additional paragraph breaks wherever the sense required. Each folio page is noted in the margin and indicated by a virgule when a manuscript page ends within any line of translation. Since Hebrew reads from right to left I have indicated the right side of the folio page as *a* and the left side as *b*: e. g., fol. 265ª, fol. 279ᵇ.

I have attempted to present a close, accurate, yet smooth prose translation without being slavish to the idiomatic Hebrew forms of expression. To avoid awkward structure or undue repetition, I have translated the Hebrew conjunction *vav*, "and," in different ways, as the sense required, e. g., "however," "yet," "when," or left it untranslated. I have often substituted pronouns where the manuscript repeats the proper noun.

The Hebrew text is published exactly as it appears in the manuscript (grammatical and spelling errors included) with the following changes: the scribe often deleted letters with a diagonal line and such deletions are eliminated in the transcription; halves of words appearing at the ends of lines are common, but when they are repeated as complete words at the beginning of the following line, they are not transcribed. Wherever errors in the text of the manuscript made the sentence incomprehensible (by the use of incorrect words, deletions, or additions of words) the Modena manuscript was used to help me decide upon a proper translation. These errors are indicated by * and the corrections, according to the Modena manuscript text, are noted in the footnotes.

Biblical words but in a manner different from the Bible, that it required "great ingenuity to detect original Biblical words in these strange changelings."

I am grateful to Dr. S. Leiter, of the Jewish Theological Seminary of America, for his opinion on the style of this narrative.

3. *Recent Major Alexander Studies*

Within the last generation, the literary legend of Alexander has received three treatments in English which are of relevance to my study. Professor F. P. Magoun Jr., in *The Gests of King Alexander of Macedon*,[8] discussed the original Greek Alexander romance, the *Pseudo-Callisthenes*, and its derivatives[9] and translations. Magoun included also an edition of two medieval English poems, *Alexander A* and *Alexander B*. The γ recension of the *Pseudo-Callisthenes*, of which our manuscript is a derivative, is in Magoun's judgment the work of a Jew.

George Cary, in *The Medieval Alexander*,[10] summarized the popular medieval conceptions of Alexander the Great, drawing the details of his picture from the romances, the chronicles, and the universal histories. He did not refer to our present manuscript except in his summary of Magoun's work.

More recently, I. Kazis, in *The Book of the Gests of Alexander of Macedon*,[11] edited a medieval Hebrew manuscript of an Alexander romance which had been translated from the Latin *Historia de Preliis Alexandri Magni*[12] itself a translation of *Pseudo-Callisthenes*.[13] Kazis included a discussion of the Hebrew sources for some of the legends, sources ancient and medieval.

Magoun and Kazis agree that: 1) the version MS. Bodl. Heb. d. 11

[8] F.P. Magoun, Jr., *The Gests of King Alexander of Macedon* (Cambridge, Mass.: 1929).

[9] See Appendix C.

[10] G. Cary, *The Medieval Alexander* (Cambridge: 1955).

[11] I. Kazis, *The Book of Gests of Alexander of Macedon* (Cambridge, Mass.: 1962).
A new study by Minoo Sassoonian Southgate, *A Study and Translation of a Persian Romance of Alexander, its place in the tradition of Alexander Romance and its relation to the English versions* appeared in 1970 (unpublished doctoral dissertation, New York University).

[12] This Latin translation of Archpresbyter Leo, done about 950 A.D. is discussed by Pfister, *Der Alexanderroman des Archpresbyters Leo, Sammlung. mittelalt. Texte*, VI (Heidelberg: 1912).

[13] *Pseudo Callisthenes*, ed. C. Muller (Paris: 1846); *Pseudo-Callisthenes*, ed J. Zacher (Halle: 1897). See also: A. Ausfeld, *Der Griechische Alexanderroman* (Leipzig: 1907); E. H. Haight, *The Life of Alexander of Macedon by Pseudo-Callisthenes* (New York: 1955).

is not derived from the Latin *Historia de Preliis*, and 2) MS. Bodl. Heb. d. 11, although it has some affinities with the Greek *Pseudo-Callisthenes* (recension γ), it cannot be attributed solely to that source. They conclude that the accessory sources of our manuscript are unknown. My study throws some light on this hitherto blank area in Alexander studies.

4. *Alexander in History and Legend*

Fearsome tyrant, philosopher, philanderer, murderous conqueror in Asia, mild confessor in Jerusalem, Alexander's private personality in poetic and Biblical legend has assumed heroic proportions in the legendary of both East and West.[14] A double-faced image emerges — fact and legend intertwined; Alexander becomes all things to all men.

Previous studies[15] have directed attention to the existence in the ancient Hebraic Talmud and Midrash of many of the legends found in MS. Bodl. Heb. d. 11, and to a long oral tradition on which both these collections rest.[16] The Talmud,[17] a commentary on the Bible and its laws and lore, had received its final form by 500 A.D., but the tradition it records extends far back to Biblical times. Midrashic literature encompassing only the lore of the Talmud received its written form from the second to the tenth century.

The name Alexander became synonymous in history with conquest. He was the cosmocreator[18] and the creator of an empire, the tyrant

---

14 See the following: I. Friedlaender, *Die Chadhirlegende und der Alexanderroman* (Leipzig: 1913); P. Meyer, *Alexandre le Grand dans la Littérature Française du Moyen Age*, 2 vols. (Paris: 1886); F. Spiegel, *Die Alexandersage bei den Orientalen* (Leipzig: 1851); M. Steinschneider, "Zur Alexandersage," *Hebräische Bibliographie*, XLIX (1869), 13–19.

15 Previous commentators have noted Talmudic echoes in the Alexander story. See: L. Donath, *Die Alexandersage in Talmud und Midrasch* (Fulda: 1873); I. Levi, "La Légende d'Alexandre dans le Talmud," *REJ*, II (1881), 273–300, and "La Légende d'Alexandre dans le Talmud et le Midrasch," *REJ*, VII (1883), 78–93; A. Wunsche, "Die Alexandersage nach jüdischen Quellen," *Die Grenzenboten*, XXXlll (1869), 269–280.

16 For a comprehensive view of the Talmud and the Midrash see H. L. Strack, *Introduction to the Talmud and Midrash* (Philadelphia: 1945).

17 See Glossary, Appendix A.

18 Alexander the Great was listed as one of the rulers of the world together with Nimrod, Solomon, etc. See *Solomonic Parallels* in this study.

whose career was prophesied in Daniel. In the Book of Daniel,[19] Alexander is the one presumed to be the he-goat that "came from the West over the face of the whole earth and touched not the ground; and the goat had a conspicuous horn between his eyes. . . . And the he-goat magnified himself exceedingly; and when he was strong, the great horn was broken; and instead of it there came up the appearance of four horns toward the four winds of heaven." Further on, the reference becomes more pointed: "The ram which thou sawest having the two horns, they are the kings of Medea and Persia. And the rough he-goat is the king of Greece; and the great horn that is between his eyes is the first king. And as for that which was broken, in the place whereof four stood up, four kingdoms shall stand up out of the nation, but not with his power."

Prominent scholars[20] have commented on the influence of Jewish tales and concepts on Islam and the Koran. In the Koran, Alexander is called "D'ul quarnaim, or Lord of Two Horns,"[21] an epithet undoubt-

---

[19] Translations from the Bible used in this study were taken from *The Twenty-Four Books of the Old Testament*, trans. Rev. A. Harkavy, 2 vols. (New York: Hebrew Publishing Company, 1916). See also Daniel 7, 8, 11.

[20] For a comprehensive view of Jewish influences on Islam see: S. D. Goitein, *Jews and Arabs: Their Contacts Through the Ages* (New York: Schocken Books, 1955); A. S. Halkin, "Judeo-Arabic Literature," *The Jews: Their History, Culture and Religion*, ed., L. Finkelstein, 2 vols. (New York: 1960); A. Geiger, *Judaism and Islam*, trans. F. M. Young (Madras, 1898); A. Guillaume, "The Influence of Judaism on Islam," *The Legacy of Israel*, ed., E. R. Bevan, and C. Singer (Oxford: 1928); J. Jacobs, *Jewish Contributions to Civilization* (Philadelphia: 1920), chap. IV; A. I. Katsh, *Judaism in Islam* (New York: 1954) and "Li-She'elat Hashpa'at ha-Talmud al ha-Koran," *Hatekufah*, XXXIV–XXXV (1950), 834–838.

[21] Note L. Ginzberg, *Jewish Folklore: East and West* (Cambridge, Mass.: 1936), p. 13. See also Daniel 8:3.
   The history of the name "D'ul quarnaim" applied to Alexander, and found as well in the Koran, is discussed fully by A. R. Anderson, *Alexander's Gate, Gog and Magog, and the Enclosed Nations* (Cambridge, Mass.: 1932), pp. 28ff. See also A. R. Anderson, "The Arabic History of Dulcarnaim and the Ethiopian History of Alexander," *Speculum*, VI (1931), 434–435, and "Alexander's Horns," *Amer. Philol. Assn. Trans.* LVIII (1927), 100–122.
   N. H. Tur-Sinai, *The Language and The Book* (Jerusalem: 1955), III, 351–353 notes that in Hebrew script of the sixth century the equivalents of *r* and *d* were written identically. A misreading of Mokdon as Mokron ("horned") by south Arabian Jews was responsible for the "D'ul quarnaim" name of Alexander used in the Koran.

edly influenced by Hebraic literature and its oral tradition. Much Islamic tradition and wisdom entered Western culture via the Jewish travelers and traders[22] known as Radanites, who voyaged freely about the known world. Active between the seventh and tenth centuries, they were the true intermediaries between the Christian and Mohammedan worlds, carrying not merely goods but the culture of Islam to the West. Another group, the Islamic storytellers, popularized the tales about figures such as Moses, Solomon, and even Alexander, which were borrowed freely from Hebraic writings and popular oral tales. As the Arabs moved westward, their literature moved with them, carrying the culture not only of Islam but of the Jews as well. Hence, the literature of the East came to the West, often via Hebrews, for many Arabic works were translated into Hebrew and then into Latin.

Earliest references to Alexander among the Jews appear in the Bible and Apocrypha: Daniel 7, 8, 11 and I Maccabees 1:1–4. The first-century Jewish historian Josephus, in *The Jewish Antiquities*,[23] records Alexander's meeting with the Jews of Jerusalem. Pfister[24] has pointed out that recension C (γ) of *Pseudo-Callisthenes* contains additions by a Jew of the first century A. D., to the stories of Alexander's adventures. The purpose of introducing material favorable to the Jews was to support the claims of Alexandrian Jews to equality of civic rights by representing Alexander as a friend of the Jews and possibly as a worshipper of the Jewish God. In Middle English literature, the portrayal of Alexander as having been kind to the Jews and worshipping their God has ancient Hebraic roots.

---

[22] L. Rabinowitz, *Jewish Merchant Adventurers* (London: 1948).

[23] Josephus, *The Jewish Antiquities*, Loeb, ed., trans. H. St. J. Thackeray and R. Marcus (London: 1930–1943), XI, 317ff.

Historically, I Maccabees covers the period 175–135 B. C., from the persecutions by Antiochus Epiphanes to the death of Simon and the winning of Judea's political independence. I Maccabees 1: 1–4 briefly relates the victories of Alexander of Macedon, son of Philip, a forefather of the tyrant Antiochus Epiphanes.

[24] F. Pfister, *Kleine Texte zum Alexanderroman, Sammlung vulgärlateinischer Texte*, IV (Heidelberg: 1910), pp. 6ff.

5. Solomonic Parallels to the Alexander Legend

Among the Jews, the Hebrew scriptures reveal a dichotomy of development: the law (*Halachah*)[25] and the lore (*Aggadah*).[26] The latter told a story which fed on the intellect as well as the imagination. Originally, these legends were transmitted orally among the people. Later, they took concrete form and were compiled in the many books of *Midrashim*.[27] The original legends were often revised in order to teach a moral lesson.

These Hebrew legends in Talmudic-Midrashic literature were codified from the second to the fourteenth centuries. Another corpus of legends, the *Targumim*,[28] was produced from the fourth to the tenth centuries. Medieval Jewish commentators and homilists also contributed to Aggadic material and long-lost legends were found in *Cabbalah*[28] writings as well. Furthermore, patristic literature contains many legends of Jewish provenance. The Apocrypha and Pseudepigrapha,[30] works which were unacceptable to the Jews, were preserved by the Church. The Pseudepigrapha contain Greek writings of Hellenist Jews, and translations of Jewish works of Palestinian or Hellenistic origin into Ethiopic, Arabic, Persian, and Old Slavic. Much of the Pseudepigrapha contains Christian interpolation so that it is often difficult to determine whether a legend is Jewish or Christian. [31]

The writings of the Church Fathers, notably in the works of Origen, Ausebius and Jerome, also show the impact of the Jewish legendary for similar legends are found earlier in rabbinic sources. Although theological differences between Christians and Jews were great, personal relations continued, thus providing a basis for the infusion of Hebrew legends into patristic literature. Many legends of saints can be traced to Talmudic-Midrashic literature.[32]

---

[25] See *Glossary of Hebrew Terms, Appendix A*.

[26] See ibid.

[27] Ibid.

[28] Ibid.

[29] Ibid.

[30] *The Apocrypha and Pseudepigrapha of the Old Testament*, ed. R. H. Charles (Oxford: 1913).

[31] L. Ginzberg, *Jewish Folklore*, op. cit., n. 21.

[32] Ibid.

Folklore studies point to the similarities of themes and tales in the folk literature of many diverse areas of the world. A single person is often the central figure who dominates the tale as it moves from nation to nation. Parallels are therefore common between folk heroes of nations of vastly different cultures.

In Hebrew legend, the figure of King Solomon looms over a wide canvas; to him were attributed great wisdom and powers beyond those of a mere mortal. In similar Hebraic legends told about Alexander, the heroic qualities of King Solomon seem to have been transferred to Alexander. Although some differences exist in the parallel tales surrounding the two kingly figures, the overall themes are usually close. These tales were then transmitted beyond the boundary of the country in which they originated. Thus, I believe, the ancient tales of Solomon became the foundation for the legendary picture of Alexander.

A summary of legendary themes involving Solomon and transferred to Alexander follows:

a. *Filicide*: A Hebrew legend tells how the mother of Solomon decides to kill him because of his slighting remark about women which he made while he was an infant of three years: "A woman's soul is not as heavy as a handful of chips of wood."[33] In the Bodleian manuscript the queen wants the child strangled at birth in order to give the throne to her son sired by Philip, her husband. The tale of strangling the infant Alexander is peculiar to this Bodleian version only.

b. *Supernatural Perception*: Solomon is known to have been endowed with the power of understanding the language of the birds.[34] In all versions of the Alexander romance appears the tale of the speaking trees which predict Alexander's early death.

c. *Cosmocreator*: Solomon is said to be one of the few monarchs to rule over the entire world. The name "cosmocreator" is given also to Alexander in Hebrew legend: "God, at the time of the creation of the

[33] L. Ginzberg, *Legends of the Jews* (Philadelphia: 1911–1938), VI, 287.

[34] Ginzberg, *Legends*, VI, 289. Ginzberg cites the Babylonian Talmud, *Sanhederin*, p. 20b which tells: that "Solomon before his fall was lord over all the terrestrials and celestials." That Solomon knew the languages of animals and trees is based on I Kings 5:13: "And he spoke of trees, from the cedar that is in Lebanon even unto hyssop that springeth out of the wall; he spoke also of beasts, and fowl, and of creeping things, and of fishes." Ginzberg also notes that Solomon's knowledge of the animals plays an important part in Mohammedan legends.

world, was the first ruler; then Nimrod, Joseph, Solomon, Ahab, Nebuchadnezzar, Cyrus, Alexander of Macedon, the Messiah, and at the end of time God, who was the first ruler, will also be the last."[35]

d. *Pride*: Solomon's pride was the subject of legend as was Alexander's. Solomon was taught the lesson that the wisest and mightiest of mortals may not indulge in pride and arrogance. Once, while riding through the air on his carpet, Solomon said: "There is none like unto me in the world, upon whom God has bestowed wisdom, intelligence, and knowledge, besides making me the ruler of the world." At that moment, the air stirred and 40,000 men dropped from the magic carpet: The king ordered the wind to cease from blowing with the word: "Return." The wind replied: "If thou wilt return to God and subdue thy pride, I, too, will return." Thus the king realized his transgression.[36]

Another legend tells that the ant reminds the great King Solomon of his earthly origin and admonishes him to humility.[37]

e. *Demonology*: Solomon's power over demons was famous in legend. It is told how Solomon contained the demons in a hollow stick and maintained his power over them even after his death by making them believe he was still alive. When they learned of his death, the power to control them was gone and they escaped.[38]

---

[35] Ginzberg, *Legends*, V, 199, n. 82. This is found in *Pirke Rabbi Eliezer*, II, in which rulers of the world are named, including Alexander.

[36] Ginzberg, *Legends*, IV, 162 and VI, 298, n. 77,78. Ginzburg cites the legend about King Solomon's seeking to enter a magnificent building. Finally, a seven-hundred year-old eagle directs him to an older brother who directs him to still an older brother and so on until he came to the brother who is 1300 years old. Entering the palace, he comes upon magnificent apartments of pearls and precious stones. Inscribed upon the doors he finds three wise proverbs dealing with the vanity of all earthly things. His final lesson was inscribed upon a statue: "I, Shaddad ben Ad, ruler over a thousand thousand provinces, rode on a thousand thousand horses, had a thousand thousand kings under me, and slaughtered a thousand thousand heroes and when the Angel of Death approached me, I was powerless." The Bodleian manuscript contains a scene in which Alexander sees a magnificent palace and is guided through it by a very old man. However, the moral is lacking in the manuscript story.

[37] Ginzberg, *Legends*, IV, 163; VI, 298, n. 79.

[38] F. W. Hasluck, *Letters on Religion and Folklore* (London: 1926), p. 289. The author tells the story of Solomon, who retained his power over the djinns after death by making them believe he was still alive. A similar story is told in J. E. Hanauer, *Folklore of the Holy Land; Moslem, Christian and Jewish* (London: 1935), pp. 49–50.

The Bodleian manuscript contains the strange episode (fol. 273ⁿ) of the headless man in the sea who refrains from harming approaching ships when the name of Alexander is uttered. The power of the kingly name is great enough to control these demons.

f. *The Mountains of Darkness*: Solomon, to whom all animals were subservient, was transported on the back of an eagle to the desert and back again in one day to build there a city called Tadmor. It is said that this city was situated near the "mountains of darkness," which was the trysting place of the spirits.[39] In the Bodleian manuscript, Alexander also journeys beyond the mountains of darkness, although in that story there is no connection with demons or spirits.

In most versions of the Alexander romance the mountains of darkness stand before the enclosed nations of Gog and Magog, the terrible peoples who, legend tells, were enclosed behind the Caspian Gates by Alexander and who will be released at the end of days.[40] However, the Bodleian manuscript does not deal with this legend of Gog and Magog, which assumed an important place in the Greek and Latin versions, *Pseudo-Callisthenes* and *Historia de Preliis*, and in the later romances which derived from them.

g. *The Magic Stone*: A famous story associated with Solomon is that of the Shamir, known as a stone (or in some tales, a magic bird), that splits rocks and aids the king in building the Temple in Jerusalem.[41] In the Bodleian manuscript such a magic stone appears in the hands of a dwarf who uses it to make himself invisible and then guides Alexander to discover which of his men are loyal to him (fol. 267ª).

h. It is told about Solomon that, at the dedication of the Temple in Jerusalem which he had built, the priests were about to place the Ark of the Lord in the Holy of Holies when the doors closed suddenly, and

---

[39] Ginzberg, *Legends*, IV, 149; VI, 291 n. 51.

[40] The subject of Alexander and Gog and Magog was treated by Anderson, *Alexander's Gate*, op. cit. Josephus, *The Antiquities*, I, 6, 1 interpreted the sons of Magog as Scythians who, in ancient geography were the barbarian peoples of the North. Neubauer, in *La Géographie du Talmud* (Paris: 1868), p. 422 notes that the invading peoples called Goths or in some sources as Germania, are close to the word Gomer (Genesis 10:2). Gomer, Magog, Madat, and Javan, etc., are called the sons of Japheth, supposed ancestors of Gog and Magog. Ezekial 38:6, mentions Gomer and all his hordes: "The house of Togarmah in the uttermost parts of the North, and all his hordes."

[41] Ginzberg, *Legends*, IV, 168; VI, 292 n. 56; VI, 299 n. 85,

12

opened only after Solomon recited the words of Psalm 24:9: "Lift up your heads, O ye gates, / Yea lift them up, ye everlasting doors; / That the King of Glory may come in."[42] The Bodleian manuscript relates that these words from Psalm 24 are engraved upon a gate which Alexander realizes leads to paradise (fol. 273[b]).

Such parallels between Solomon and Alexander merit the observation that the provenance of the portrait of Alexander was the literature of the Talmud and the Midrash. The attributes of King Solomon, real and imaginary, were transferred to Alexander the Great by the ancient Jewish sages who, in gratitude for his real or imagined kindness to the Jews, likened him in fondness to their king, Solomon.

6. *Alexander References in Middle English Literature*

Allusions to Alexander in Middle English reflect, uniformly, his reputation as the ideal warrior-king, generous and wise, the successful world conqueror, as well as a victim of excessive pride and overweening ambition.

No attempt has been made to list every Middle English text which refers to Alexander; however, the sampling here presented reveals that the conventional picture had already assumed the status of a cliché. The Bodleian Hebrew manuscript, Heb. d. 11, the subject of our study, is relevant and pertinent because, like the English texts, it, too, contains legends exemplifying these dominant themes: pride and the desire for world conquest.

World mastery was Alexander's overwhelming ambition. A "cosmo-creator," wise and barbaric, Alexander set forth to subjugate the nations of the world, the sky above and the depths below.

The Bodleian manuscript reports Alexander's victories, the historical as well as the fanciful. These are tales of battles and the conquests of bizarre peoples, mysterious antagonists, strange men and stranger beasts.

It may be well to summarize briefly some of Alexander's more notorious exploits. The famous oft-told tale of Alexander's visit with the queen of Anshiq (Amazons) as told in MS. Bodl. Heb. d. 11 finds its prototype, albeit shorter and with none of the elaborations found in the

---

[42] Babylonian Talmud, *Shabbat*, p. 30a.

Bodleian manuscript, in the Babylonian Talmud, *Tamid*, 32 a b.[43] The Middle English: *The Prose Life of Alexander*[44] and *The Wars of Alexander*[45] also deal with the visit of Alexander to this mighty queen, and his psychological defeat at her hands.

Another popular episode, Alexander's visit to Jerusalem, and his supposed subsequent kindly treatment of the Jews, is related in great detail in the Bodleian manuscript and in ancient and medieval Hebraic texts.[46] Middle English references to this episode appear in *The Wars of Alexander*[47] and *The Prose Life of Alexander*;[48] in each version Alexander bows to the priest who appears before him, declaring that the priest is the one whom he has seen in visions as leading him to victory against the Persians. In the Temple in Jerusalem, the priests show Alexander the prophecy of Daniel, foretelling that Alexander will be the destroyer of Persia. The priests then ask that the Jews be allowed to practice their religion in freedom — a request which is granted. Alexander then makes a generous donation of gold, silver, and precious stones to the Temple and departs.

Works about Alexander during the Middle Ages, whether romances or biographies, and the allusions to him in other writings show both praise and blame heaped upon the great king. Only a select few of the many references are listed here. Particularly noteworthy, however, is the hostile attitude of some of the later medieval English writers toward Alexander: They condemn the king's lust, a lust which brought discord among mankind. His sordid death they accepted as proof that evil

---

[43] It was pointed out earlier in this study (n. 18) that previous scholars have noted these sources. *Midrash Rabbah* (*Leviticus Rabbah*, XXVII, 1) published in Hebrew (Warsaw: 1877–1890) and with an English translation (London: Soncino Press, 1939), IV, 342–344. All page references in this study to *Midrash Rabbah* are to the Soncino edition. See also: *Midrash Tanhuma* (*Vayikra*, *Emor* 9) ed. S. Buber (Vilna: 1885); *Pesikta d'Rab Kahana*, ed. S. Buber (Lyck: 1868).

[44] *The Prose Life of Alexander*, ed. J. S. Westlake, EETSOS 143, pp. 65ff.

[45] *The Wars of Alexander*, ed. W. W. Skeat, EETSES 47, Passus XVI, pp. 214–216.

[46] See: *Megillat Ta'anit*, chap. 9 (Warsaw: 1874); Babylonian Talmud, *Yoma*, p. 69a; *Midrash Rabbah* (*Genesis Rabbah*, LX 1, 7) op. cit., vol. 2, pp. 545–548; Josephus, *The Antiquities*, op. cit., II, viii, 3–5; *Yossippon*, ed. D. Ginzberg - A.Kahana (Berditschev, 1896–1913), pp. 32–34.

[47] *The Wars*, op. cit., Passus VI, VII, pp. 58–96.

[48] *The Prose Life*, op. cit., pp. 20ff.

14

forces and paganism cannot win against the justice of God. John Lydgate's *Fall of Princes*,[49] using Alexander as an example of the tragedies that befall great men, admonishes the princes not to trust in martial policy as did Alexander, for everything may suddenly change, as witness Alexander's death by treachery.

In another incident,[50] Lydgate points to Alexander's mighty career, yet even that did not last forever. By contrast Diogenes, the philosopher, representing truth, lived to an old age.

Chaucer's monk[51] cites a catalogue of famous people in a non-dramatic narrative. He praises Alexander's courage and character as the flower of knighthood. However, despite great conquests of both women and nations, Fortune turned her back on him and he died treacherously.

John Gower violently attacked Alexander as the archetype of modern conquerors. In his work, *In Praise of Peace*,[52] Alexander is contrasted to that earlier great king, Solomon, who sought peace, whereas Alexander brought destruction in his wake. In *Confessio Amantis*[53] Gower tells the famous tale of the pirate and King Alexander, emphasizing with hostile vigor the wanton cruelty Alexander displayed in his conquests. The pirate justifies himself by saying that he only did on a small scale what Alexander did worldwide. It is not surprising that Alexander came to a tragic end, for his appetite was insatiable; his death, by treacherous poisoning was the expression of God's justice.

In another episode,[54] Gower uses Alexander's wars and conquests as an example of pride, teaching the lesson that no man should kill others, for one day he is above all and the next day he is nought.

Alexander's overweening pride, his incontinence, and his desire to aspire to the Godhead also impressed writers whether of Alexander or non-Alexander romances. The Bodleian manuscript likewise contains

[49] John Lydgate, *Fall of Princes*, ed. H. Bergen, 3 vols. (Washington: 1923), III, 753.

[50] *Fall of Princes*, I, 176–177. cf. John Gower, *Confessio Amantis*, ed. G. C. Macaulay, Bk. III, lines 1201ff., pp. 259–261.

[51] Geoffrey Chaucer, *The Poetical Works of Chaucer*, ed. F. N. Robinson, 2nd ed. 1957 (Cambridge, Mass.: 1933), pp. 234–5.

[52] John Gower, *The Works of John Gower*, ed. G. C. Macaulay, 4 vols. (Oxford: 1899–1902), Bk. III, p. 482.

[53] *Confessio Amantis*, ed. G. C. Macaulay, p. 291.

[54] Ibid., pp. 292–293.

15

tales of Alexander's pride. Often repeated in many different ways, is the tale of Alexander's trip to the earthly paradise which concludes with the exhortation that the king's eyes will not be satisfied (with riches or conquests) until he dies. The same tale is also related of Alexander in the Talmud, *Tamid* 32b. Middle English references to this episode and to its moral are numerous. Among the most famous are those in Higden and Lydgate. Higden's *Polychronicon*[55] relates a tale of Alexander and his knights in India. Although instead of the eye, a stone is placed on the scale, the moral implication is the same as that in the Bodleian manuscript.[56] Lydgate's "Mesure is Tresour"[57] repeats the same theme. King Alexander is mentioned as an example of one who comes to misfortune because he did not control his desires. In *Gologros and Gawane*[58] reference is made to Alexander in order to warn Arthur against attempting to subjugate a marvelous city built on a river's bank. Synagrose, his guide, warns him of the pitfalls of pride and points to the history of Alexander. Here the image of a leaf blown down by the wind is used. This recalls the dust or the feather that overbalances the eye-stone in the scales found in other versions of the tale.[59] The lovely descriptions of the earthly

[55] *Polychronicon*, trans. R. Higden, ed. J. R. Lumby, *Rolls Series* IV (London: 1865–1886), III, XXX, 7.

[56] In the Western world the earliest form of the legend of Alexander and the earthly paradise appeared in the Latin text (c. 1100) *Iter ad Paradisum*, ed. Julius Zacher (Königsberg: 1859), which was later incorporated into the French *Roman d'Alexandre*. See A. Hilka, in L. P. G. Peckham and M. S. La Du, ed., *The Prise de Defur and the Voyage au Paradis Terrestre* (Princeton University Press, 1935; Elliot Monographs, 35), pp. xli–xlviii.

P. Meyer, "Etude sur les Manuscrits du Roman d'Alexandre," *Romania*, XI (1882), p. 245 comments that the voyage tale as noted by I. Levi, "La Légende d'Alexandre dans le Talmud," *REJ*, II (1881), 293–300, came from Jewish sources and was used in the literature of the Middle Ages.

[57] John Lydgate, *The Minor Poems of John Lydgate*, ed. H. N. MacCracken, EETSOS 192 (London: 1934), p. 777.

[58] *Gologros and Gawane*, ed. F. J. Amours, *Scottish Alliterative Poems in Rhyming Stanzas*, STS 27, 38 (Edinburgh: 1891–1897), 27, 10–11.

[59] I am grateful to Professor John Fisher (New York University) for drawing my attention to the study by Wm. Matthews, *The Tragedy of Arthur* (Berkeley: 1960). Matthews discusses the Arthurian romance "Morte Arthure" against a background of the Alexander legends, and he finds that much of the Arthur legend is derived from the legends surrounding Alexander. See also M. Gaster, "The Legend of the Grail," *Studies and Texts*, II (1925–1928,) pp. 879ff.

paradise similar to that found in the Bodleian manuscript appear in *Mandeville's Travels*[60] and *Kyng Alisaunder*.[61]

Alexander's pride is further exemplified by his desire to visit the heavens and the depths of the sea. Three versions of Alexander's celestial journey occur in Talmudic literature.[62] One can well imagine why the amazing sight of Alexander's ascent into the air became a favorite subject for iconographers during the Middle Ages.[63] Combined with stories of

An Alexander romance entitled *The Buick of King Alexandre the Conqueror* (c. 1450) by Sir Gilbert Hay, unpublished except as a study by Dr. A. Hermann: *The Taymouth Castle Manuscript of Sir Gilbert Hay's Buik of King Alexander the Conqueror* in *Wissenschaftliche Beilage zum Jahresbericht der II. Städtischen Realschule zu Berlin* (Berlin: 1900), existing in a manuscript in the British Museum (Add. MS. 40/32) contains the entire version of the French *Roman d'Alexandre* translated from the French. M. Lascelles, "Alexander and the Earthly Paradise," *Medium Aevum*, V (1936), 79–104, 173–188, notes that the story of the voyage to paradise occupies three quarters of the Taymouth manuscript.

G. V. Smithers, ed. *Kyng Alisaunder*, EETSOS 227, 237 (1952–1957) notes in vol. II, p. 16 that in one of the manuscripts of *Roman de Toute Chevalerie* by Thomas of Kent (c. 1250) which is the source for *Kyng Alisaundre* there appears an interpolation which is peculiar to that manuscript. The episodes are: Alexander's dealings with the inhabitants of Jerusalem and Alexander's meeting with the old man who brings him a stone from the Earthly Paradise. These episodes do not appear in *Kyng Alisaunder*.

[60] *Mandeville's Travels*, ed. P. Hamelius, EETS 153, 154 (London: 1919–1923), chap. XXXIV, lines 10ff., p. 203.

[61] *Kyng Alisaunder*, ed. G. V. Smithers; also in *Metrical Romances*, I, ed. H. Weber (Edinburgh: 1810). M. Lascelles, op. cit., 178, points out that the Earthly Paradise theme is associated with the Holy Rood legends. Seth, Adam's son, sees four rivers and a mighty tree. Seth is given three branches from the apple tree and told to bury them with Adam. Thus, from a wonder tree sprung from Adam's grave the cross was made.

For a comprehensive survey of Alexander romances see J. E. Wells, *A Manual of the Writings in Middle English* (New Haven, Conn.: Yale University Press, 1916–1951, with nine supplements).

[62] Jerusalem Talmud, 6 vols. (Vilna: 1911–1917), *Avodah Zarah*, III, I, 42c; *Midrash Rabbah*, Eng. trans., Soncino Press, vol. 6, pp. 526–531 (*Numbers Rabbah*, XIII, 14); *Yalkut Shimoni*, ed. Lewin-Epstein (Jerusalem: 1952), I Kg., 18, sec. 211, p. 758; *Pirke Rabbi Eliezar* (New York: 1946), XI, 28b, 29a; *Midrash Aseret Melakim* in H. M. Hurwitz ha-Levi, *Bait Eked ha-Agadot* (Frankfurt a.M.: 1881), pp. 44–45 and in J. D. Eisenstein, *Ozar Midrashim* (New York: 1915), II, 463.

[63] This theme was a favorite subject in iconography during the Middle Ages. See: R.S. Loomis, "Alexander the Great's Celestial Journey," *Burlington Magazine*, XXXII (1918), 177–185; D.J.A. Ross, *Alexander Historiatus: A Guide to Medieval*

his famous ascent are stories of Alexander's descent into the sea noted also in Talmudic literature[64] and, particularly, in the *Pirke Rabbi Eliezer*, XI and *Yalkut Shimoni*.

In the Middle English *The Wars of Alexander*, the episode of the ascent of Alexander into the air is similar to the narration in the Bodleian manuscript with only the slight difference that in *The Wars* the episode begins as Alexander sees a mighty mountain which he assumes reaches to God. Desiring to be lifted to the heavens, he orders his smithies to forge an iron chair, bind it with chains and fasten meat above the contraption. As eagles soar, with the meat as bait over their heads, they will bear Alexander to the clouds.[65] *The Prose Life of Alexander*[66] describes the ascent in a similar manner, with the chair, four griffons fastened with iron chains and meat hanging over them, and Alexander borne up into the air from where he sees the earth.[67] He comes down after ten days. When he descends into the sea in a glass cage he sees the wonder of the depths. In this version, he is drawn up by his knights.

Illustrated Alexander Literature (London: The Warburg Institute, University of London 1963); A.L. Meissner, *Bildliche Darstellungen der Alexandersage in Kurchen des Mittelalters, Archiv. für des Studium der neueren Sprachen und Literaturen*, LXVIII (1882), 177–190; J. Berzunza, *A Tentative Classification of Books, Pamphlets and Pictures Concerning Alexander the Great and the Alexander Romances*, privately printed, (1939).

64 *Midrash Tehillim*, ed. S. Buber (Vilna: 1891), Ps. 93, 5, English trans. *The Midrash on Psalms*, trans. Wm. G. Braude, 2 vols. (New Haven: Yale Judaica Series, 1959), II, 126–127; I. Kazis, op. cit., p. 20.

65 M. Gaster, *Ilchester Lectures on Greeko-Slavonic Literature and its Relation to Folklore of Europe During the Middle Ages* (London: 1887), pp. 112ff. points out a parallel Oriental fable which tells how Solomon flew through the air carried by a demon; from this developed the flying carpet, a flying chest and even a flying horse.

G. Millet, "L'Ascension d'Alexandre," *Syria*, IV (1923), 85–133, discusses the popularity of this legend and notes its parallel in the Babylonian myth of Etana and his ascent to heaven, and to the Oriental tale of the Persian king, Kaikus, a contemporary of Solomon, who also wanted to rule the world. This legend was used in two ways: for amusement and for edification (like the eye symbol).

66 *The Prose Life*, op. cit., pp. 105ff.

67 Note the opinion of R. S. Loomis, "The Youth of Alexander the Great," *Medieval Romances* (New York: 1957), p. 233ff. who feels that this incident has been treated with an eye toward the comic rather than to illustrate the sin of pride. "The Youth of Alexander" is a translation of an anonymous French author of about 1270 whose work was based on Alberic's romance written c.1100. In all other versions of this legend Alexander ascends in his mature years; in this version the episode was transformed to his youth.

18

Alexander's pride is further illustrated in Middle English works in an episode of his encounter with the Brahmins, the wise men of India. In the Talmudic account, *Tamid*, 31–32b, somewhat akin to the Bodleian manuscript version, Alexander poses ten questions to the elders of the South. The similarity between this dialogue and one found in Plutarch has been noted by Dr. Kazis.[68]

Alexander B or *The Letters of Alexander to Dindimus*[69] contains two relevant episodes, one in which Alexander is shown to be powerless to grant the people everlasting life, and a second in which the life of Dindimus, the life of a contemplative philosopher, is shown to be preferable to that of the proud conqueror, Alexander.

Similar to the Bodleian version of this tale is *The Wars of Alexander* in which the life of the Brahmans, their extreme moderation, abstinence, and love of peace is condemned by Alexander.[70] The episode of the people requesting immortality which Alexander cannot grant[71] recalls *Alexander B* as well as the Bodleian manuscript narratives.

Again, in *Mandeville's Travels*[72] this theme is repeated when Alexander is asked, by the residents of the isle called Gymnosophe, for immortality, which he confesses he cannot grant. The people admonish him reminding him that since he is not a god and does not know when he will die, he must cease subjecting all the world to his will.

On the other hand, Alexander's wish to learn wisdom from Dindimus and the latter's answers to Alexander listing precepts, found in *The Prose Life of Alexander*,[73] give a picture of Alexander as a philosopher-king — a portrait which also emerges from medieval writings.

However, G. Cary feels that this legend was interpreted during the Middle Ages as a condemnation of Alexander's pride. He notes particularly the German works, *History-Bible I* and Enikel's *Weltchronik* in which a severe condemnation of Alexander appears. In these works the story relates that Alexander is deterred from ascending further when he reaches a certain height. A voice warns him that no man may ascend who has not deserved to do so by good works. G. Cary, *The Medieval Alexander*, pp. 134–135.

[68] Kazis, op. cit., p. 15.

[69] *Alexander and Dindimus*, ed. W. W. Skeat, EETSES 31 (London: 1878); *Alexander B* (Together with *Alexander A*), ed. F.P. Magoun, Jr., *The Gests of King Alexander of Macedon*, op. cit.

[70] Passus XIX–XXI, pp. 231–245.

[71] Passus XVIII, pp. f. 223

[72] *Mandeville's Travels*, EETSOS 153 (London: 1919), pp. 194–197.

[73] *Prose Life*, op. cit., pp. 77ff.

19

TALES OF ALEXANDER
THE MACEDONIAN

ספר אלכסנדרוס מוקדון

Ms. Bodl. Heb. d. 11

fol. 265–278

TEXT, NOTES AND ENGLISH TRANSLATION

21

ו׳ה׳ ב׳נ׳ים ההם׳ ויהי מלך בארץ מצרים ושמו פוליפוס. ויהי המלך ההוא רחב לב
ורחב ידים² ואוהב משפט וצדקה³ אשר לא קם כמוהו⁴ בכל ארץ מצרים וכל עמו
אהבו אותו. ושם אשתו גולפירא המלכה והיא היתה אשה יפה אשר לא קם כמוה.

* Exodus 2:11; Job 19:1; I Samuel 28:1 "And it came to pass in those days. . ."	¹ "ויהי בימים ההם"
Psalms 104:25 "So is this great wide sea . . ."	² "זה הים גדול ורחב ידים."
Psalms 33:5 "He loveth righteousness and judgment."	³ "אוהב צדק ומשפט."
II Kings 23:25 ". . . neither after him arose there any like him."	⁴ "ואחריו לא קם כמוהו."

* Translations from the Bible used in this study may be found in *The Twenty-Four Books of the Old Testament*, trans. Rev. A. Harkavy, 2 vols. (New York: Hebrew Publishing Company, 1916).

22

Once upon a time there lived a king in the land of Egypt[1] named Philip. He was good-hearted and open-handed and loved justice and mercy. None could compare with him in all Egypt, and all his people loved him. His wife, the queen Golofira,[2] was of surpassing beauty. In that country there was also an unrivaled magician Bildad the Wizard,[3] who surpassed

[1] In this version of the Alexander romance, the tale begins in Egypt and Macedonia is mentioned only towards the end of the romance. Arabic writers considered Macedonia a Greek name for Egypt or a name of a single Egyptian region. See A. Harkavy, "Neizdannya Versiya romana obu Alexandrê," *Akademiya nauk. Otdeleniye russkovo yazyka i slovesnosti. Sbornik*, LIII (1892), 65–155; his comments on names and places were helpful to me. I am grateful to Professor S. Riddlich of the University of Washington for translating this article for me from the microfilm copy. See also M. Gaster, "An Old Hebrew Romance of Alexander," op. cit., 486–488, who points out that the presence of a different version of the Alexander legend than the *Pseudo-Callisthenes* tradition in the Syriac and Ethiopian literatures points to the theory that two traditions of the Alexander romance existed. He notes that many of the tales found in the fantastic group of Alexander tales as represented by the Bodleian manuscript are also present in the later medieval romances of the West. See also the Ethiopic version of the Alexander romance, *The Life and Exploits of Alexander the Great*, ed. Sir E. W. Budge (Cambridge; 1896).

[2] P. Meyer, *Alexandre le Grand dans la Littérature du Moyen Age*, (Paris: 1886), pp. 132ff. notes that the Paris manuscript of the *Historia de Preliis* records Galiopatra for the second wife of Philip. The Modena manuscript Liii (transcribed by I. Levi, "Sefer Alexandrus Mokdon," in *Festschrift zum achzigsten Geburtstage Moritz Steinschneiders* (Leipzig: 1896), pp. 142–163, similar in most of its details to MS. Bodl. Heb. d.11, gives the name of the queen as Galopatra. As such, it is similar to Cleopatra. During Alexander's lifetime there lived two well-known women called Cleopatra. One was the niece of Attalus, one of the generals of Philip. Philip married her when he divorced Olympias in 337 B. C. She was put to death by Olympias. Her infant child perished with her, being looked upon as a rival to Alexander. Another Cleopatra was the daughter of Philip and Olympias and a sister of Alexander the Great. She married Alexander, King of Epeirus, her uncle on her mother's side. Wm. Smith, *A Dictionary of Greek and Roman Biography and Mythology* (London: 1844), I, 799.

[3] Bildad is mentioned in Job 2:11. He was one of Job's three friends who came to mourn with him and comfort him. In the Greek and Latin versions of the Alexander romance, it is Nectanebus who is the seducer of the queen.

23

ויהי באו ף ההוא מכשף אחד ושמו בלדד המכשף אשר לא קם כמוהו בכל ארץ
מצרים. ויעש בכישופיו כל מה שלבו חפץ. ויפול לבו על גולפירא אשת פוליפו׳
המלך וימת לבו בקרבו⁵ מרב אהבה אשר אהבה.⁶ ויחל בלדד ג׳ ימים ויתחזק בלדד
ביום השלישי וישען על מקלו לראות היועיל תוחלתו אם לא. ויקבור העשבים ט׳
ימים רצופים ויפול גורלו על המלכה וישמח בלדד שמחה גדולה. ויהי ביום השלישי
ויבא מכתב אל המלך פוליפוס אם לא יציל את ארץ תוגרמה מיד מלך כוס יפסיד כל
המלכות כי סמך מלך כוס עליהם בחיל כבד. ויצו המלך פוליפוס ויעבר קול בכל
ארץ מלכותו⁷ להיות מוכנים כל איש שולף חרב⁸ לבא לעזרת המלך להציל את ארץ
תו׳ תוגרמה. ויבואו כולם כאיש אחד ויצא המלך פוליפוס עם כל עמו להציל ארץ
תוגרמה. ויהי כצאת המלך פוליפוס עם כל עמו ויתחזק בלדד המכשף ויבא אל גול־
פירא המלכה ויאמר: "שמעיני המלכה! הנה דיגוניא אלהיך שלחני אליך לדבר דבר."
ותקם המלכה מעל כסאה ותפול לפניו ארצה⁹ ותאמר: "מה אדוני דובר אל שפחתו?"
ויאמר בלדד: "הנה דיגוניא אלהיך חיפש בכל העולם למצא אשה שהיא מזרע מלוכה
יפה וצנועה לבא אצלה ושהוליד בן ממנה שיהיה מושל תחת הכיפה ולא מצא דמותך
בכל העולם." ותאמר: "תנה לי אות."¹⁰ ויעש לפניה כמה אותות ותאמן המלכה
לדבריו ותתן לו ממון גדול. ותאמר לו: "מה דמות אדם אלהי בבואו בלילה?" ויאמר
לה בלדד: "בבואו בלילה יתמלא כל החדר אור ונר דלוק במצחו ושני קרנים במצחו
האחד של זהב והאחד של כסף הפוך כנגד השמים. זה סימן שהבן תלד ימשול עד
לשמים משושט והמלך בכל העולם. זה סימן שימלוך בכל העולם." ויהי בלילה ההוא¹¹
ויעש בלדד המכשף

---

⁵ "וימות לבו בקרבו."
I Samuel 25:37
" ... that his heart died within him."

⁶ "מאהבה אשר אהבה."
II Samuel 13:15
" ... than the love wherewith he had loved her."

⁷ "ויעבר קול בכל ארץ מלכותו."
Ezra 1:1
II Chronicles 36:22
" ... that he made a proclamation throughout all his kingdom ... "

⁸ "כל איש שולף חרב."
Judges 8:10; 20:15,
17, 46
" ... men that drew sword."

⁹ "ותפול על כפיה ארצה."
II Samuel 14:4
" ... she fell on her face to the ground."
   See also: I Samuel 17:49; Joshua 7:6

¹⁰ "ונתתם לי אות [אמת]."
Joshua 2:12
" ... and give me a (true) token."
   See also: Judges 6:17

¹¹ "ויהי בלילה ההוא."
Judges 6:25, 7:9
II Samuel 7:4; II Kings 19:35; I Chronicles 17:3
"And it came to pass the same night ... "

24

everyone in the land for he could achieve anything his heart desired by his magic. His heart fell on Phillip's wife, Golofira, and it seemed that his heart was dying within him from the greatness of the passion he felt for her. After three days Bildad took courage and leaning on his staff,* waited to see whether his wizardry would be effective. For nine successive days he buried herbs and he rejoiced greatly that his lot revealed that the queen would be his.

On the third day a letter came to King Philip stating that the King of Kos had descended upon the land of Togarma[4] with a great army and if he did not rescue it, he would lose his entire kingdom to the King of Kos. King Philip issued a proclamation to the effect that all able-bodied men should be ready to come to his aid to save Togarma. They rallied as one man to his call and King Philip led them forth to save that land.

As soon as King Philip went out with his entire people Bildad the Wizard summoned his courage and approaching Golofira, the queen, said to her:

"Hear me, O Queen! Behold! Digonia,[5] your god, sent me to you with a message." The queen rose from her seat and prostrated herself before him saying:

"What does my lord say to his maid-servant?"

Bildad replied: "Behold! Digonia, your god, has sought all over the world for a beautiful and modest woman of royal birth in order that he may come to her and beget a son who would reign on earth, and he has not found one like you anywhere."

"Give me a sign," she said.

Then he performed wonders before her eyes and she believed him and rewarded him generously. Then she asked: "How will my god appear?" to which Bildad replied: "When he comes at night the entire room will

---

* The word ויחל could also mean "sick" in which case the translation would be: "After three days of feeling ill, Bildad gathered strength and on the third day, he leaned on his staff and waited to see. . . ."

4 This is the same name as a grandson of Japhet in Genesis 3. In the later Hebrew literature, an interchange of letters would give the name Turkey. Togarma is one of the seventy peoples listed in Genesis 10. The country has been identified with Togarma on the Central Euphrates mentioned in Hittite inscriptions. The Armenians and Georgians were traditionally descended from the people of Togarma. *The Standard Jewish Encyclopedia*, ed. Cecil Roth (New York: 1959), p. 1822.

5 In the *Pseudo-Callisthenes* the god is Ammon.

וּיָבֹא אֵל אוון חדרה ונר דלוק במצחו ושני קרנים במצחו האחד של זהב והאחד של
כסף כאשר אמר לה. וישכב עמה בלילה ההוא ותהר ממנו. ותאמר לו: "אדוני אלהי
דיגוניא וכי אני הרה?" ויאמר לה: "הן". ותאמר: "מה יהיה שמו של הנער?"[12] ויאמר
לה: "אלכסנדרון." ותאמר לו: "מה זה אלכסנדרון?" ויאמר לה: "אדון על כל."[13]
ויהי אחרי כן ויבא המלך פוליפוס והוא הציל את ארץ תוגרמה מיד מלך כוס ויבוא
בשמחה גדולה כי נצח במלחמה. ותבא המלכה לקראתו ותאמר לו: "איש טוב אתה
וטוב תבשר"[14] כי דיגוניא אלהינו שכב עמי והנה אנכי הרה לו." ויגער בה המלך
כי איש חכם היה ויבן כי בלדד המכשף בא עליה בכישופיו נצחה. ולכן גער במלכה
כדי שלא יבינו עמו מה דיברה. ויאמר לה המלך בכעס: "וכי דרכה / של נשים לצאת
מאוהלם?"[15] ויהי אחרי אכלו המלך[16] וילך עם המלכה בחדר ויאמר לה: "שתקי
וסתרי הדבר כי בלדד המכשף בא עלייך והנך הרה לו[17] ואין עליך משפט מות[18] כי
בכשופיו נצחייך." ותבך המלכה בכי גדול ותגד למלך את כל ארע לה והיאך עשה
לה אותות. ויבן המלך את כל דבריה והנה אמיתים כי ניכרים דברי אמת. וישלח
המלך בכל ארץ מלכותו לחפש את בלדד ולהמיתו. ויברח בלדד מאת המלך וישב
במערה עד יום מותו.

ויהי אחרי כן ותכרע המלכה ללדת ויהי באשר המליטה והנה ילדה בן. ותאמר לה
המילדת: "אל תיראי כי ילדת בן."[19]

Judges 13:12   [12] "מה יהי משפט הנער."
" . . . what shall be the proceeding with the child . . . ?"

Genesis 45:9   [13] "לאדון לכל מצרים."
" . . . lord of all Egypt."

I Kings 1:42   [14] "איש חיל אתה וטוב תבשר."
" . . . for thou art a valiant man and bringest good tidings."

Some references in the Bible pertaining to women remaining "in their tents" are: [15]
Genesis 18:10, 24:67, 31:33, 18:9; Judges 5:24

I Kings 13:23   [16] "ויהי אחרי אכלו לחם."
"And it came to pass after he had eaten bread . . . "

Genesis 16:11   [17] "הנך הרה וילדת בן."
"Behold thou art with child, and shalt bear a son. . . . "
See also Judges 13:5.

Deut. 19:6   [18] "ולו אין משפט מות"
" . . . whereas he was not worthy of death."
See also Jeremiah 26:16.

I Samuel 4:20   [19] "אל תיראי כי בן ילדת"
"Fear not, for thou hast borne a son."
See also Genesis 35:17.

26

be illuminated. On his forehead are a burning candle and two horns, one of gold and the other of silver. The silver horn is pointed toward the skies and is a sign that the son you will bear will reign over the entire world." Later that night, Bildad the Wizard came into her room with a burning candle upon his forehead and two horns, one of gold and the other of silver, as he had prophesied. He lay with her that night and she conceived by him.

She said to him: "My lord god Digonia! Am I pregnant?"

He replied: "Yes."

"What will the boy's name be?" she asked.

"Alexander," he replied."

"What does Alexander mean?" she inquired.

"Lord over all," he answered.

Some time later Philip returned rejoicing because he had succeeded in the war and had preserved Togarma from the King of Kos. The queen went forth to greet him, saying: "You are a good man and you bring good tidings. Digonia, our god, has lain with me and behold I have conceived by him." The king rebuked her, for being a clever man he understood that Bildad the Wizard had come to her and by his witch-craft had seduced her. Therefore, he rebuked her so that his people should not understand what she had said. The king said in anger: "Is it the way / of women to leave their tents?"[6] After having eaten he took her aside and said: "Mention this matter to no one. Conceal it. It was Bildad the Wizard who came to you; it was by him you conceived. Because he seduced you by his witchcraft you will not be punished by death." The queen wept bitterly and told the king all that had happened and of the wonders he [Bildad] had performed before her eyes. The king understood her words; they had the aspect of truth and were believable. The king sent messengers throughout his kingdom with orders to find Bildad and to slay him. Bildad fled from the king and hid in a cave until his dying day.

f. 226[a]

And it came to pass that the queen entered into labor and bore a son. The midwife told her: "Have no fear, for you have borne a son."

---

6 The king does not wish to show his anger against the queen in public, before all his people, so he uses this phrase, ordering her back to her tent, for she had come out to greet him.

ותאמר לה המלכה: "חינקי אותו ואני אתן לך משקלו של זהב." ותאמר לה המילדת: "חלילה לי לשלוח ידי בבן מלך[20] כי אני רואה בו סימני מלכות וכי הוא ימשול בכל העולם כולו ואימתו ומוראו יהיה על כל העולם כולו." וזה דמות הנער: בעל שער היה מרגלו עד טיבורו ובין כתיפיו סימן אריה וכנגד לבו סימן נשר ועינו אחת כמו אריה מביט כנגד שמים

ועינו אחת כעין חתול ובו מביט לארץ. וכעיניייו זה נמלט אלכסנדרון. ותאמר המי־לדת: "עוד אני רואה בו בארץ נכרי ימות."

ותאמר המלכה אל המלך: "עוץ עיצה איך נהרג זה הממזר ואל יירש עם שאר בנינו"; כי ד' בנים היו להם לבד מאלכסנדרון. ויאמר המלך: "חלילה לנו להורגו אך נטיב לו כשאר בנינו." ובעניין נמלט הנער ויגדל הנער[21] עד כי גדל מאד[22].

ויהי היום וילך הנער אלכסנדרון בגן ויראהו מכשף אחד ויאמר לו המכשף: "רואה אני בך שתמלוך בכל העולם כולו ובארץ נכריה תמות ובארץ מצרים תקבר. ועוד תהיה עולה בגדולה ועמקי מצולה תרד ובין כוכבים שים קניך[23] ואל מקום יראי הש' תבוא בחייך." וישמח הנער אלכסנדרוס מאד ויאמר אל המכשף: "אם אמת דברת הרי אני עושה אותך ואת משפחת אביך ואמך חופשים[24] ואתה תהיה לי למשנה." וישתחו המכשף ויתן מתנות גדולות אל הנער למען יהיה לו לאות ולזכרון[25].

ויזקן פוליפוס ויחלה וידלו חוליו אשר מת בו[26]. וישלח לקרוא את כל חרטומי מצרים ואת כל חכמיה[27] וישאל מהם להודיע לו באמת מי ימלוך אחריו. ויענו כולם ויאמרו: "תן לנו זמן עד הבקר ונגידה למלך" ויעש המלך כן. ויהי בבקר ויבואו החרטומים וחכמי המזלות ויאמרו בפה אחד אל המלך:

I Sam. 26:11.   "הלילה לי מה' משלח ידי במשחי ה'."[20]
"The Lord forbid that I should stretch forth mine hand against the Lord's annointed."

Judges 13:24; I Sam. 4:21   "ויגדל הנער"[21]
". . . and the child grew."

Genesis 26:13   "עד כי גדל מאד"[22]
". . . until he had become very great."

Obadiah 4   "ואם בין כ כבים שים קנך."[23]
"Though thou exalt thyself as the eagle, and though thou set thy nest among the stars . . ."

I Samuel 17:25   "ואת בית אביו יעשה חפשי בישראל"[24]
". . . and make his father's house free in Israel.,,

Exodus 13:9,16   "והיה לך לאות על ידך ולזכרון"[25]
"And it shall be for a sign unto thee upon thine hand and for a memorial . . . "

II Kings 13:14   "ואלישע חלה את חליו אשר ימות בו"[26]
"Now Elisha was fallen sick of his sickness whereof he died."

Genesis 41:8   "וישלח ויקרא את כל חרטמי מצרים ואת כל חכמיה"[27]
". . . and he sent and he called for all the magicians of Egypt."

The queen said: "Strangle him' and I shall give you his weight in gold."

The midwife replied: "Far be it from me to harm a king's son for I see in him signs of royalty. He will reign over the entire world and will be dreaded and feared everywhere."[8]

In appearance, the child was covered with hair from his feet to his navel. There was an imprint of a lion between his shoulders and upon his heart the imprint of an eagle. One eye resembled a lion's peering towards the sky and the other eye a cat's peering toward the ground. So it was that Alexander's life was saved. The midwife continued: "Moreover, I foresee that he will die in a strange country."

The queen said to the king: "Tell me how we can kill this bastard so that he does not share in the inheritance together with our other sons"; for they had four other sons in addition to Alexander.

"It is wrong for us to kill him," the king replied. "No, we will be as good to him as to our other sons." Thus, the child escaped death and grew to manhood.

One day, as Alexander was walking in the garden a wizard met him and said: "I foresee that you will rule over the entire world and will die in a strange country and will be buried in Egypt. And furthermore, you will ascend to great heights and descend to great depths. Your fame will be eternal as the stars and, in your lifetime, you will come to the dwelling-place of the Lord." At this, the lad rejoiced greatly and said to the wizard: "If you have spoken the truth, lo, I will make you and your father's and mother's families free and you shall become my viceroy." The wizard bowed and presented Alexander with valuable gifts so that there would be proof of his promise to the wizard.

Philip grew old and suffered from that illness from which he was to die. He summoned all the magicians and wise men of Egypt and besought them to tell him truthfully who would inherit his throne.[9] They answered as one: "Give us time until morning and we shall tell you." The king agreed, and in the morning the magicians and astrologers came

---

[7] A parallel to this incident is found in the old French poem of Alberic de Besançon (early twelfth century).

[8] In the Greek and Latin versions the description of the future greatness of Alexander is given by Philip.

[9] This version stresses that Alexander acted only upon the advice of his mother and advisors. This is not the view of the hero Alexander in other versions.

"זֶה הַנַּעַר אלכסנדרוס ימלוך אחריך ויגדל כסאו מכסא אדונינו המלך ובכל אשר יעשה
יצליח.״²⁸ וירגז המלך מאד ויבך בכי גדול כי רבים בנים היו לו ואין מלוכה לאחד
מהם ואף כי ידע המלך כי אלכסנדרוס לא יצא מחלציו.

ויקרא המלך לכל בניו ויאמר אליהם: ״שמעוני בניי! אתם שמעתם מכל החכמים כי
נגזרה המלוכה לאלכסנדרוס על כן שמעו לעצתי ואל תלחמו עם אלכסנדרוס כי
מאת השם יצא הדבר²⁹ ואתם אל תרגזו ואל יחר אפיכם ואל תפרקו עול אלכסנדרוס
מעל צואריכם פן תהיה לכם למכשול ולפוקה³⁰ כי המלוכה והממשלה ביד מלך מלכי
המלכים והוא נותן מלוכה ומעבירה ובידו / לגדל ולחזק לכל.״³¹ ויהי ככלותו לצות
בניו ויאסוף רגליו³² וימת בשיבה טובה³³ בן תשעים ושלוש שנים ויקברוהו בכבוד
גדול ויעשו בנין גדול ומופלא על קברו.

ויהי אחרי מות פוליפוס ויבקשו בניו להרוג אלכסנדרוס בסם המות ויוגד לאלכסנד־
רוס ויאמר אל אחיו: ״מה חטאתי ומה פשעי³⁴ כי תבקשו להמית אותי ולשפוך דם
נקי? הלא ידעתם שמעתם כי המלוכה ניתנה לי מן השמים ואף כי המלך צוה לכם
לתת לי המלוכה.״ ויהי כאשר שמעו שנודע לו הדבר ויאמרו איש אל אחיו: ״לשוא
אנו טורחים כי כל החרטומי׳ וחכמי המזלות אומרים שהוא ימלוך אחר אבינו אם
נמליך אותו ויטיב לנו כי אחינו ובשרינו הוא³⁵ ואם נקשה עורף כנגדו כאשר
חזקה ידו במלוכה ימית את כולנו.״ ויקראו בני המלוכה לכל השרים וידברו
באזניהם ובאזני החכמים וחכמי המזלות לאמר: ״אתם שמעתם את אשר ציוה
אבינו להמלי׳ את אלכסנדרוס. ולמה זה אתם מתאחרים את הדבר? הלא מאת
השם ניתנה לו המלוכה כאשר אומרים כל החרטומים והחכמים?״ ויענו
השרים ויאמרו אליהם: ״כדברכם כן הוא³⁶ אך יראים היינו להמליך אותו;
ועתה ראה ראינו כי אתם חפצים בו ואנו לא נעכב וחפצים אנו בו.״ ויקבצו
השרים כל עם הארץ וימליכו את אלכסנדרוס ויאמרו: ״יחי המלך! יחי המלך!״³⁷

Psalms 1:3   ²⁸ ״וכל אשר יעשה יצליח״
"... and whatsoever he doeth shall prosper."
Genesis 24:50   ²⁹ ״מה יצא הדבר״
"The thing proceedeth from the lord ..."
I Sam. 25:31   ³⁰ ״ולא תהיה זאת לך לפוקה ולמכשול (לב)״
"That this shall be no grief unto thee, nor offence of heart ..."
I Chron. 29:12   ³¹ ״ובידו לגדל ולחזק ולכל״
"And in thine hand it is to make great, and to give strength unto all."
Genesis 49:33   ³² ״ויאסף רגליו אל המטה״
"... and he gathered up his feet unto the bed ..."
I Chron. 29:28   ³³ ״וימת בשיבה טובה״
"And he died in a good old age."
Genesis 31:36   ³⁴ ״מה פשעי מה חטאתי.״
"What is my trespass? What is my sin?"
Genesis 37:27   ³⁵ ״כי אחינו ובשרינו היא.״
"... for he is our brother and our flesh."
Genesis 44:10;   ³⁶ ״כדברכם כן הוא.״
Joshua 2:21
"Now let it be according unto your words."
I Sam. 10:24; I Kings 1:25;   ³⁷ ״יחי המלך! יחי המלך!״
I Kings 1:34, 39
"God save the King!"

to him and said. "Young Alexander will inherit your throne, and his reign will be greater than yours, our lord king, and he will be successful in all that he undertakes." At this, the king grew very angry and wept loudly, for he had many sons, none of whom was destined to reign and he knew that Alexander had not come from his loins.

The king summoned all his sons[10] to him and said to them: "Listen my sons! You have heard from the wise men that it is decreed that Alexander shall inherit the kingdom. Since God so decrees it, I advise you not to wage war against Alexander nor give way to depression. Do not remove Alexander's yoke from your neck lest he become your ruination, for the kingdom and the dominion belong to the King of Kings and it is He alone who grants and takes away kingdoms and it is in His hands / to elevate and strengthen all." After he had exhorted his sons he f. 266[b] pulled his feet into the bed and died at the venerable age of ninety-three. He was buried with great honor, and a large, magnificent mausoleum was erected over his grave.

After Philip's death, his sons sought to kill Alexander with deadly poison. Alexander was warned of this and he said to his brothers: "What is my sin and my transgression that you seek to kill me and shed innocent blood? Surely, you are aware that heaven granted me the kingdom and even the king commanded you to give me the kingdom." When they realized that he was aware of their intention they said to each other: "Our efforts are in vain, for all the magicians and astrologers state that he shall reign after our father. If we crown him he will be good to us for he is our brother and of our flesh, but if we resist him he will slay us all as soon as the kingdom is in his hands." The king's sons then summoned all the princes and in the presence of the wise men and astrologers they addressed them thus:

"You know that our father commanded that Alexander be crowned. Why do you delay? Was not the kingdom given to him by God, as the magicians and wise men have said?"

The ministers replied: "What you have said is true, but we were afraid to crown him. Now that we know your wishes we shall delay no longer. We, too, wish him for our king." So the ministers assembled

---

[10] This episode is close to the Biblical story of Joseph and his brothers in Genesis 50:15–21. In MS. Bodl. Heb. d. 11, there is no mention of the campaigns and conquests of Alexander until after the death of Philip.

ויעש לו המלך אלכסנדרוס רכב ופרשים[38] ויהי מצליח בכל דרכיו. ויאמר המלך אל
אמו: "אם ייטב בעינייך אבנה היכל חדש לדיגלנייא אלוה שלנו." ותאמר לו אמו:
"אל יעלה על לבבך לבזבז את אוצרותיך אך שמע בקולי והעבר קול בכל מדינות
מלכותיך כל איש מבן שלושים שנה ומעלה שיבא אליך וילך עמך להלחם ולכבוש
כל הממלכות תחתיך.

ואתה תאזור מותניך[39] ותהיה לבן חיל והלחם מלחמות בבחרותיך וייטב לבך בזק־
נותיך."[40] וישמע המלך אלכסנדרוס את דברי אמו וייטב בעיניו ויעשה ככל אשר
אמרה לו והוא לא ידע כי תואנה היא מבקשת עליו[41] להפילו ביד אויביו כי הייתה
מתכוונת לתת המלוכה לבנה הגדול אשר ילדה מפוליפוס המלך. ויקבוץ המלך
אלכסנדרוס את השרים ויועציו ותהי עצתם כעצת המלכה כי היא הסיתם בדברים.
וישלח המלך אלכסנדרוס ויקבוץ את כל חילו ויעשו לו רכב ברזל הרבה מאד. ויצא
בראש החיל ויקח דגלו בידו ויצאו כולם אחריו.

ויבאו ביער אחד גדול וימצא שם אחו יפה ובתוך האחו באר יפה. ויחן שם אלכסנדרוס
עם כל חילו. וילך אלכסנדרוס אנה ואנה וירא הוא לבדו נס רוכב על סוס קטן
ומכוסה היה הסוס במעיל ומשובצים בו אבנים טובות ומרגלית ואוקיפו של אבן
טובה והפרומיא של זהב. ויהי כראות אלכס' הננס וירץ אלכסנדרוס לקראתו ויאמר
לו: "מי אתה או מה מעשיך או מאין תבא אשר אתה רוכב כן לבדיך ומטוכסט ככה?
והידעתה כי יש פריצים בעמי אשר הם חומדים ממון?" ויען הננס ויאמר: "שמי
אנטלוניא ואני מלך ורבים הם אשר רוכבים עמי מאשר רוכבים עמך ואין אנו
מתראים משום אדם/ואנו מוליכים כלה לבית חמיה." אמר לו אלכסנדרוס: "והלא
איני רואה שום אדם כי אם אותך." אמר לו הננס: "כל אחד ואחד מוליך אבן
תעלומה בידו וכל מי שיש לו אחד אין שום בריה יכול לראותו ולכבודך הראיתיך[42]
כדי להזהירך." ונתן לו

I Kings 1:5
"ויעשו לו רכב ופרשים".
"...and he prepared him chariots and horsemen..."

Jeremiah 1:17
"ואתה תאזור מותניך".
"Thou therefore gird up thy loins..."

Ecclesiastes 11:9
"שמח בחור בילדותיך ויביטך לבך בימי בחרותיך".
"Rejoice, O young man, in thy youth; And let thy heart cheer thee in the days of thy
youth..."

Judges 14:4
"כי תואנה הוא מבקש מפלשתים".
"...that he sought an occasion against the Philistines..."

Deuteronomy 34:4
"הראיתיך בעיניך".
"I have caused thee to see it with thine eyes..."

f.267ᵃ

32

all the people of the land and crowned Alexander exclaiming: "Long live the king!"

King Alexander ordered prepared chariots and horsemen and he was successful in everything. The king then said to his mother: "If it please you, I will build a new temple to Digonia, our god." "Do not waste your treasures but listen to my advice," she said. "Issue a decree throughout all the provinces of your kindgom declaring that every man from the age of thirty years and up should come to you and join you in battle so that you may bring all kingdoms under your rule. As far as you yourself are concerned, gird your loins, become a warrior and wage battles in your youth so that you may prosper in your old age."

King Alexander heeded his mother's advice, for it appealed to him. He did all that she advised without realizing that she was seeking to trap him and cause his downfall at the hands of his enemies, for she intended to give the kingdom to the eldest son whom she had borne to King Philip. When the king consulted the princes and his advisors he received the same counsel as the queen's, for she had already influenced them. Accordingly, King Alexander assembled his army and prepared many iron chariots. He set out with his banner borne aloft in his hands, at the head of his troops.

Entering a vast forest, they came upon a beautiful clearing with a lovely fountain in it and camped there. As Alexander was walking about, he alone noticed a dwarf riding on a pony. Its caparison was studded with precious stones and pearls, and its saddle contained precious stones and its stirrups were made of gold. Seeing the dwarf, Alexander ran towards him and said:

"Who are you? What do you do? Where do you come from riding alone, so richly bedecked? Don't you know that there are desperate men among my company who covet riches?".

He answered: "I am King Antalonia. Many more ride with me than with you, and we are not afraid of anyone. / We are escorting a bride to   f. 267a her parents-in-law."

Alexander said: "But I see no one but you."[11]

---

11 Gaster notes that this tale is reminiscent of the popular legends of fairies and pixies and the cap of invisibility well-known in German medieval romance. He gives the following references: Grimm, *Deutsche Mythologie*, chap. xvii; Plato, *Republic*, ii; they cite the legend of gyres and the ring that makes one invisible. See M. Gaster, "An Old Hebrew Romance of Alexander," op. cit., p. 821.

אבן תעלומה מיד. ויאמר לו אלכסנדרוס: "במטו מנך הזהירני.". ויאמר לו: "יש לך
יועצים ומשרתים המבקשים את נפשיך.[43]", ויאמר לו אלכסנ': "מי הם?", ויאמר
המלך אנטלוניא: "לא אחד ולא שנים אך למחר שב אתה על הבאר שבאחו ואני
אשב אצלך על הבאר ואבן תעלומה בידי. ואתה אדוני המלך קרא לכל עבדיך ומשר-
תיך ולכל מי שאכנו על צוארו הוא מן המשרתים המבקשים את נפשך ולאחר כן
תעשה כחכמתך.[44]" ויאמר אלכסנ': "אשריך אנטלוניא! איש טוב אתה וטוב תבשר.[45]
בא למחר. האמנם לא אוכל כבדיך![46]" ויאמר לו הננס: "כדבריך כן אעשה ויאמר לו
הננס: "תן לי רשות לרכוב" ויאמר לו: "רכוב והשם יצליח דרכיך.[47]" וירכוב הננס
עם עמו.

וישכם אלכסנ' בבקר ויפן כה וכה[48] אם הננס שלו ויראאהו והנה יושב על האבן על הבאר
כדבריו, וישמח אלכסנ' מאד ויחבקהו וינשק לו.[49] ויהי בעת האוכל ויבא המשרת לפניו
ויכהו הננס אשר הקול נשמע בכל. ויאמר לו המשרת: "אדוני המלך על מה הכיתה
את עבדך?[50] מה פשעי ומה חטאתי?[51]" ויאמר לו המלך: "לא הכיתיך חלילה לי מלה-
כותך. ההסכן הסכנתי[52] להכות את עבדיי?" והנה משרת אחר בא וישתחו לפני המלך
ויכהו הננס על הצואר ויפול מלא קומתו ארצה. ויאמר העבד אל המלך: "על מה
הכית את עבדך?" ויאמר לו המלך: "לא הכיתיך." ויאמר לאשר עמד אצלו: "רשע:
למה הכיתני?[53]" וכך עברו כמה וכמה שהכם הננס ותהי הריגה גדולה על השדה
וכל אשר בקשו לשלח יד במלך[54] הכם הננס. ולא דבר המלך מאומה ביום ההוא.
אך נתן טביעת עין במוכים.

Exodus 4:19;
Jeremiah 11:21
"...which sought thy life."   43 "המבקשים את נפשיך."

I Kings 2:6
"Do, therefore, according to thy wisdom."   44 "ועשית כחכמתך."

See n. 14 .   45

Numbers 22:37
"...am I not able indeed to promote thee to honor!"   46 "האמנם לא אוכל כבדיך."

Genesis 24:21
"...to know whether the Lord had made his journey prosperous or not."   47 "ההצליח ה' דרכו (אם לא)."

Exodus 2:12
"And he looked this way and that way."   48 "ויפן כה וכה."

Genesis 29:13
"...and he embraced him and he kissed him..."   49 "ויחבקהו ונשק לו."

Numbers 22:32
"...wherefore hast thou smitten thine ass..."   50 "על מה הכית את אתנך."

See n. 34.   51

Numbers 22:30
"Was I ever wont to do so unto thee?"   52 "ההסכן הסכנתי לעשות לך כה."

Exodus 2:13
"...and he said to him that did the wrong,
Wherefore smitest thou thy fellows?"   53 "ויאמר לרשע למה תכה רעך."

Esther 6:2
"...who had sought to lay hands on the King Ahasuerus."   54 אשר בקשו לשלוח יד במלך אחשורוש."

The dwarf said: "Each and every one of us holds in his hand a stone that makes him invisible. Anyone holding this stone cannot be seen by another, but I have appeared to you in order to warn you." And he immediately gave Alexander a stone.

Alexander said: "I beg of you, give me the warning."

"You have advisors and servants who seek to kill you, " said the dwarf.

Alexander asked: "Who are they?"

King Antalonia replied: "There are many. Tomorrow, my lord king, sit by the fountain in the meadow, and I shall join you there with this stone in my hand. Then summon all your slaves and servants. I shall strike on the neck all of them that seek to kill you. Then you may do as you see fit."

Alexander said: "Bless you, Antalonia. You are a good man, and you bring good tidings. Come tomorrow. I cannot possibly repay you for this."

The dwarf replied: "I will do as you wish. Permit me to ride on."

"Ride on and may the Almighty grant you success in your endeavors," the king replied. The dwarf rode on with his people.

Upon arising the next day, Alexander looked about for the dwarf and noticed him sitting by the fountain, as he had promised. Alexander rejoiced greatly, and he embraced and kissed him. When a servant appeared before him at mealtime, the dwarf struck him so hard that the sound resounded through the camp. The servant said to him: "My lord king, why did you strike your servant? How have I sinned or transgressed? "Far be it from me to hit you," replied the king. "Have I ever resorted to striking my servants?" At this moment another servant appeared and bowed before the king. The dwarf struck him on his neck and he fell to the ground. He said to the king: "Why did you strike your servant?" The king replied: "I did not strike you." The servant turned to the one standing beside him saying: "O, wicked one! Why did you strike me?" In a like manner the dwarf struck many. There were a great many lying as if dead[12] on the field, for all those who sought to harm the king were struck down by the dwarf.

The king remained silent, carefully noting those who were struck. On the following day, after much deliberation he deposed those princes who had been struck and appointed others in their stead. Addressing

12 Literally, the translation reads: "There were a great many dead lying on the field..."

ויהי ממחרת ויועץ המלך בלבו ויחלל את שריו המוכים וישם אחרים תחתם. ויאמר
להם: "שמעוני שריי ועבדיי! הנה ארץ מצרים ארצי עומד כצאן אשר אין להם רועה[55]
ואין מי עצר בהם להצילם מאויבם. לכו וחזרו למצרים והביאו זאת העטרה לקניטור
אחי הגדול וקחו עמכם עבדים." ויתן להם לאכסנ׳ העבדי׳ אשר הכה מלך אנטלוניא.
וכל העם אשר נשארו אצל אלכסנ׳ אהבו המלך כגופם וגם המלך אהבם. וישמח
המלך ביום ההוא שמחה ויחדש האמרכולים והמשרתים ותהיי שמחה גדולה על הבאר
וינוחו שם עשרה ימים.

ויהי אחרי כן ויסע המלך וכל חילו ויבואו ביער גדול וימצא שם אנשים גוצים ובעלי
שער וקטנים. היו עד מאד וישחיתו רבים מעמו. ויצו המלך לירות אותם בחיצים
ויקבלו החצים בידם ולא חששו ויצו המלך להדליק היער עליהם וי׳ וישרפם ביער.
ויהי כאשר יצא מן היער בא לפני הר גדול וגבוה מאד ועליו בניין גדול ומפואר.
ויאמר המלך: "מי ילך עמי לעלות על ההר?" ויצאו מאתם איש מתוך חילו ויאמרו
לו: "עלה נעלה עמך."[56] ויעלו אל ראש ההר וימצאו שם שער גדול ורוחב מאד לפני
השער היה יושב זקן אחד. וכראות הזקן/ את המלך רץ לקראתו לחבק לו ולנשק לו
ויירוצו הגבורים כנגד הזקן. ויתפשו אותו ולא הניחוהו ליגע אל המלך. ויען הזקן
ויאמר להם: "למה זה שאינכם מניחים אותי לחבק ולנשק את אדוני המלך אלכסנ-
דרוס?" ויאמרו הגיבורים אל הזקן: "מי הגיד לך אשר שמו אלכסנדרוס?" ויען
הזקן ויאמר להם: "כי שמו וצורתו חקוק בהיכלי ואני ישבתי בהר זה הרבה ימים
ושנים לשמור לו כל המבצר הזה." ויענו הגבורים ויאמרו אל הזקן מה כח ומה
גבורתך אשר אתה לבדך יושב הנה? הלא אנו מתי מספר תפשנוך ולא הנחנוך ליגע
אל המלך." ויחר אף הזקן בגבורים ויאמר להם: "וכי עלה על רוחכם שאתם נצחתם
אותי כי לולא מורא מלך ת עלי לא הייתי חושש עליכם כלום כי נצטויתי ככה לבלתי
עשות דבר כנגד המלך."

Numbers 27:17
I Kings 22:17; II Chronicles 17:16
". . . as sheep which have no shepherd . . ."

[55] "כצאן אשר אין להם רועה."

Numbers 13:30
'Let us go up at once and possess it."

[56] "עלה נעלה וירשנו."

f. 267[b]

them he said: "Listen to me, my princes and my servants. Egypt, my country, stands like a flock without a shepherd. There is no one to guide it and save it from its enemies. Go, return to Egypt and bring this crown to my eldest brother, Quanitor, and take servants along with you." Alexander gave them those servants whom King Antalonia struck. The servants who remained with Alexander loved him as they loved themselves, and the king loved them, too. That day he rejoiced and appointed new princes and servants. There was a great rejoicing at the fountain and they remained there ten days.

After this, the king and his army set forth and came to a large forest. They encountered many fat, hairy pygmies who attacked and killed many of Alexander's men. At first, the king ordered them shot with arrows, but when they fearlessly stopped them with their hands, he ordered the forest set on fire and had them burnt to death.

Leaving the forest, he arrived at a very high mountain upon which stood a large and magnificent building. The king asked: "Who will climb the mountain with me?" In response two hundred men volunteered saying: "We shall climb the mountain with you." They climbed to the top of the mountain where they found a large, wide gate before which sat an old man. When the old man saw the king / he ran towards him f. 267ᵇ to embrace and kiss him, but the warriors intercepted and seized him and prevented him from reaching the king.

Addressing them, the old man said: "Why do you prevent me from embracing and kissing my lord, King Alexander?"

The warriors asked the old man: "Who told you that he is called Alexander?"

The old man replied: "His name and image are engraved in my temple, and I have been sitting on this mountain for many years and guarding this entire fortress for him."

Then the warriors asked: "What is the source of your strength and prowess that you can remain here alone? Behold, it took only a few of us to seize you and prevent you from approaching the king."

The old man retorted angrily: "Do you really believe that you overcame me? Were it not that I respect royalty, and was ordered to desist from doing anything against the king, I would not have paid attention to you at all."

At this, the warriors said to him: "If it please you, reveal to us the source of your strength."

37

ויאמרו הגיבורי' אל הזקן: "אם נא מצאנו חן בעיניך הראינו נא את כחך."[57] ויאמר להם: "אם המלך יתן לי רשות אודיעכם את כחי וגבורתי." ויאמר לו המלך: "הרשות נתון לך."[58] ויהי כשמוע הזקן כן ויצעק צעקה גדולה[59] עד אשר לא היה כח בגבורים לעמוד ויפלו כולם על פניהם[60] ואף המלך נפל על פניו. ויאמר המלך אל הזקן: "רב לך אל תוסף[61] כי אין בי ובגבוריי כח לעמוד מפני כח קולך." ויען הזקן ויאמר אל המלך: "אם אתה חפץ אודיעך עוד את גבורתי בדבר אחד." ויאמר: "לא" ויאמר הזקן אל המלך: "בא עמי ואנשיך העומדים לפניך ואראך את יופי המבצר הזה ואת כל בניינו מקטן ועד גדול."[62] כי מופלא הוא ונחמד למראה." ויאמר המלך אל הזקן: "אם ייטב בעיניך ירד נא את אחד מגבורי ויקרא לאחד מסופריי ויכתוב כל אשר יראה בהר הזה." וירד אחד מן הגבורים מן ההר ויביא את מנחם היהודי ראש סופרי המלך. וילך המלך עם הזקן בתוך המבצר וילכו אחריו גבוריו ומנחם ראש הסופרים. ויבוא המלך וגבוריו בחדר אחד של זכוכית אדומה גבוה ורחבה ובה הי' תשעים וחמש חלונות ובתוך כל חלון וחלון היו כל מיני עופות טמאים וטהורים וכל אחד ואחד מצפצף בקולו ונשמע קולם למרחוק. ובחלון העליון היה כושי אחד זקן והוא מניף עליהם בסודר ולא ענו עוד.

ויצא המלך וגבוריו מחדר ההוא ויבואו בחדת אחר בנוי מזכוכית ירוקה ובה שוכ־ נים כל מיני חיות טהורות וטמאות ובתוכם חיה משונה. וזאת דמות החיה: מכף רגלה ועד קדקדה[63] לה היה בה בה שער אך חלקה מכף רגלה ועד קדקדה. ורגליה דומים לרגלי אריה ופניה כפני עוף ועיניה גדולות ורחובות כמאתים וגובה החיה כחמש אמות וזנב החיה ירוק מאוד ואורך כשלש אמות, ושיניה ארוכים כאמה וחצי.

Exodus 33:18   "הראיני נא את כבדך." [57]
"I beseech thee, show me thy glory."

Esther 3:11   "הכסף נתון לך." [58]
"The silver is given to thee."

Genesis 27:34   "ויצעק צעקה גדולה." [59]
"... he cried out with a great and exceeding bitter cry ..."

Leviticus 9:24   "ויפלו על פניהם." [60]
"... and fell on their faces."
See also Numbers 17:22

Deuteronomy 3:26   "רב לך אל תוסף." [61]
"Let it suffice thee" (speak no more unto me of this matter).

I Samuel 5:9   "מקטן ועד גדול." [62]
"Both small and great ..."
See also: Jeremiah 8:10.

Deuteronomy 28:35;II Samuel 14:25 Job 2:7.   "מכף רגל ועד קדקדה." [63]
"... from the soul of thy foot unto the top of thy head."

He answered: "With the king's permission, I shall acquaint you with the source of my strength and prowess."

The king said: "I grant you permission."

Hearing this, the old man screamed so loudly that the warriors had no strength to withstand it and all of them, including the king, fell flat on their faces.

Then the king said to the old man: "Stop! Do not continue, for neither my warriors nor I have the strength to withstand the power of your voice."

"If you wish," the old man replied, "I will demonstrate my strength to you in a different way." But Alexander answered: "No!" The old man then said to the king: "Come with me, and let your men who stand before you come and I will show you the beauty of this fortress, and all its buildings, large and small, for it is a wondrous and pleasant sight to behold."

The king answered: "If it please you, one of my warriors will descend the mountain and bring back a scribe to record all that we see here." One of the warriors went down the mountain and brought back Menachem, the Jew,[13] chief of the king's secretaries. The king entered the fortress accompanied by the old man and followed by his warriors and Menachem, chief of the secretaries. They entered a high spacious room of red glass with ninety-five windows. On each window were perched all kinds of birds, clean and unclean,[14] and each of them chirped. Their sounds carried far and wide. In the uppermost window an old dark man sat waving his scarf at them, thus silencing them.

Leaving that room, the king and his men entered another chamber built of green glass in which dwelt all kinds of creatures, clean and unclean, and among them a strange creature which was smooth and hairless from the sole of its foot to the top of its head. Its legs resembled a lion's, its face a bird's, and its eyes were large and wide as two cubits. It was about five cubits tall. It had a green tail about three cubits long and

[13] The Jewish scribe is apparently similar to Simon, notary, as well as Clerc Symon in other Western versions of the Alexander stories. There is speculation that Simon is the same as Eumenes, the real secretary of Alexander. Menahem is the Hebrew form of this known Alexander scribe, Eumenes.

P. Meyer, *Alexandre le Grand*, op. cit., II, 395, notes that Simon may be connected with "Salomon didascalus Judaeorum" of the Pavia manuscript.

[14] Leviticus 11 and Deuteronomy 14 give the laws pertaining to clean and unclean animals.

ויחמה המלך מווד. ויוומר לו חזקן. "אל' ותומה כ' עוז אראך פלא גדול מזה."
הזקן ויקח עשב אחד ויתן בפי החיה ויצא ממנה חיה משונה והיא מלאה שער
לבן וקולה כקול בני אדם ושיניה ירוקים. ויאמר הזקן: "שער של חיה זאת טוב הוא
מאד לנצחון כי כל הנושא עליו במלחמה ינצח ואויביו יפלו לפניו חללי'." וילעג המלך
בדבריו ויהי כמצחק בעיניו 64 ויחר אף הזקן ויאמר אל המלך: "איך נשאך לבך להיות
לועג על דברי? ועתה ידוע תדע כי מרה יהיה לך באחרונה. 65 וירא המלך רוגז אפו
וידבר אליו דברים רכים למען ינוח חמת הזקן. ויאמר/לו: "אם נראה בעיניך שדברתי
כנגדך דבר אשר לא יישר בעיניך מחול על כבודך וחלוק כבוד למלכות." ויען הזקן
ויאמר אל המלך: "גם לדבר הזה שמעתיך רק אל תוסיף לדבר כדברים האלה."
ויאמר המלך אל הזקן: "אם נא מצאתי חן בעיניך הראיני נא את יופי המבצר הזה."
ויאמר לו הזקן: "בא עמי ואראך פלא גדול ומופלא." וילך המלך עם הזקן ויבואו
בחדר יפה מאד בנוי מאבני שיש אדומים ובו כל מיני בשמים. ויכנס הריח בחוטם
המלך ויפלא מאד מאד ויהי לו כח וגבורה כפולאה מבראשונה.

וישא המלך את עיניו וירא אבן שיש יפה ובו היה מונח כלי זכוכית אדומה. ויאמר לו
המלך: "מה זאת?" ויאמר לו הזקן: "זהו שמן בלסמון אשר הובא מיריחו עיר התמ־
רים." ויסף המלך וישא את עיניו וירא אבן שיש ירוקה כעין קברת מלכים וישאל
אל הזקן מה זאת. ויאמר לו: "באבן הזאת נקבר אלטינוס המלך והוא נמשך בשמן
אפרסמון ועדיין גופו קיים." ויאמר לו המלך: "הידעת כמה שנים יש שנקבר בו?"
ויאמר הזקן: "המתן מעט ואקרא את המכתב אשר חקוק על האבן." ויקרא הזקן את
המכתב וימצא מאתים ושמונים וחמש שנים.

Genesis 19:14   "ויהי כמצחק בעיני חתניו." 64
"But he seemed as one that mocked unto his sons-in-law."

II Samuel 2:26   "כי מרה תהיה באחרונה." 65
"Knowest thou not that it will be bitterness in the latter end?"

40

teeth about one and a half cubits long. The king was astonished at the sight of it, but the old man said to him: "Do not be amazed for I shall show you a wonder even greater than this." He then took an herb and placed it in the beast's mouth, and a strange beast emerged from it covered with white hair. Its voice was human and its teeth were green. The old man said: "Whoever carries this beast's hair into war will be victorious and his enemies will fall before him wounded." The king scoffed in ridicule at these words whereupon the old man became angry and said to the king: "How dare you ridicule my words? Now you may well know that you will come to a bitter end."

When the king saw the anger of the old man, he spoke kind words to calm him: / "If I offended you by my words please pardon me and honor the king."   f. 268ª

At this, the old man said to him: "I grant you this request but do not utter such words again."

Then the king said to him: "If I found favor in your eyes please show me the beauty of this fortress."

"Come with me," replied the old man, "and I shall show you a great and wondrous thing."

The king accompanied the old man and they entered a beautiful room of red marble, and in it were all kinds of spices. He marveled greatly as the fragrance entered his nostrils and felt as if his strength and prowess were increased twofold.

Gazing about he saw a beautiful marble stone on which was a red vessel of glass. The king said to him: "What is this?"

The old man replied: "This is balsam from Jericho, the city of palms."[15] The king then noticed a green marble sarcophagus resembling a royal sepulchre and asked the old man what it was. "King Altinos[16] is buried here. He was annointed with balsam; his body is preserved from decay," the old man told him.

"Do you know how many years have elapsed since he was buried here?" asked King Alexander.

---

[15] Jericho is mentioned in Deuteronomy 34:3 as famous for balsam. Note: Josephus, *The Jewish Antiquities*, Loeb ed., trans. H. St. J. Thackeray and R. Marcus (London: 1930–43), chap. XIV.4.1, chap. XV.4.2 and *The Jewish Wars*, Loeb ed., trans. H. St. J. Thackeray (London: 1927), chap. IV.8.3.

[16] A similar name, Latinus or Lotinus appears in *Yalkut Shimoni, Vayishlach*, chap 140.

ויומר חמלך אל וותקן: אם נא מצאתי חן בעיניך הראיני נא את הגוף את המלך אל-
טינוס וראה כי האמת אתך את אשר אמרת שגופו קיים עדיין." ויען הזקן ויאמר
אל המלך: "את שאילתך אמלא אך השמר בנשפך שלא תיגע בגופו אם באת הלילה
הזאת אל אשה." ויאמר לו המלך: "לא באתי אל אשה בלילה הזאת," ויכזב לו.
ויאמר לו הזקן: "אמור לאנשיך שלא יגעו אל גוף המלך אם לא נטהרו ממשכבי
אשה." ויאמר להם המלך: "הנוגע בבשר המלך מות יומת. [66] ויקרב הזקן ויגל את
האבן העליון מעל השייש ויסר המכסה מעל המת. ויראו המלך וגבוריו את המת
ויתמהו האנשים איש אל רעהו. ויאמר המלך אל הזקן: "האגע בבשר המת?" ויאמ'
הזקן: "לא!" ועוד הדבר בפי המלך ויקרב פתאום ויגע אל המת ויפול המלך לאחוריו
ויזע זיע גדול, ומשונה במראיתו. ויראו הגבורים ויצעקו זעקה גדולה ומרה ויפלו
כולם לפני הזקן וישתחוו לו אפים ארצה ויאמרו לו: "בי אדוני! [67] מה נעשה מאדונינו
המלך?"

ויאמר הזקן: "הלא אמרתי לכם אל תגעו בבשר המת כי מות תמותון. [68] ויוסיפו
הגבורים ויבכו בכי גדול ויבקשו שנית את פני הזקן ויאמר להם: "לולי נשאתי
פניכם לא נטפלתי במלככם. ועתה התיצבו וראו מה אעשה לו. [69] ויענו כולם פה
אחד ויאמרו: "הננו ועשינו כאשר אדונינו מצוה." ויאמר הזקן: "אל תיראו כי
יש תקוה [70] לאחרית המלך." ויקח הזקן קרן שחור מקרן התיש ויביא גחלת לוחשה
ויתן בקרן וישם על פדחת המלך אלכסנדרוס. ויעמוד המלך על עומדו כבראשונה
ויאלם ולא היה בו יכולת להוציא דבר מפיו. ויראו גבוריו ויבכו ותהפך שמחתם
לקינה. ויאמר להם הזקן: "אל תיראו!" ויקח הזקן עשב אחד וישם באוזן שמאלית
המלך ויפתח את פיו וידבר לגבוריו וישמחו כולם שמחה גדולה ויאמר הזקן אל המלך:
"איך לא יראתה [71] ליגע בגוף המת ולא שמעת אלי ותמר את פי?

Exodus 19:12 — "הנוגע בהר מות יומת."
"Whosoever toucheth the mount shall be surely put to death."

I Samuel 1:26 — "בי אדוני."
"O, my lord . . ."

Genesis 3:4 — "לא מות תמותון."
"Ye shall not surely die."

Exodus 14:13 — "התיצבו וראו את ישועת ה' אשר יעשה לכם (היום)."
" . . . stand still, and see the salvation of the Lord, which he will show you today."

Proverbs 19:18 — "כי יש תקוה."
" . . . while there is hope . . ."
See also: Jeremiah 31:17.

II Samuel 1:14 — "איך לא יראת לשלוח ידך."
"How wast thou not afraid to stretch forth thine hand . . ."

"Wait a moment and I will read the inscription engraved on the sepulchre," replied the old man. "The inscription reads two hundred and eighty-five years." Then the king said to the old man: "If it please you, show me the body of King Altinos so that I may see for myself that you are right in saying that it has been preserved from decay."

"I shall grant your request," said the old man to the king, "but take care not to touch the corpse if you have been with a woman this night."

"I was not with a woman this night," replied the king, but he lied.

The old man said to him: "Instruct your men not to touch the king's corpse if they have lain with a woman and have not cleansed themselves afterwards."

The king declared: "He who touches the king's flesh shall die."

The old man drew near the marble sarcophagus and lifted the top slab and removed the covering from the corpse. The king and his warriors gazed upon the corpse and turned to each other in astonishment. The king asked the old man whether he could touch the dead man's flesh and the answer was "No!" No sooner had the king spoken than he suddenly approached the coprse and touching it fell backwards in a great sweat and a peculiar look came over him. When the warriors saw this, they cried out and, kneeling before the old man, their faces to the ground exclaimed:

"May it please our lord, what has happened to our master, the king?"

The old man replied: "I warned you not to touch the dead man's flesh for you would die."

The warriors continued to weep and again implored the old man, who said: "It is only as a favor to you that I shall bother with your king. Now stand up and witness what I will do for him."

They all said: "We shall do exactly as our master commands."

The old man said: "Do not worry for there is still hope for the king's future." The old man then took a black ram's horn and inserting a glowing coal in it placed it on King Alexander's forehead. The king again rose to his feet but was dumb and unable to speak. At this his warriors wept and their joy turned to lamentation.

"Do not be afraid," said the old man. He took some grass and inserted it in the left ear of the king who then opened his mouth and spoke to his warriors, and they rejoiced greatly. Then the old man said to the king: "How dared you touch the dead body? You disregarded and dis-

נכשל[ו] בחי! ו[ל]א צויין ל[אמו] : ״השמו בנפשך[ם]⁷² מליגע בו.״ ויאמר לו המלך: ״מה אומר לך? פי כסיל מחיתה לו.״⁷³

ויאמר המלך אל הזקן: ״בי אדוני! תמדוד לי מדת המת.״ וימצא את מדתו/תשעים אמות ויתמה המלך מאוד וכל גבוריו ויאמר המלך אל הזקן: ״שים נא את המכסה על המת,״ ויעש הזקן כן.

ויהי אחרי זאת ויאמר הזקן אל המלך: ״בא עמי בחדר אחר ואראה אותך את מחמד עיניך.״ וילך המלך עם הזקן ויבואו שניהם בחדר אחד וימצאו שמה נערה יפה מאוד. ורימת לב המלך בקרבו על הנערה ותהפך מראיתו לכמה מראות. ויאמר לו הזקן: ״מה לך כי נבהלת?״ ויאמר המלך: ״לא אכחד ממך⁷⁴ כי נשבר לבי בקרבי⁷⁵ על יופי הנערה הזאת.״ ויאמר לו הזקן: ״השבע לי שלא תשגנה לפילגש ואני אתננה לך לאשה.״ וישמח המלך וישבע לו שלש שבועות. ויאמר: ״לך לדרכך וקח אותה ותהי לך לאשה כאשר נשבעת.״ ויקרב המלך אל הנערה ויחזק בידה ויביאה אל אהלו. ויאמר אל עבדיו וגבוריו: ״קחו את אשתי הראשונה והוליכוה ארץ מצרים עד שובי שלום.״ ויקחוה ויביאוה ארץ מצרים ויגידו לאמו את כל הקורות אותו לאמר. ותשמח המלכה ותאמר אל לבה: ״ולמה אשנא את בני אשר יצא ממעי?⁷⁶ מה לי מאישי המלך מה לי מאיש אחר הלא בני הוא ואכבדה בו.״ ותשלח המלכה סוס אחד אל בנה ושמו בוספל והוא קל לרוץ וחזק ואין כמוהו בכל ארץ מצרים. ויביאו את הסוס אל המלך וישמח מאד וינסה הסוס וימצא בו כל תאות לבו. אז אמר המלך לעשות משתה גדול לכל שריו ועבדיו⁷⁷ וישמחו המלך וכל גבוריו ויקח המלך את הנערה לאשה ויאהביה. ויתן לו הזקן אבן יקרה לרוב מאוד, ויברך את המלך ויוצי׳ כלי חמדה ויתן אל המלך ויצא וכל חילו מן המגדל ההוא.

---

⁷² ״השמר בנפשכם.״

"Take good heed unto yourselves . . ."
See: Deuteronomy 4:9, 15; Joshua 23:11; Jeremiah 17:21.

⁷³ ״פי כסיל מחיתה לו.״

Proverbs 18:7
"A fool's mouth is his destruction . . ."

⁷⁴ ״לא נכחד ממני.״

Genesis 47:18
"We will not hide it from my lord . . ."

⁷⁵ ״נשבר לבי בקרבי.״

Jeremiah 23:9
"Mine heart within me is broken . . ."

⁷⁶ ״הנה בני אשר יצאה ממעי.״

II Samuel 17:11
"Behold, my son which came forth from my bowels . . ."

⁷⁷ ״עשה משתה לכל שריו ועבדיו.״

Esther 1:3
" . . he made a feast unto all his princes . . ."

obeyed my orders. Thus you stumbled, for didn't I command you: 'Be careful not to touch it'?"

"What can I say to you?" answered the king: 'A fool's mouth is his destruction.'"[17] The king continued: "If it please you, my lord, measure the length of this corpse." It measured / ninety cubits which surprised   f. 268ᵇ the king and his warriors. "Cover the corpse again," the king requested of the old man, and he did so.

Then the old man said to the king: "Come with me into another chamber and I will show you a sight to delight your eyes." The king accompanied the old man and they entered a chamber where they found a most beautiful maiden. The king's heart pined at the sight of her and his face changed color.

"What has frightened you?" asked the old man.

The king replied: "I will not conceal from you the fact that I long for this beautiful maiden."

"Swear to me," said the old man "that you will not make her your concubine, and I shall give her to you as a wife."

The king rejoiced and swore a triple oath. "Go and take her for your wife, as you have sworn," said the old man. The king approached the maiden and taking her by the hand brought her into his tent. Then he said to his servants and warriors: "Take my first wife and bring her to the land of Egypt until I return in peace." They took her to Egypt and told his mother of all that had happened to him. The queen rejoiced saying to herself: "Why should I hate my son who came forth from my womb? It does not matter to me whether he is from my husband, the king, or from another man. He is my son and through him I shall be honored." The queen sent a horse called Busifal to her son. It was very swift and strong and none could match it in all Egypt. When the horse was brought to the king he rejoiced greatly. He tested it and found it fulfilled his greatest expectations. Then the king prepared a banquet for his ministers and servants and they all rejoiced. The king took the maiden as a wife and loved her. The old man presented the king with many precious stones, and other beautiful gifts, and blessed him. Then the king and his army departed from that fortress.

Afterwards they passed through the land of Quartigonia,[18] whose

---

[17] Proverbs 18:7.

[18] Possibly Carthage, known as a city of women. "Carta" means city, a word of

ויעבור ארץ קרטיגוניא והיא כמהלך שלשים יום ובכל הארץ ההיא אין אשה על
הארץ כי אם תחת הקרקע.

וישאל להם המלך לשלום ויביאו לו מאה אלף ככר זהב ואבן יקרה לרוב מאד.
ויביאו לפניו דג גדול ומשונה וזה דמות הדג קשקשים שלו אדומים ואין לו כי אם
עין אחד. במצחו ושיניו שחורות כזפת. ולא רצה המלך לאכול ממנו ויצו להשליכו
לכלבים וכאשר אכלו אותו מתו. וירא במלך ויחר אפו מאד ויאמר להם: "למה זה
אתם מבקשים להרוג אותי ואת כל עמי." ויחרישו ולא מצאו מענה. ויצו ה' המלך
לכל עמו לאמור: "החלצו[78] והלחמו על האנשים האלה אשר בקשו לשלוח יד בכם.[79]"
ויעשו וילחמו אלה מול אלה ותהי ביניהם מלחמה גדולה שלשה ימים ושלשה לילות
ותגבר יד המלך עליהם ויהרוג לאין מספר. ויצאו הנשים מן הקרקע וילחמו במלך
וכל חילו ויחזק המלך מהם ויהרגם עד מתי מספר אשר נתחבאו בקרקע.

ויצא המלך משם וילחם באנשי אנטיפיא ויהרוג מהם כשלשים אלף ויקח את כל כלי
זיינם מהם. ויפלו לפניו ארצה וירחם המלך עליהם ויאמר להחיותם.

ויביאו לו חמש מאות ככרי זהב וילך המלך מעליהם וישימם למס עובדי'.

ויצא המלך משם ויבא בארץ אלציל והיא שחורה כזפת וילחמו עם המלך. ויאמר להם
המלך: "למה אתם מקשים עורף כנגדי?" ויאמרו לו: "כי מעולם לא היה עלינו לא
מלך ולא שר כי אנו חופשים מכל עמי הארצות." ויאמר להם המלך: "איני מבקש
מכם לא כסף ולא זהב, אך כל הנערים הילודים בזה השנה תנו למנה לאכילה לכלביי."
ויענו ויאמר לו: "לא נכון לעשות כן[80] לתת בנינו למאכל לכלביך. אם תחפוץ קח
ממנו כסף וזהב לרוב ואם לאו הננו נלחמים בך."

Numbers 31:3
[78] "החלצו."
"Arm ..."

Esther 6:2
[79] "אשר בקשו לשלח יד במלך."
" .... who had sought to lay hands on the king Ahasuerus."

Exodus 8:22
[80] "לא נכון לעשות כן."
"It is not meet so do so ..."

length measured a thirty-day march. Not a woman was to be seen since they all lived underground. The king offered them peace and in return they brought him 100,000 talents of gold and precious stones in abundance. They also brought him a large, strange-looking fish with red scales, a single eye in its forehead and teeth black as pitch. The king refused to eat it and ordered it thrown to the dogs, who devoured it and died. At this, the king became very angry and said: "Why did you seek to kill me and all my people?" They were silent and could not reply. So the king commanded his army saying: "Take up your arms and make war against these people who sought to harm you." So they did, and a fierce battle was fought lasting three days and three nights; and the king overpowered them and slaughtered countless of their numbers. The women then emerged from beneath the ground to fight against Alexander and his army, but they were all overcome and slain save for a handful who sought refuge underground.

The king left that place and fought against the people of Antifay, killing some 30,000 of them and capturing all their armaments. The survivors knelt before him and the king had mercy on them and spared them, whereupon they brought him 500 talents of gold and became his subjects.

He departed and came to the land of Altzil,[19] which was as black as tar and whose inhabitants fought against him.

The king said: "Why are you stiff-necked?"

They replied: "We are an independent people and have never been ruled by a king."

"I do not want from you your silver or gold," said the king "but all your sons born this year as food for my dogs."

"It is not right to give our sons to you as food for your dogs. If your wish, you may have any amount of silver or gold, and if this does not please you, we will fight you."

The king sought the counsel of his wise men / who told him: "Do not   f.269a
accept their gold and silver, but rather fight against them and your name

Semitic origin. Carthage was located on the northern coast of mid Africa and was founded in 853 B. C. (Carthago). Wm. Smith, *A Classical Dictionary of Greek and Roman Biography, Mythology and Geography* (London: 1848), p. 199. Dido was the legendary founder and queen of Carthage.

19 Possibly Alsium, one of the most ancient Etruscan towns on the coast near Caere. Wm. Smith, *Dictionary of Biography, Mythology and Geography*, op. cit., p. 56.

וייעץ המלך/ויאמרו לו חכמיו: "אל תקח מאתם לֹא כסף ולֹא זהב אך הלֹחם כנגדם ויצא לך שם בגויים." ⁸¹ וישמע המלך לקולם וילח ¦ עמהם ותגבר יד המלך ויהרוג מהם לאין מספר. ויקח מהם כסף וזהב וכל שכיות החמדה עד אשר מאסו בזהב ובכסף ויקחו רק אבן יקרה.

ויצא המלך משם ויבא ארץ ארמניא ויצאו לקראתו כל איש חיל וילחמו עמו ויהרגו רבים מחיילותיו. ותגבר יד המלך עליהם ביום השני ויהרוג מהם לאין מספר. ויצא המלך עם דגלו ויבא בחוזקה על מגדל מלכם. וימצא שם אבן יקרה לרוב מאד ויקח כל שכיות חמדתם ויחלק לכל עמו ויעש משתה לכל עבדיו. וינח שם תעשה ימים. ויהי בלילה ההוא ותצא צפרדע אחת לפני מיטת המלך ובתוך פיה עשב אחד. ויאמר המלך בלבו: "אין זה בחינם." וישלח חרבו על הצפדר׳ ותסרח סרחון גדול וימותו מעמו הרבה מאוד וגם המלך חלה חולי גדול על אודות הסירחון ההוא ויבואו רופאיו וירפאוהו.

ויצא המלך משם ויבא ארץ עופלה. ויצאו כנגדו כל עם הארץ וישחיתו רבים מעמו. ותגבר יד המלך עליהם ותשחת בהם כארבעים אלפים ויקח מהם זהב ואבן יקרה לרוב."

Ezekial 17:14

⁸¹ "ויצא לך שם בגויים."

"And thy renown went forth among the nations ... "

will be famous among all the nations. The king heeded their advice, fought and overpowered them, killing countless numbers. He confiscated so large a quantity of their silver, gold, and other precious objects that his men despised them[20] and then took only precious stones.

The king went from that place to the land of Armenia.[21] There all the brave men came forth and fought him killing many of his soldiers. On the second day, the king overcame them, killing many of their number. Bearing his standard, the king led a mighty offensive against their king's tower. There he found many precious stones. He took all their prized possessions and distributed them among his men and made a great feast for all his servants. They camped there for nine days.

That night a frog came near the king's bed holding in its mouth an herb.[22] The king thought to himself: "This means something," and he struck the frog with his sword. It emitted so foul a stench that many of his men died. Even the king became ill from it, but his physicians came and healed him.

Leaving that place, the king came to the land of Olpa.[23] All the inhabitants of this country attacked him and annihilated many of his people, but the king overpowered them and slaughtered some 40,000 of them seizing large quantities of gold and precious stones.

The king then proceeded to the land of Nanasia[24] and was greeted by the king, Antalonia. Alexander bowed before him and said:

---

[20] The connotation is that the men considered these precious objects valueless, since they had so much of them.

[21] Armenia, a country of Asia lying between Asia Minor and Caspian, a lofty tableland backed by a chain of the Caucasus and containing the source of the Tigris and Euphrates rivers. Wm. Smith, *Dictionary of Biography Mythology, and Geography*, op. cit., p. 119.

[22] The word "herb" is used as "an herb" and "a bitter herb".

[23] Possibly Olpae (Olpa) a town of the Amphilichi in Acarmania on the Ambracian gulf, northwest of Argus Amphilochicum. Wm. Smith, *Dictionary of Biography, Mythology and Geography*, op. cit., p. 623.

[24] Nanasia, from the Hebrew word *nanas* meaning "dwarf." Antalonia, the dwarf was mentioned earlier in the story.
    Possibly Naisus, an important town of Upper Moesia, on the eastern tributary of Margus and birthplace of Constantine the Great. Wm. Smith, *Dictionary of Biography, Mythology and Geography*, op. cit., p. 585.

ויצא המלך משם ויבוא אל ארץ נגסיא ויצא המלך לקראתו. ואנטלוניא מלך עליהם.
וישתחו אלכסנדרוס על אפיו ארצה ויאמר: "האתה זה אדוני המלך אנטלוניא?
תגזור אומר ואני אעשה.[82]" ויאמר לו המלך אנטלוניא: "וכי אתה חפץ כסף אתן
כסף וזהב לרוב עד בלי דיי.[83]" ויאמר אלכסנדרוס: "איני מבקש ממך אך עשבים
אשר הם טובים לרפוא." והגידו למלך אלכסנדרוס כל כח העשבים. ויהי שם אלכסנ־
דרוס עם כל עמו שלשה ימים ויצו המלך למנחם הסופר לכתוב כל כח העשבים.

ויהי אחרי כן ויאמר אלכסנדרוס לאנטלוניא: "לאיזה דרך אפנה מכאן כי יצאתי חוץ
כדי לכוף כל העולם." אמר לו אנטלוניא: "יש כמה מלכיות סביבותי וכולם משו־
עבדים לי. וכולם יהיו עבדיך אם אתה חפץ למלחמה וכן לעלות מס על שולחן אדוני
המלך." ויאמר אלכסנדרוס: "חלילה לי לשלוח ידי בעמך, אך יעציני על איזה צד
אפנה." ויאמר: "לתוך הרי חשך ואני אתן לך אבנים טובות אשר יאירו כאור השמש."
ויתן לו אבנים טובות ויכין לו מאכל ולכל עמו לשבעה ימים. ויעבור אלכסנדרוס
הרי חשך. ויהי כאשר יצאו לאור העולם ויאמר אלכסנדרוס: "פה ניחן שני ימים או
שלשה." והנה שם עומדים שני אילנות אדומים גדולים ועליהם יושבים שני זקנים
אחד מהם היה סומא והאחד אלם. ויאמר המלך: "מה אתם יושבים כאן?" ויען לו
הזקן ויאמר לו: "לשמוע עתידות מן האילנות האלה." ויאמר לו המלך: "הנהיה כדבר
הגדול הזה[84] שאילנות מדברים?" ויאמר לו הזקן: "אדוני המלך כי האמת אגיד לך
שהאילנות אילו מדברי שעה שלישית ביום וכל מה ששואלים מהם מגידים מיום
המות." ויתמה המלך ויתקע את אהלו שמה.[85] ויהי ממחרת ביום השעה השלישית ויצא
קול מן האילן האחד ויקרא אל המלך ויאמר לו: "אדוני המלך שאל נא את את אשר
תחפוץ ואגידה לך חוץ מדבר אחד." וישאל המלך ויאמר: "האמלוך עשר שנים?"
ויען ויאמר: "תמלוך עשר ויותר." ויאמר המלך: "האמלוך עשרים שנים?"

Job 22:28   "ותגזר אמר ויקם לך." [82]

"Thou shalt also decree a thing, and it shall be established unto thee . . . "

Malachi 3:10   "עד בלי די." [83]

" . . . there shall not be room enough (to receive it)."

Deuteronomy 4:32   "הנהיה כדבר הגדול הזה." [84]

" . . . whether there hath been any such thing as this great thing is . . . "

Genesis 31:25   "תקע את אהלו בהר." [85]

" . . . pitched his tent in the mount . . . "

"Are you my lord, King Antalonia? Command and I will obey."

King Antalonia replied: "If you desire silver, I shall give you endless amounts of silver and gold."

"I ask nothing of you," replied Alexander, "but information about herbs that are beneficial for healing." They told Alexander of the special virtues of the herbs. Alexander and his men remained there three days, and he ordered Menachem, the secretary, to record the healing powers of the different herbs.

Afterwards, Alexander asked Antalonia: "Whither shall I go, for I set out to encompass the entire world?"

Antalonia answered: "Several kingdoms surround me and are subject to me. They can be your subjects when you go to war, as well as bring tribute to you, my lord king."

Alexander said: "Far be it from me to lay my hands on your people, but only advise me which way to turn."

"Into the mountains of darkness,"[25] he said, "and I will give you precious stones as brilliant as the sun."

He gave Alexander the precious stones and prepared seven days provision for all his men. Alexander passed through the mountains of darkness. When he emerged into the light of the world he said: "Let us camp here for two or three days." There were two large red trees standing there on which sat two old men, one blind, and the other dumb.

The king said: "Why are you sitting here?"

"To hear the future from these trees," the old man answered.

"Can trees possibly speak?" the king asked.

The old man replied: "In truth, my lord, king, these trees speak on the third hour of the day and answer every question put to them except one. They will not answer a question concerning the day of death."

The king was astonished and camped there. On the third hour of the following day, a voice was heard from one of the trees calling to the king: "My lord, king, you may ask all you wish and I will tell you all, except for one thing." The king asked: "Will I rule for ten years?" It answered: "You will rule for ten years and more." "Will I rule for twenty years?"

25 Several versions of this story attributed to Alexander are found in Hebraic literature: Jerusalem Talmud, *Baba Mezia*, II, 5, 8c; *Midrash Rabbah* (Soncino ed.), I, *Genesis Rabbah* XXXIII, 1, pp. 257ff.; *Midrash Rabbah*, IV, *Leviticus Rabbah* XXVII, 1, pp. 340ff.; *Pesikta d'Rab Kahana*, IX, 24; *Midrash Tanhuma, Emor*, 6; *Yalkut Shimoni*, Ps. 36, sec. 727.

ויען ויאמר: ״תמלוך עשרים ויותר.״ ויאמר המלך: ״האמלוך שלשים שנה?״ ויען
ויאמר: ״תמלוך שלשי׳ ויותר.״ ויאמר המלך ״האמלוך ארבעים?״ וישתוק הקול ולא
ענהו. ויוסף המלך/וישאל: ״האמלוך שלשים וחמש?״ ויען ויאמר: ״שלשים וחמש
ויותר.״ ויאמר המלך: ״וכמה יותר?״ וישתוק הקול ולא ענהו. וידע כי לא ימלוך עד
ארבעים. וישאל עוד המלך ויאמר: ״האחזור עוד לארץ מצרים?״ ויען ויאמר לו:
״על ארץ נכריה תמות ובארץ מצרים תקבר.״ וישאל עוד המלך: ״הימלוך בני
אחרי?״ ויאמר לו: ״ולא ימלוך בנך אחריך אך מלכותך תחלק לארבע אבוסים.״
וישאל המלך עוד דברים אחרים ולא ענהו עוד.

ויצא המלך משם ויבא מעבר להרי חשך על ידי ה׳ מרגלית אחת אשר האירה לפניו.
ויצא המלך ההוא לקראתו ויכבדהו מאד ויעש לו ככל אשר אמר. ויהי היום וישבו
שני המלכים יחד וכתרם בראשם ויבאו שני אנשים לפני המלך.
ויאמר האחד אל המלך: ״בי אדוני![86] אני קניתי קרקע אחד מן האיש הזה ורציתי
לבנות עליו בניין, וחפרתי בו חפורה ומצאתי מטמון ואוצר לרוב מאד. ואני אמרתי
לו: ״קח לך האוצר כי לא קניתי ממך כי אם הקרקע והאוצר לא קניתי.״ ויען השני
ויאמר אל המלך: ״בי אדוני, כשמכרתי הקרקע, שלי מכרתי לו כל מה שבקרקע מתהום
ארעא ועד רום רקיעא וכשם שהוא מרחיק מן הגזל כך אני פורש מן הגזל.״

Genesis 44:18
"O, my lord"

[86] ״בי אדוני.״

he asked and it answered: "You will rule twenty years and more."
"Will I rule for thirty years?" The reply came: "You will rule for thirty
years and more." Then the king asked: "Will I rule for forty years?"
but there was no reply. The voice remained silent. The king continued to
question it. / "Will I rule for thirty-five years?" The voice came back: f. 269b
"Thirty-five years and more." So the king said: "But how many more?"
The voice did not answer but remained silent, and the king knew he would
not reign for forty years. He questioned further: "Will I return to the
land of Egypt?" It answered: "You will die in a foreign land, but will
be buried in the land of Egypt." "Will my son rule after me?" he asked
further. "Your son will not rule after you, but your kingdom will be
divided into four states." The king asked about other matters, but it
did not answer any more.

From there, the king passed again through the mountains of darkness,
using a pearl to light the way. The king of that land greeted him and
showed him great honor and did all that he asked. One day as the two
kings sat together with their crowns on their heads,[26] two men came
before them. One said to the king: "O my lord! I purchased a piece of
land from this man intending to erect a building upon it. While digging
a ditch I found a tremendous cache of hidden treasure. I told him:
'Take the treasure, for I did not purchase it from you, but only the land.'"
The second man answered: "Please, my lord! When I sold him my
land, I sold him all that was in it from the depths of the earth to the

[26] This story is found in the Jerusalem Talmud, *Baba Mezia* I, 6, 8c in connection with
the question as to who is to be looked upon as the rightful owner of a treasure. A
second aspect of this story is the point the foreign king makes, i.e., the guiltless
man is the center of creation. See L. Wallach, "Alexander the Great and the Indian
Gymnosophists in Hebrew Tradition," *Proceedings of the American Academy for Jewish
Research*, XI (New York: 1941), 47–83.

    A similar tale appears in M. Gaster, *The Example of the Rabbis* (London: 1924),
No. Va. Gaster points out that this tale also appears in *Bocados de Oro* of Ibn Fatikh.
See "An Old Hebrew Romance of Alexander, " op. cit., p. 822.

L. Ginzberg, *Legends*, IV, 235, tells the tale of the contrition of the Ninevites, as follows:
"A man found a treasure in a building lot he acquired from his neighbor. Both buyer
and seller refused to assume possession of the treasure. The seller insisted that the
sale of the lot carried with it the sale of all it contained. The buyer held that he had
bought the ground, not the treasure hidden therein. Neither rested satisfied until the
judge succeeded in finding out who had hidden the treasure and who were the heirs,
and the joy of the two was great when they could deliver the treasure up to its legitimate
owners."

ויאמר המלך לאחד מהם: "יש לך בן אחד?" ויאמר לו: "כן אדוני." וישאל גם את
השני: "יש לך בת אחת?" ויאמ' לו "כן אדוני" ויאמר לו המלך: "תן בנך לבתו וכל
האוצר תנו לשניהם." ויעשו כן.

וישחק אלכסנדרוס. ויפלו בעיניו ויאמר לו המלך: "מה אתה שוחק לא יפה דנתי?
ולא יפה עשיתי?" ויען אלכסנדרוס ויאמר אליו: "יפה דנת ויפה עשית, אבל במל־
כותי לא הייתי דן לכך." ויאמר לו המלך: "האיך היית דן?" ויאמר לו המלך: "אם היה
כך במלכותי היה המלך הורג שניהם ונוטל כל הממון." ויתמה המלך מאד ויאמר לו:
"וכי זורח השמש במלכותך?" ויאמר לו: "כן" ויאמר לו: "וכי יש טללים במלכו'
ויאמר "כן." ויאמר לו: "וכי יש בהמה דקה ובהמה גסה במלכותך?" ויאמר לו: "כן."
ויאמ' לו המלך: "בזכות הבהמות אתם חיים ובזכות הבהמות אתם נזונים שנאמ'
אדם ובהמה תושיע השם.[87]"

ויצא אלכסנדרוס משם ויבא אל ארץ אפריק ויכבשה ויכבשו תחתיו ויתנו לו מאה ושמונים
ככרי זהב ואבן יקרה הרבה. ויצא המלך משם ויבא ארץ אנשיק ולא מצא בו כי אם
נשים ומעבר הנהר ישבים האנשים. ולעולם אין האנשים עוברים את המים אך הנשים
עוברות תמיד את המים כדי להתעבר מן האנשים. ואם האשה תלד זכר היא מביאה
אותו מעבר למים והאנשים מגדלים אותו, ואם היא יולדת נקבה היא מגדלת אותה
עד חמש שנים ומלמדת אותה מלחמה. והמה רוכבות סוסים ועוברות תמיד ומתלחמות

Psalms 36:7
"O Lord, thou preservest man and beast."   [87] "אדם ובהמה תושיע ה'."

height of the heavens.[27] Just as he refuses to accept this hidden booty, so do I." Then the king asked one of them: "Do you have a son?" "Yes my lord," he replied. He asked the other: "Do you have a daughter?" "Yes, my lord." The king said: "Give your son to his daughter and give the entire treasure to both." And so it was done.

At this, Alexander laughed.

Surprised, the king said: "Why are you laughing? Did I not judge properly? Did I not do well?"

"You acted justly, and did well," replied Alexander. "However, I would not have decided so in my kingdom."

"How would you have judged?" asked the king.

"If this had happened in my kingdom," he said, "the king would have killed both of them and confiscated the entire treasure." The king was amazed at this and said: "Does the sun shine in your kingdom?"

"Yes."

"Is there dew in your kingdom?"

"Yes."

"It is because of the cattle that you are living and because of the cattle that you are fed," said the king, "as it is written: 'O Lord, Thou preservest man and beast,'."[28]

Leaving there, Alexander came to the land of Afriq[29] and conquered it. He was given 180 talents of gold and many precious stones. From there he came to Anshiq[30] where he found only women, for the men dwelt apart on the other side of the river. The men never crossed the river, but the women always did in order to become pregnant. If a woman bore a son, she brought him to the men on the other side of the river and they

---

[27] This famous story is told about a King Kazia and King Alexander and is found in the aforementioned sources noted in n. 26. The legal phrase "from the depths of the earth to the height of the heavens," is quoted in the Babylonian Talmud, *Baba Batra*, p. 53b.

[28] Psalms 36:7.

[29] This is the name under which the Romans (after 146 B.C.) erected into a province the whole of the former territory of Carthage. Wm. Smith, *Dictionary of Biography, Mythology and Geography*, op. cit., p. 32.

[30] Anshiq comes from the Hebrew "ha-nashim" meaning "the women," or from the Aramaic "d'nashi" meaning "land of women" or Amazons. Afriq or Africa is known in rabbinic sources as a place of women. Carthage, Anshiq, Amazons and Africa all refer to lands of women. Cf. Virgil, *Aeneid*, Bk. IV and opening book.

In Talmudic literature this tale is found in the Babylonian Talmud, *Tamid*, p. 32a–b.

עם כל סביבותיהם כי עושות בכל שנה פעמים ושלש. וישלח המלך אלכסנדרוס אל
המלכה לאמר: "אל נא תמנעי מלבא אלי עם שרות׳ ועם כל שכיות חמדתך ואל
תקשי עורף כנגדי פן יהי לך למכשול ולפוקה.

ות׳(ען)* המלכה ותאמר למלאכי אלכסנדרוס ותאמר אליהם: "מה כח אדוניכם כי
בא אל ארצי להלחם בי לקחת את ארצי מידי?" ויענו ויאמרו לה: "הוא משפיל כל

f. 270ᵃ

אויביו תחת כפות רגליו ואין חומה אשר שגבה ממנו[88] וממלכות ועמים/נפלו תחתיו
וכל אשר יעשה יצליח.[89]

ותען ותאמר: "אמרו לאדוניכם שאינו נראה בעיני חכם אך ששעתו עומדת לו."
ויאמרו לה: "ולמה את אומרת כך על אדונינו?" ותען ותאמ׳ להם: "כי נכרים דברי
אמת, שאם היה אדוניכם חכם לא היה בא להלחם עם הנשים. שאם ינצח את הנשים
יאמרו העולם: "מה בכך שנצח את הנשים? הלא אדם קל ממנו יכול לנצח אותם.
ואם הנשים ינצחו אותו מה יאמרו העולם: "מלך כזה נצחוהו נשים! נמצא שכל
המלחמות שעשה ינצח בהם לא יהיו לו לשם ולתהילה, אך קלונו ירבה ויגדל ויסגא
בעיני כל השומעים." וישובו המלאכים אל אלכסנדרוס ויאמרו לו כזאת וכזאת דיברה
המלכה. וייטבו דבריה בעיני אלכסנדרוס ובעיני כל עמו. ויאמר להם אלכסנדרוס:
"ומה אעשה אם אלך מהם בלא מלחמה ובלא נצחון יאמרו כל השומעים נשים נצחוני."
ויאמר המלך: "לא אלך מכאן עד אשר אראה את פני המלכה ואדבר אליה פה אל פה.[90]
ותשמע המלכה כי המלך בא לראות פניה ותלך ותקבץ חמשים אלף נערות בתולות
ותלבישם שש ומשי ורקמה, ותרכבנה על הגמלים ותבואנה לקראת המלך.

ויהי כאשר קרבה המלכה אל מחנה אלכסנ׳ ותאמר אל נערותיה: "ממני תראו וכן
תעשו.[91] ותמהר המלכה ותגלה אחת מדדיה ותעשינה כולן ככה. ויבט המלך וכל עמו
ויתמהו מאד וימהר המלך וירכב כנגדה ויחבקה וינשקה ויאמר לה המלך: "למה זה
עשית ככה?" ותאמר לו: "כה חק ומשפט[92] במלכות הזה להקביל את פני המלך.
להראות לו את יופיי[93] גופינו."

---

* Only the first two letters of this word appear in the manuscript. Comparison with
MS. Modena Liii gave the complete word.

Deuteronomy 2:36   "קריה אשר שגבה ממנו."[88]
"...there was not one city too strong for us..."

Psalms 1:3   "וכל אשר יעשה יצליח."[89]
"And whatsoever he doeth shall prosper."

Number 12:8   "פה אל פה אדבר בו."[90]
"With him I will speak mouth to mouth..."

Judges 7:17   "ממני תראו וכן תעשו."[91]
"Look on me and do likewise."

Exodus 15:12   "שם שם לו חוק ומשפט."[92]
"There he made for them a statute and an ordinance...'

Esther 1:11   "להראות העמים והשרים את פיה."[93]
"...to show the people and the princes her beauty...."

reared him. But if she bore a daughter she herself reared her for five years and taught her the art of war. The women rode horses and often invaded their neighbors' territories and fought with them two or three times a year. King Alexander sent word to the queen: "Do not refuse to come to me with your princesses, and bring all your precious possessions, and do not oppose me lest it prove to be your downfall."

The queen answered the messengers of Alexander: "What right has your master to come to my land to fight me and take my land from me?"

They answered: "He subdues all his enemies. No wall has withstood him. Nations and kingdoms/have fallen before him, and he will suc- f. 270ᵃ ceed in all he undertakes."

She answered: "Tell your master that he appears not wise, but fortunate."

"Why do you say this about our master?" they asked.

"Because it is evident," she replied. "If your master were wise he would not come to fight women. For if he were to conquer them, the world would say: 'What is it to conquer women? A lesser man could have subdued them.' If, on the other hand, the women were to win the victory, what would the world say? 'Imagine such a king being defeated by women!' In that event, all his past triumphs in war will no longer bring him glory or renown but, rather, he will be disgraced before all who hear of it."

The messengers returned to Alexander and told him what the queen said. Her words pleased Alexander and all his people. "How can I leave without waging war and achieving victory? All who would hear of my departure would say that the women had triumphed over me. No," said the king, "I will not depart until I see the queen and speak to her personally."

When the queen heard that the king was about to visit her, she assembled 50,000 maidens arrayed in fine linen, silk, and lace and, with them all riding on camels, went to meet King Alexander.

As they approached his camp, she said to them: "Observe what I do and do likewise." The queen swiftly bared one of her breasts, and they did likewise. The king and all his people viewed this in amazement. He quickly rode up to her, embraced her and kissed her.

"Why did you do this?" he asked.

"It is our custom to expose the beauty of our bodies whenever we welcome a king," she told him.

ויאמר המלך: "ומה אעשה לכם?" ותאמר לו המלכה: "לא תעשה לנו דבר אך תלך
מעלינו ולא תחריב את ארצינו." ויאמר לה המלך: "אם תקבלי המלכות ממני אלך
מעליכם ואם לאו אחריב את כל ארצכם." ותאמר לו: "ולמה זה תחריב את
ארצי ותוסיף פשע ועון על עונך? שהרי כבר נשבענו מימי קדם שלא נקבל עול
מלך עלינו אך אם אתה חפץ אני אתן לך כסף וזהב ואבן יקרה לרב מאד אשר
לא ראית כמותה אתה ואבותיך ואבות אבותיך." ויאמר לה המלך: "אם אלחם
עמך ואתגבר עליך אקח ממך אבן יקרה וזהב וכסף כל אשר לך." ותאמר המלכה:
"נסכלת בזאת כי אמרת אם תתגבר עלי תקח ממני כל כספי וזהבי ושכיות חמדתי
הלא אצרתה כבר עם כל נערותי כל שכיות החמדה במקום אשר לא תוכל למצא
אפילו אם תהפוך כל הארץ מה שלמטה למעלה." ויאמר לה המלך: "אם לא תגלה
כל אוצרותיך." ותאמר לו המלכה: "כבר נשבענו אנחנו ואבותינו שלא לגלות
כל שכיות חמדתיך לשום אדם, על כן כלה דבריך כי לא יועיל לך." ויאמר
לה המלך: "מה אעשה כבר נתחכמת יותר ממני ואני לא דברתי כדברים האלה כי
אם לנסותך ועתה תני לי זהב ואבן יקרה כאשר דברתך ואלך מארצך בשלום."
ותמהר המלכה ותתקע בשופר קטן ומשונה למראה ותבא אליה נערה יפה מאד.
ותאמר לה המלכה: "קחי עמך את נערותיי והביאו לי זהב ואבן יקרה שאצרתי
במקום אשר גיליתי לך. ותמהר הנערה ותלך ותבא אל המלך זהב ואבן יקרה לרוב
מאד אשר תמהו בה כל רואיו. וגם המלך תמה מאד ויאמר לה המלך: "עשי נא את
שאלתי ואראה כי מצאני חן בעיניך." ותאמר לו המלכה: "כל אשר תאמר לי אעשה
רק שלא אקבל את מלכותי ממך/ולא אטעון עולך." ויאמר לה המלך: "זה איני שואל
f. 270^bממך אך אכן אשכב עמך הלילה." ותען המלכה ותאמר לו: "גם לדבר הזה שמעתיך
אך השבע לי שלא יבואו אנשיך לנערותיי כי לא נעשה כדבר הזה[94] בכל ארצי."
ויאמר המלך: "אנכי אעשה כדבריך,"[95] וישבע לה. ויעבור קול וכל מחנהו[96] לאמר:
"כל הנוגע בנערות המלכה מות יומת."

Genesis 47:30   [94] "כי לא נעשה כדבר הזה."
"I will do as thou hast said. . . ."

Ibid.   [95] "אנכי אעשה כדבריך."

Exodus 36:6   [96] "ועברו קול במחנה."
". . .and they caused it to be proclaimed throughout the camp. . ."

"What may I do for you?" asked the king.

She answered: "Nothing — only leave us without destroying our country."

"I will leave if you accept my rule. If you do not, I will destroy your whole country."

"Why need you destroy my country and add sin and iniquity to your transgressions?" she said. "Long ago we swore that we would never be ruled by a king. But if you wish, I will give you silver, gold, and man precious stones such as were never seen before by you, your fathers and your forefathers."

"If I fought and overcame you," he answered, "I would confiscate your precious stones, silver, and gold, and everything else you own."

She said: "How foolish of you to say that if you overcame me you would confiscate all my silver, gold, and precious possessions. My maidens and I have hidden them all in a place you could not discover even if you overturned the entire land."

"If you do not reveal where your precious possessions are hidden," he said, "I will torture you and all your maidens until you do so."

The queen said: "We are bound by an ancestral oath not to disclose the whereabouts of our precious possessions to any one. Therefore, say no more, for it is of no avail."

The king said:" What can I do? You have outwitted me and the only reason I spoke to you in this way was to test you. Now, give me the gold and precious stones you spoke of and I will leave your country peacefully."

The queen quickly blew a strange-looking miniature horn and a lovely maiden came up to her. The queen said: "Take my maidens and fetch the gold and precious stones stored in the place I have revealed to you." The maiden quickly brought the king an abundance of gold and precious stones, and all who viewed them were astonished. The king said: "Please honor my request, and I will know that I have found favor in your eyes." "I will do everything you request of me," the queen answered "so long as I am not compelled to accept your rule / or bear your yoke." "I do not ask this," he said, "but only that I may lay with you tonight." She said: "I grant this request, but give me your word that none of your men will come to my maidens, for such things are not done in my country." "I agree," he said, and swore to her. He commanded his camp: "Anyone who molests the queen's maidens will be executed." That

f. 270^b

ויהי בלילה ההוא וישלח המלך להביא את המלכה אל אהלו. ותמאן המלכה לבא
אל המלך[97] כי אמרה: "לא נכון שתלך האשה אחרי האיש." ויאמר המלך: אמת
כדבריה כן הוא."[98] ויקם המלך וילך אל המלכה ויבא אליה ותהר לו.[99] ויהי בבקר
ותאמר לו המלכה: "אנכי הרה ממך." ויאמר לה המלך: "במה את יודעת?" ותאמר
אליו: "כי ראיתי במזלות הלילה שאנכי הריתי ממך והוא יהיה גיבור חיל ואיש
מלחמה ורבים חללים יפיל[100] ולעת זקנתו יהרג."

עודנה מדברת אל המלך[101] ותבא נערה אחת מנערותיה ותצעק אל המלך לאמר: "אחד
מאנשיך שכב עמי בעל כרחי." ויחר אף המלך ויאמר: "מי האיש אשר עשה את הדבר
הזה?" ויגידו לו לאמר: "זה הוא געתן שומר אוצרותיך." ויאמר: "מהרו והביאו
אותו אליי!" וימהרו ויביאוהו אל המלך. ויאמר לו המלך: "למה זה עברת על דבריי
אשר צויתי לאמר הנוגע בנערות המלכה מות יומת ותמר את פי ולא השגחת על דברי?"
ויען געתן ויאמר אל המלך: "מה אאריך בדברים? אך דע לך אם לא תשבע לי שלא
תעשה לי מאומה כל אוצרותיך המסורים בידי לא תראה מהם עוד כי כבר גנזתי אותם
במקום אשר לא תמצא אותם לעולם." וירגז המלך מאד ויחר אפו מאד ולא ידע מה
לעשות. ויאמר אל געתן: "למה הרעותה לי?[102] מה עולתה מצאת בי?" ויען געתן אל
המלך: "כי יצרי תקף עלי ולא היה בי כח לעצור." ויאמר המלך: "אנכי אשבעך[103]
וישבע לו. ויאמר לו: "הראיני את אוצרותיי!" ויראם אליו ויקחם המל דْממנו וישם
על אוצרו את אצן סריסו.

ויהי ביום ההוא וישב המלך לאכול על שולחנו וישא את עיניו והנה געתן בא ועיני
מפולמות על המלך. ויבהל המלך ויצעק: "הסירו את זה ממני!" עוד הדבר בפי
המלך והנה געתן בא בסכינו ויתקע ויתקע המלך. ויראו אנשי המלך וירגזו ויקומו ויתפשו
את געתן ויבא אנטיפל רופא המלך ויקח עשב אחד וישם על המכה וירפאהו מיד.

Esther 1:12   "ותמאן המלכה ושתי לבוא בדבר המלך."
"But the queen Vashti refused to come at the King's commandment. . ."

Genesis 44:10; Joshua 2:21   "כדבריכם כן הוא."
". . .let it be according unto your words. . ."

Genesis 38:18   "ויבא אליה ותהר לו."
". . .and he came in unto her and she conceived by him."

Proverbs 7:26   "כי רבים חללים הפילה."
"For she hath cast down many wounded. . ."

I Kings 1:22   "עודנה מדברת עם המלך."
". . .while she yet talked with the king. . ."

Exodus 5:22   "למה הרעתה לעם הזה."
". . .wherefore hast thou done so much evil to this people?"

Genesis 21:24   "אנכי אשבעך."
"I will swear (to you)."

night the king summoned the queen to his tent, but she refused to go to him saying: "It is not proper for a woman to go to a man."

"She speaks the truth," he said, and he arose and went to the queen and she conceived by him. In the morning she said: "I am pregnant by you." "How do you know?" he asked. "Because," she said "I saw in the constellations, last night, that I have become pregnant by you. He will be a mighty warrior and will slay many and he will be slain himself in his old age." As she was speaking to the king, one of her maidens approached in tears, and said to the king: "One of your men has lain with me and has raped me." The king grew angry and said: "Who did it?" He was told: "It was Ga'atan,[31] the keeper of your treasuries." The king ordered him brought before him at once and they immediately did so.

"Why did you disobey my command that whoever molested the queen's maidens would be executed. You disregarded this and did not heed my words," said the king.

Ga'atan replied: "Why should I speak at length? I warn you that unless you swear not to harm me, you will never see again any of the treasures you deposited with me, for I have hidden them in a place where you could never find them." The king grew very angry and did not know what to do.

He said: "Why have you brought this end upon me? What fault have you found in me?"

Ga'atan said: "Because my evil inclination overcame me and I was unable to resist it."

"I swear,"[32] said the king and he did so. "Show me my treasures," he said. When he brought them, the king took them away from Ga'atan and appointed his eunuch, Etzin, to guard them.

One day, as the king was eating at his table, he looked up and noticed Ga'atan approaching him with a crazed look in his eyes. The king was startled and cried out: "Take him away!" As the king spoke Ga'atan charged at him with a knife and wounded him. When the king's men saw this, they were enraged and seized Ga'atan. Antipol, the king's physician, came and placed some herbs on the wound, which healed

---

[31] Ga'atan is mentioned in Genesis 36:11, 16 as one of the descendents of Esau and a chief in his own right.

[32] By this is meant, "I will not harm you."

ויתן לו המלך מתנות רבות ויצו המלך לחתוך את געתן לפני כלביו. ויעשו לו ויחתכוהו איברים איברים וחמת המלך שככה.״[104]

ויהי אחרי זאת ויסע המלך עם כל חילו מן האר׳ ההיא וישם פניו לבא ללכת ארץ הגר. ויוגד לו לאמר: ״הנה מלך הגר בא להלחם כנגדך.״ וישחק המלך ויהי כמצחק בעיניו. וישלח מלאכים אל מלך הגר לאמר: ״מה ראית כי הקשית עורף כנגדי ותעש לך חיל להלחם כנגדי? הלא ידעת הלא שמעת[105] הלא הוגד לך את אשר עשיתי בכח ידי כי ממלכות ועממים השפלתי תחת ידי?״ ויבאו המלאכים ויגידם כדברים האלה דיבר אלכסנדרוס. ויען מלך הגר אל מלאכי המלך: ״אמרו אל אדוניכם! באת להלחם בארצי מה פשעי ומה חטאתי כנגדך?[106] ויגידו למלך את דבריו ויאמר אל כל עמו: ״הכינו את כל כלי מלחמתיכם ויבואו להלחם עם המלך.״ ומלך הגר ציוה קודם לכן לחפור בורות ושיחין ומערות בכל ארץ מלכותו ויכסום בתבן ובקש למען יכשלו ויפלו בו אלכסנדרוס וחילו. ויוגד הדבר אל אלכסנ׳ וחילו וירע הדבר מאד בעיניו, וייירא לבא בארץ מפני עומק הבורות אשר כרו עבדי המלך הגל.*

f. 271ᵃ וישלח מלאכים שנית אל מלך הגר ויאמר לו: ״שמע לעצתי/אל תקשה עורף כנגדי ובוא נא אלי והבא לי מס ואצא לשלום ולא אשחית את ארצך.״ ויאמר המלך הגר אל מלאכי אלכסנדרוס: ״אנכי אעשה כדברי אלכסנדרוס ואבזבז לו מאוצרותי רק אם ילך מארצי.״ וישובו המלאכים ויגידו למלך את דבריו ויאמר לעשות כן. ויבא ויבא מלך הגר עם מבחר גבוריו ועמו אבן יקרה לרוב מאד ויתן אל המלך ויקבלם המלך ויסע המלך מארצו.

Esther 7:10
[104] ״וחמת המלך שככה.
"Then was the king's wrath assuaged."

Isaiah 40:28
[105] ״הלא ידעת אם לא שמעת.
"Hast thou not known? Hast thou not heard. . ."

Genesis 31:36
[106] ״מה פשעי ומה חטאתי.
"What is my trespass, what is my sin?"

* Should read: הגר

62

immediately. The king rewarded him with many presents. He ordered Ga'atan's body to be dismembered and thrown to the dogs. So it was done. Ga'atan's body was dismembered and the king's anger subsided.

After this, the king and his entire army journeyed from that land toward the country of Hagar.[33] It was reported to him: "The king of Hagar has set out to fight against you." At this the king laughed for it seemed absurd. He dispatched messengers to the king of Hagar, saying: "What stubborness has possessed you to assemble an army and fight against me? Have you not heard of my power to subdue kingdoms?" The messengers related this to the king of Hagar who answered: "Tell your master: 'What sin or transgression have I committed against you that you have come to fight in my land?'" When Alexander heard this, he ordered his army to prepare their weapons and wage war against the king of Hagar. The king of Hagar had already ordered pits, ditches, and caverns dug throughout his kingdom and covered them with straw or chaff so that Alexander's army would stumble and fall into them. When Alexander and his army learned of this, they were greatly disturbed and Alexander feared to enter the country because of the depth of the pits dug by the servants of the king of Hagar.

So, once again, he dispatched emissaries to the king of Hagar saying: "Heed my advice! / Do not oppose me, but bring me tribute and I will f. 271ª depart peacefully without destroying your land." The king of Hagar told Alexander's emissaries: "If King Alexander will depart from my country, I will do his bidding and empty my treasuries for him." The emissaries returned to the king and related these things to him and he said to act accordingly. The king of Hagar, accompanied by his chosen warriors, came to Alexander. They brought many precious stones with them and gave them to Alexander who accepted them.

Then Alexander traveled from that land towards Jerusalem,[34] for he

---

[33] In Genesis 16, Hagar is mentioned as the mother of Ishmael. In Hebrew, Hagar means Arabia or Arabs. The Arabs begin their calendar from the year Mohammed fled from Mecca to Medina (622 A.D.) called *Hegira* which comes from the same root as Hagar.

[34] This tale is found in several ancient Hebraic sources: *Scholium* to *Megillat Ta'anit*, chap. 3, 9; the Babylonian Talmud, *Yoma.* p. 69a; *Midrash Rabbah* (Soncino ed.), II, *Genesis Rabbah* LXI, 7, pp. 545–548. A more detailed version appears in Josephus, *Antiquitis*, XI, viii, 3–5. In both Talmudic literature and Josephus, Alexander appears friendly to the Jews and attributes his victories to the God of the Jews.

וישם את פניו ללכת דרך ירושלים כי הגידו לו לאמר את כח היהודים ואת
עוצם גבורתם ויאמר: ״אם לא אנצח את היהודים אין כבודי לכלום.״ ויסע
משם המלך וילך עשרים וששה ימים עם כל מחנהו ויבא עד דן וישלח מלאכים
אל אנשי ירושלים לאמר: ״כה אמר המלך הגדול אלכסנדרוס: כבר ישבתם כמה
שנים אשר לא עבדתם אותו לא במסים וגולגליות וארנוניות. ועתה בבא מכתבי
אליכם הקבצו ושלחו לי מסי. וזה הוא המס אשר אני שואל מכם: כל אוצרות בית
אלהיכם אשר אצרתם בבית מקדשו זה כמה ימים ושנים!״ וישמעו אנשי ירושלים
וייראו מאד ויתכסו שקים ויקדשו צום.[107] וייוועצו יחדיו[108] הזקנים והחכמים אשר

Jonah 3:5
See also Jonah 3:8.
"... and proclaimed a fast and put on sackcloth ... "

[107] ״ויקראו צום וילבשו שקים.״

Isaiah 45:21
"... ye, let them take counsel together ... "

[108] ״אף יועצו יחדיו.״

64

had heard of the strength of the Jews and of their valor and heroism. "If I do not defeat the Jews, all my glory is as nothing," he said. For twenty-six days the king and his entire army journeyed and arrived at Dan.[35] From there he sent ambassadors to the people of Jerusalem with this message: "Thus speaks the great King Alexander: You have dwelt many years without serving him by bringing tribute, taxes nor gifts. Now, having received my letter, gather, and send me my tribute. This is the tribute I expect of you: All the treasures in the house of your God, which you have accumulated in His temple over the past days and years." When the people of Jerusalem heard this, they were very fearful, put on sackcloth,[36] and declared a fast. The elders and wise men of Jerusalem planned how to answer King Alexander. Annani, the High Priest,[37]

V. Tcherikover, *Hellenistic Civilization and the Jews* (Philadelphia: 1959), chap. 1, discusses the historical inaccuracies in the Josephus account. He points out that Alexander did not linger in Palestine, but went from Egypt to Tyre, to northern Syria and Mesopotamia. He further notes that Josephus wrote that Alexander visited Jerusalem after he captured Gaza. From Arrian and Curtius we know that Alexander journeyed from Gaza to Pelusium in Egypt in a week. Thus, he could not have come to Jerusalem. Josephus also relates that Alexander was shown the prophecy in the Book of Daniel which was interpreted to refer to Alexander. However, this is not chronologically accurate, since Daniel was written one hundred and fifty years later. Thus, Tcherikover concludes that the Josephus narrative is a historical myth. See also Josephus, *The Collected Works*, trans. R. Marcus, VI (London: 1930–43), Appendix C, p. 528 in which Marcus also states that he feels that Alexander did not visit Jerusalem. None of the old Greek and Latin sources mention such a visit. Therefore, Josephus may have drawn this portion of his history from apologetic literature of the Jews of Alexanderia. I. Levi also feels that the incident as recorded in the Talmud reflects the apologetic literature. See: I. Levi, "La Dispute entre les Egyptiens et les Juifs devant Alexandre," REJ, LXIII (1912), 210–215 and "Alexandre le Grand et les Juifs," in *Gedenkenbuch zur Errinnerung an David Kaufmann* (Breslau: 1900), 346–354.

The Talmudic story of the meeting of Alexander and the priests mentions Antipatris as the site. This is also chronologically inaccurate, since the city of Antipatris, founded by Herod, did not exist in Alexander's day. Scholars place the possible meeting of Alexander and the Jewish representatives as Kfar Saba, a settlement near the shore. It is known that Alexander traveled along the coast on his way back from Tyre to Gaza and back. *The Jewish Encyclopedia*, 12 vols. (New York, 1901–1912), I (1901), 340–343.

[35] Judges 20:1 and Samuel 3:20. Dan was and still is the northern boundary of Israel.

[36] See the similarity in Jonah 3:5; Esther 4:3.

[37] Historically, the High Priest at the time of Alexander was Simon the Just. Josephus

דירווזל׳ מה להיטיב למלך **ודאכסנדרוס. ו**יכתוב ענני׳ ולשון הגדול׳, כמוב אל׳ אלכסנ־
דרוס: ״כה אמרו אנשי ירושלים: כבד מהם הדבר אשר שאלת[109] כי לא יוכלו לעשות
את הדבר הזה. כי האוצרות אשר בבית האלהים אין כח בידם להוציאם משם ולשלח
אליך כי אבותיהם הקדישום לצורך אלמנות ויתומים ולכושלי ברך ולמטי יד להחזיק
בידם. ואם אתה חפץ הם יתנו לך מכל בית ובית שבירושלים דינר זהב אבל אוצרו׳
שהקדישו אבותיהם אין בידם כח להוציא מבית המקדש בית האלהים.״

ויהי כקרוא המלך אלכסנדרוס את מכתב אנשי ירושלים ויחר אפו מאד וישבע
בתועבת שלו שלא יצא מירושלים עד ישים את ירושלים ומקדש האלהים תל שממה.

ויהי בלילה וישכב המלך על מטתו ושנתו נדדה עליו ויפתח את חלון אהלו וישא את
עיניו וירא והנה מלאך אלהים עומד עליו וחרבו שלופה בידו.[110] ויבהל המלך מאד
ויאמר אל המלאך: ״למה זה אדוני יכה את עבדו?״ ויען המלאך ויאמר לו: ״הלא אני
הכובש מלכים תחתיך ומדבר עמים תחתיך[111] ולמה זה נשבעת לעשות הרע בעיני יי׳
להשחית את ארצו ואת עמו.״ ויען המלך ויאמר אל המלאך הדובר בו. ״בי אדוני, כל
אשר תאמר אלי אעשה.״[112] ויאמר לו המלאך לבוש הבדים:[113] ״השמר בנפשך לבלתי
עשות רעה[114] לאנשי ירושלים, אך בבואך ירושלים תשאל בשלום והטיב תטיב להם
ומאוצרותיך תאצור בבית אלהים. ואם תמרה את פי דע כי מות תמות אתה וכל אשר
לך.״

ויען אלכסנדרוס ויאמר אל המלאך לבוש הבדים: ״קשה לי מאד להשפיל את כבודי
ולעשות את הדבר הזה. אבל אם רע בעיניך אשובה לי[115] ולא אבוא ירושלים.״ ויאמר
לו המלאך: ״השמר בנפשך! אם תשוב עד אשר תבא ירושלם ושם תתן אוצרותיך
בבית מקדש האלהים.״

Exodus 18:18
"... for this thing is too heavy for them."
[109] ״כי כבד ממך הדבר.״

Genesis 18:2.
"And he lifted up his eyes and looked, and lo ... "
[110] ״וישא עיניו וירא והנה.״

Psalms 47:4.
"He shall subdue the people under us ... "
See also Psalms 18:48.
[111] ״ידבר עמים תחתינו.״

Numbers 22:17.
"... and I will do whatsoever thou sayest unto me ... "
[112] ״כל אשר תאמר אלי אעשה.״

Ezekial 9:11
"... clothed with linen ... "
[113] ״ויאמר לו המלך לבוש הבדים.״

Leviticus 18:30.
"... that ye commit not anyone ... "
[114] ״השמר בנפשך לבלתי עשות רעה.״

Numbers 22:34
"... if it displease thee, I will get me back again."
[115] ״אבל אם רע בעיניך אשובה לי.״

wrote a letter to Alexander: "Thus say the people of Jerusalem: 'Your request places too heavy a burden upon them and they cannot honor it. They are powerless to remove the treasures of the house of God and send them to you because their forefathers consecrated them to the support of widows, orphans, the lame, and the crippled. If you wish, they will give you a gold dinar for every household in Jerusalem, but they cannot remove the treasures of the Temple which were dedicated by their ancestors.' " King Alexander grew very angry when he read the letter from the people of Jerusalem. He swore by his idols that he would not wihdraw from Jerusalem until he had reduced it and its temple to rubble.

During the night, as the king lay awake on his bed, he noticed through the open window of his tent an angel of God standing with a drawn sword.

Terrified, the king exclaimed: "Why would my lord strike his servant?"

The angel replied: "It is I who conquer kings for you and trample nations beneath you. Why did you swear to do evil in the eyes of God by destroying His land and His people?"

The king said: "Please my lord, I will do whatever you say."

"Beware of your soul and do no harm to the people of Jerusalem," answered the angel dressed in linen, "but when you arrive there be concerned with their welfare, treat them well and deposit your treasures in the house of the Lord. If you disobey me, you and yours will die."

Alexander said to the angel dressed in linen: "It is very difficult for me to humble myself in this way. However, if it displeases you, I will turn back and not enter Jerusalem."

The angel answered: "Beware, lest you turn back before coming to Jerusalem and bringing your treasures to the House of the Lord."

Morning came. The king and his entire army arrived in Jerusalem. When he came before the gate of the city, he was welcomed by Annani, the High Priest, accompanied by eighty priests dressed in holy garments. They came to plead with him to spare the city. When Alexander saw Annani, the High Priest, he dismounted from his horse, / and prostrated   f. 271ᵇ
himself before him, embracing and kissing the priest's feet.

Alexander's warriors were displeased at this and said: "Why did you do this? Why did you degrade yourself before this man? Dukes and

calls the priest Jaddeus. The writer of this manuscript did not know the rabbinic stories of Simon the Just or the Josephus tale that the priest showed Alexander the prophecy of Daniel.

ויהי בבקר ויסע המלך עם רל חילו ויריא ירושלים ורשייר רז לסני יער חעיר
וילך ענני הכהן עם שמונים כהנים לבושי בגדי קדש להקביל פני המלך ולהתחנן על
העיר לבלתי השחיתה. ויהי כראות אלכסנדרוס ענני הכהן הגדול וירד מן הסוס/ויפול
לפניו ארצה ויחבק את רגלי הכהן וינשק להם. וירא גבורי אלכסנדרוס וירע בעיניהם
ויאמרו אל המלך: "מה זאת עשית ותשפיל את כבודך לפני האיש הזה? הלא דוכסים
ואפרכסים משתחוים לפניך ואתה זלזלת את כבודך בזה הזקן שהשתחוית לפניו
וירדת מן המרכבה." ויען המלך ויאמר להם: "אל תתמהו כי האיש הזקן הזה אשר
יצא כנגדי זה דמות המלאך האלהים אשר הולך לפניו בעת המלחמה ואשר ירודה
עמים תחתיי, על כן כבדתיו את כל הכבוד הזה." וכשמע ענני הכהן את דברי המלך
ויקד וישתחו לאלוהי ישר׳ ויברך השם בקול גדול. ויאמר אל המלך: "אם נא מצאתי חן
בעיניך[116] אל תעש מאומה ליושבי ירושלם כי הם עבדיך לעשות רצונך." ויאמר לו
המלך: "עד שאתה מצויני על אנשי ירושלים צוה עלי ועל אנשי מלחמתי כי לא
אוכל לעשות רעה לאנשי ירושלים כי מלאך האלהים הזהירני לבלתי עשות רעה."
ויבואו כל גיבורי ירושלים וזקניה וחסידיה וחכמיה ויביאו את המלך על הבירונה
העליונה אשר בירושלים ויהי שם ימים שלשה. ויהי ביום הרביעי ויאמר המלך אל
ענני: "הראיני נא את האל הגדול הרודה עמים תחתיי[117]." ויבא המלך וגיבוריו בבית
המקדש האלהים וישא עיניו וירא והנה מלאך לבוש הבדים עומד כנגדו. וימהר
המלך ויפל מלא קומתו ארצה וישתחו ארצה. וישא את קולו ויאמר: "זה הוא בית
אלהים וכמוהו אין בעולם." ויוצא המלך כלי כסף וכלי זהב ואבן יקרה הרבה מאד
ויתן באוצר בית אלהים. ויבקש המלך מענני הכהן ומשאר כהני השם אשר יקחו זהב
הרבה ויעשו תבניתו במקדש השם למען יהיה לו לאות ולזכרון. ויאמרו לו ענני
והכהנים: "לא נוכל לעשות את הדבר הזה לחקוק פסל כל תמונה בבית האלהים.
אך שמע נא לעצותינו. אותו זהב שאמרת לעשות ממנו פסל תבנית דמותך תן אותו
לאוצר בית השם למען יתפרנסו בו עניי העיר וכושלי ברך. ואנחנו נעשה לך שם

Genesis 18:3   "אם נא מצאתי חן בעיניך."[116]
"... if I have found favor in thy sight ... "

Psalms 144:2   "הרודד עמים תחתי."[117]
"... who subdueth my people under me."
See also: Psalms 18:48; II Samuel 22:48.

lords have prostrated themselves before you, and now you have lowered yourself by descending from the chariot and bowing before this old man."

"Do not be amazed," said the king. "This old man who came toward me resembles the angel of God who leads me at the time of battle and who tramples nations beneath me. Therefore, I have bestowed all this honor upon him."

Hearing these words, Annani, the priest, knelt and bowed to the God of Israel and blessed the Lord in a loud voice. He turned to the king saying: "If it please you, do not harm the people of Jerusalem for they are your subjects and will do your will."

"Instead of pleading with me for the people of Jerusalem," said the king, "entreat them on my behalf and that of my warriors, for I could not harm them since the angel of God warned me not to do evil against them."

The soldiers, the elders, the holy men, and the wise ones accompanied the king to the highest castle in Jerusalem and he stayed there for three days. On the fourth day the king said to Annani: "Please show me the house of the great God who tramples nations beneath me." The king and his warriors entered the temple of God. Alexander lifted his eyes and saw the angel, clothed in linen, standing opposite him.

The king prostrated himself, raised his voice and said: "This is the house of the Lord and there is none like it in the world."

Then the king took vessels of gold and silver and a large quantity of precious stones and deposited them in the treasury of the house of God. The king asked Annani and the other priests of the Lord to take a large quantity of gold and make a statue of him and place it in the temple of the Lord as a sign and a remembrance of him.

Annani and the priests said: "We are forbidden to engrave a statue or an image in the house of the Lord. However, heed our advice. Give the gold that you wanted us to use to make your statue to the treasury of the house of the Lord so that it may be used to maintain the poor and crippled of the city. We will commemorate your good name by naming all the boys born this year after you."[38]

---

[38] A similar tale is found in a chronicle of 1166, *Sefer Ha-Kabbalah*, in which it is related that the priests also promise Alexander to begin the calendar from this time. Cf. "Sefer Ha-Kabbalah," ed. A. Neubauer, *Medieval Jewish Chronicles*, II (Oxford, 1887), 47–84. Comments on the author, David of Toledo, are found in the Preface, xiiff.

עוד ל**זכרון** כל חנע־״־ים ח־ל־י־ם בשנו, ואת כולם יקראו על שמך.״ וייטב הדבר בעיני
המלך ויאמ׳ לעשות כן. וישקול ארבעים ככר זהב טוב ויתן ביד ענני הכהן ושאר
הכהנים ויאמר אליהם: ״התפללו בעדי תמיד.״[118] ויוסף המלך ויוצא כלי כסף וכלי
זהב ואבן יקרה לרוב לענני הכהן ויתן לו ויאמר לו: ״אם נא מצאתי חן בעיניך התפלל
בעדי תמיד.״ ויאמר ענני לעשות כן.

ויהי אחרי זאת ויצא המלך מן המקדש ויתן בירושלים עם כל חילו שלשה חדשים
ויתן את הכסף ואת הזהב בירושלים כאבנים[119] אשר אמרו חכמי העיר וזקניה מימי
שלמה בן דוד לא היה כזה בירושלם. וכל העם אשר סביבות ירושלים שמעו את
אלכסנדרוס ויביאו לו משתה ומאכל לרוב מאד ויתן להם המלך ככל אשר שמעו
שאלו ממנו ותמלא כל ארץ ישר׳ מכסף וזהב ותעשר הארץ.
ויהי אחרי כן ויסע המלך משם מירושלים וילך ויעבור ארץ הגליל ומארץ הגליל
עבר דרך קרדוניייא והארץ טובה ושמינה מאד.
והמה חונים באהלים, ואין להם בתים ואין להם מלבושים זולתי מלבוש העשוי
משער גמלים ומרוב חמימות הארץ אינם יכולים לסבול שום מלבוש אחר. וישמעו
את שמעת אלכסנדרוס ויצאו לקראתו וישתחו לו. ויקבלם המלך וידבר עמהם וינסה
בחידות[120] ובכל מיני חכמות כי הם חכמים מחוכמים מאד וישמח המלך על רוב חכ־
מתם. ויאמר אליהם: ״כל אשר תשאלו ממני/אתן לכם,״ ויצעקו כולם ויאמרו:

f. 272ᵃ

[118] ״ויתפללו בעדו תמיד.״
Psalms 72:15
“. . . prayer shall also be made for them continually . . .”

[119] ״ויתן את הכסף ואת הזהב בירושלים כאבנים.״
II Chronicles 1:15
“And the king made silver and gold at Jerusalem as plenteous as stones . . .”

[120] ״מביא לנסותו בחידות.״
I Kings 10:1.
“. . . she came to prove him with hard questions.”

This pleased the king and he agreed that it be done. He weighed forty talents of fine gold and placed it in Annani's hands, saying: "Pray for me always." The king brought forth more objects of silver and gold and an abundance of precious stones and giving them to Annani, the priest, said: "If I have found favor in your eyes, pray for me always." Annani promised to do so. After this, the king left the sanctuary and camped for three months in Jerusalem with all his army. He distributed silver and gold as if they were stones, and the wise men and elders of the city said that never had such riches been seen in Jerusalem since the days of Solomon, son of David. The people from the environs of Jerusalem heard of Alexander's fame and brought him an abundance of food and drink and he gave them all that they requested of him, and the land of Israel was filled with silver and gold and prospered.

Afterwards, the king traveled from Jerusalem passing through the Gallil[39] and from there through Kardonia,[40] a prosperous and fertile land. The inhabitants dwelt in tents for they did not own houses.[41] Because of the intense heat of the country they could not tolerate any type of garment except those made of camel hair. Having heard of Alexander's fame, they came to greet him, bowing before him. The king received them and spoke to them, testing them with all kinds of riddles and all matters pertaining to wisdom, for they were known to be very wise men. He rejoiced at their wisdom and said: "Whatever you request of me / I will grant," and they all cried out: "O lord King, grant us f. 272^b

---

[39] A district at the northern border of Israel from ancient times to the present.

[40] Possibly refers to Kurds, located in northern Babylonia and Iraq, near the Ararat mountains.

[41] Apparently the writer of this story was not familiar with the rabbinic tale of the wise men of the South, or Brahmins, as told in the Babylonian Talmud, *Tamid*, pp. 31b–32a. In this version, Alexander put ten questions to the elders of the South (Negev).

Another opinion states that the Ten Wise Men of the South are not the elders of Israel, but were the wise men of India and Ethiopia. See: S. J. L. Rapoport, *Erich Millin* (Warsaw: 1914), p. 69 and A. de Rossi, *Meor Eynayim* (Warsaw: 1899), p. 126.

In this tale of the wise naked men, a possible echo of the Rechabites is found. This religious group existed during the period of the First Temple. They lived a nomadic life; they did not live in houses, sow seeds, or plant vineyards. This group sought a return to the simple, sober ways of the desert, in opposition to the idolatry and immorality of the Canaanites. *The Universal Jewish Encyclopedia* (New York: 1939–1943), IX (1943), 93–94.

"אדוניי המלך תן לנו חיים עולם." ויבהל חנוך ויאמר אליה: "אין, אין בידי
לעשות." ויענו ויאמרו לו: "אם אין בידך לעשות זה לתת לנו את שאילתינו לא נשאל
ממך דבר אחר". ויאמרו אל המלך: "שאל ממנו מה נתן לך." ויאמ' המלך: "לא אשאל
מכם דבר זולתי עשבים המועילים שאתם בקיאים בהם ובכח גבורתם."

ויאמרו אל המלך: "כדברך כן נעשה," וילכו ויביאו אל המלך עשבים הרבה ויגידו
לו כל כחם ואת כל שימושם ואת כל רפואתם. וילך המלך אחרי העשבים לחפש אנה
ואנה כתבניתם וכדמותם למען יזכור את העשבים במקום אחר. ויצו המלך ויכתבו
רופאיו את כל העשבים ואת כל שמושם ויצו להביא את הספר אל בית גנזיו. אחרי
הדברים האלה חלה המלך אלכסנדרוס חולי גדול ויצו להביא את ספר הרפואות אשר
בבית גנזיו. ויביאו אותו ויבקשו בו את תחלואי המלך וימצאוהו וירפאו הרופאים
את המלך.

ויהי בין הרופאים רופא אחד אשר היה שונא את המלך, וילך הרופא ההוא ויגנב
את ספר הרפואות וישרפהו באש. ויוגד למלך כי נשרף הספר ויצר לו מאד ויקרע
שמלותיו ויצו להביא את הרופא אשר שרף את הספר ויברח הרופא ויתחבא ולא
נמצא.

אחרי זאת נסע המלך עם כל חילו ויבא ארץ קרטיניא ויקבלהו המלך ארדוס בכבוד
גדול. ויוליכהו בתוך עיר ממלכה שלו ושמה עמק. ושם היתה אשה יפה מאד אשר
כל רואיה יאשרוה ומעידים עליה שלא היתה כמותה בכל העולם. ומדי חודש בחדשו
היה חק משפט לאשה הזאת ללכת פעם אחת להיכל אצילין או"ה שלהן, ולזבוח זבח
תועבה ומדי עוברה דרך רחובות העיר היו בעלי מלאכה מרפים ממלאכתם ורצין אחריה
להסתכל ביופיה. כה עשתה האשה הזאת תמיד עוברת להיכל ומקטורת. ויהי היום וירא
אותה מתן כהן אצילין וכמעט אשר נשתגע אחריה. וכאשר באתה האשה לקטר לבעל
ויאמר אליה מתן "בי אדונתי! שלוח שלחתי אליך לאמר מאת אצילין קדש שלנו."

everlasting life." The king was bewildered and said: "This is not within my power to grant." They said: "If you cannot grant us this, we will ask nothing more of you." Then they said to him: "Tell us what you want us to grant you." "I will ask nothing of you except your knowledge of the beneficial herbs in whose potential and strength you are skilled," he answered. "We shall do as you request." And they brought him many herbs and disclosed their virtues and their healing power to him. The king searched for similar herbs everywhere so that he could recognize them if he ever saw them again. He ordered his physicians to record the uses of these herbs and commanded them to place the book in his treasury. Subsequently, King Alexander became very ill and ordered the *Book of Remedies*[42] brought to him from the treasury. They looked up the king's illness and finding it, the physicians were able to cure the king.

Among the physicians there was one who hated the king and he stole the *Book of Remedies* and burnt it in the fire. When the king was told that the book had been burned he was greatly saddened. He tore his garments and ordered the physician who had burned the book to be brought to him, but the physician had fled and could not be found.

The king and his army set forth again and arrived at the land of Kartinia and were received by King Ardos with great honor. Alexander was led in to Amak,[43] the capital city. There lived in that city a very beautiful woman. All who saw her praised her, saying that there was no one who surpassed her in beauty in the whole world. Once a month this woman went to the temple of their god, Atzilin,[44] to offer sacrifices. Whenever she passed through the city streets, the craftsmen ceased their work and ran after her to gaze upon her beauty. This woman regularly went to the temple to burn incense. One day, Matan, priest of Atzilin, saw her and almost went out of his mind because of her. When she came to offer incense to the idol, Matan said to her: "Please, my lady, I have been sent to speak to you by our holy Atzilin."

---

[42] The *Book of Remedies* was used by King Hezekiah 720–692 B.C., who finally had it hidden so that people, in case of sickness, would rely on God and not on the *Book* for their cure.

[43] Amak and Jerusalem and Ayuna are the only capital cities in this story.

[44] Similar to Asilin and possibly comes from Apolon or Avulon; the Arabs interchange *p* and *v*.

ותשמח האשה ותזנמר זל מתן. "חגידה נא לי מה ונמעשה, אל תכחד ממני."121 ויאמר
אליה מתן: "דעי כי אצילין מתאוה לבא אליך ותלדי ממנו בן קדש כמותו כי אין אשה
בכל העולם הראויה למשכבו זולתי את." ותשמח האשה ותאמר: "כל אשר יצוה עלי
אצילין אעשה לא אפיל מכל דבריו ארצה."122 ויאמר מתן אל האשה: "אם את שומעת
לדברי אצילין, לכי וקחי לך רשות מבעליך ואם טוב בעיניו בואי הלילה בהיכל
אצילין ותלדי ממנו." ותמהר האשה ותלך אל ביתה ותגד לבעלה את כל דברי מתן.
ויאמר לה בעלה: "עשי כטוב בעיניך אך תביאי עמך בהיכל אצילין כרים וכסתות
ומצעות ומעילין ובגדי משי להציע עליהם." ותעש האשה כן, ותשלח כרים וכסתות
ובגדי משי אל מתן ויקבלם ויעשו מצע בתוך ההיכל אחורי*. ויהי בלילה ההוא ותבא
האשה אל היכל אצילין ותלך שפחתה עמה. ויאמר מתן אל האשה: "לא נכון שתהיה
שפחתך עמך בהיכל כי אינה ראויה לכך ותאמר האשה אל שפחתה: "לכי צאי מן
ההיכל ושכבי פתח ההיכל עד/אור הבקר." ותעש שפחתה כן.

f. 272^b

ויהי בחצי הלילה ויבא מתן אל ההיכל דרך פתח השיני דרך מבואו. ותשמע השפחה
את קול ציר הדלת וירע בעיניה ותקם ממשכבה ותבא בלט ותרא והנה מתן בא בהיכל
והיא יראה לדבר פן יהרג אותה מתן ולא דברה דבר. ותרא את מתן מחבק את גבירתה
ומנשק אותה ועשה עמה כדרך כל הארץ עד תשע פעמים. והיא ממתינה עד אשר
תשש כחו ותבא בלט ותקח את פסל אצילין ותך אותו על ראשו וימות על מצע גביר-
תה. ותאמר השפחה: "מה זאת עשית כי נטמאת עם האיש אחר זולתי בעליך?" ותרגז
האשה ותבהל כי ידעה כי נטמאת ותשא את קולה ותבק.123 ותאמר לה שפחתה: "אל
תבכי, מה שנעשה אין להשיב124 אלא שתקי ולכי לביתך ואל תגידי את הדבר הזה."

Joshua 7:19   "והגד נא לי מה עשית אל תכחד ממני."121

" . . . tell me now what thou hast done; hide it not from me."
See also Jeremiah 38:25.

I Samuel 3:19   "ולא הפיל מכל דבריו ארצה."122

" . . . and did let none of his words fall to the ground."
See also II Kings 10:10.

Genesis 21:16   "ותשא את קולה ותבך."123

" . . . and lift up her voice and wept."

Missing word: הבמה.*

The woman rejoiced and said: "Please tell me everything; do not withold anything from me."

He said: "Know that Atzilin desires to come to you and beget by you a holy son like himself for there is no other woman in the entire world worthy to be with him."

The woman was overjoyed and said: "Whatever Atzilin commands I will do and I will not omit anything."

"If you heed the words of Atzilin " said Matan to the woman, "go and obtain permission from your husband and if he agrees, come to-night to the temple of Atzilin and you will give birth by him."[45]

The woman hurried to her house and told her husband all that Matan had said. "Do as you see fit," her husband said, "but take pillows, coverings, and mattresses, cloaks, and silken garments to the temple of Atzilin to spread over the ground." The woman did this, sending pillows, coverings, and silken garments to Matan, who received them and made a bed behind the altar in the sanctuary. That night the woman came to the temple of Atzilin accompanied by her maid.

Matan said: "It is not proper that your maid stay with you in the temple, for she is not worthy."

So the woman told her maid: "Leave the temple and lie down at the entrance until / daybreak."

f. 272[b]

Her maid did so. At midnight, Matan came to the temple through a second entrance. When the maid heard the noise of the door hinge she became suspicious and arose from her bed and entered silently. She saw Matan enter the temple but was afraid to speak lest he kill her; so she did not utter a word. She saw Matan embracing and kissing her mistress, and he had intercourse with her nine times. She waited until he had exhausted his strength, and then, grabbing the statue of Atzilin, she softly approached and struck him on the head and he died on the bed of her mistress.

The maid said: "What have you done? You have been defiled by a man other than your husband." The woman was disquieted and grew frightened for she knew she was defiled and she wept bitterly.

Her maid said: "Do not weep, for what is done cannot be undone. Remain silent, return, home, and do not reveal this to anyone."

---

[45] Note the striking parallel to the conversation between Bildad and Golofira preceding the conception of Alexander.

וחזן האשה ויאמר לה: "אל תאמרי לי לשתוק כי לו ווּּפֵל לְעֲעוּר בְּמִילִין"[125] כי מן
הדבר כי נטמאתי כי מעולם לא נגע בי אדם זולתי בעלי ועתה נטמאתי ואיך תאמרי
שתקי ואל תגידי." ותלך האשה ותשם ידה על ראשה ותלך הלוך וזעקה עד אשר
באה אל ביתה. ויאמר לה בעלה: "מה לך?" ותגד לו כל הדברים האלה ולא היה לה
פתחון פה[126] לבעלה לעשות לה מאומה כי הוא בעצמו נתן לה רשות ללכת אל היכל
אצילין.

ויבא בעלה אל המלך ויספר לו כל אשר עשה מתן לאשתו ואף כי שפחתו הרגתו
ויאמר המלך אל אלכסנדרוס: "איזה דין אעשה?" ויאמר אלכסנדרוס: "לא תוכל
לעשות למתן כי כבר נהרג ומשפטו חרוץ. אבל אם היה במלכותי הייתי מפיל
את היכל אצילין כי נטמא ואין נכון להתפלל בתוכו." ויצו המלך ויהרסו את היכל
אצילין וערו ערו עד היסוד[127] ואת מתן הנהרג שרפו באש. ויאמר אלכסנדר' אל המלך:
"אם נא מצאתי חן בעיניך תשלח אחרי האשה ההיא ואראה את יופיה. וישלח המלך
אחריה ותבא האשה לפני המלך. וירא אכלסנדרוס את יופיה ויתמה ויפלא בעיניו.
ויאמר אל המלך: "תן אותה לי לאשה." ויאמר לו המלך: "חלילה לך לעשות כדבר הזה
לקחת אשה מבעלה בעוד שהוא חי ותמלא הארץ זימה." ויאמר המלך אלכסנדרוס
אל המלך: "אם לא תתן לי את האשה הזאת לאשה דע כי מלחמות גדולות יתגרו בכל
מלכותיך." ויאמר לו: "עשה מה שתוכל כי לא אתן לך את האשה כי כל מלכותי
מתכבד בה.

ואם יוצאה ממלכותי תעשה בו רושם גדול." וירא אלכסנדרוס כי לא רצה המלך לתת
לו את האשה ויערוך כלי מלחמתו וילחם עם המלך. ותגבר יד אלכסנדרוס וישחת
רבים מגיבוריו ויתפש המלך חי ויצו לקשור אותו בכבלי ברזל. ויקח אלכסנדרוס את
האשה ההיא בחזקה ויאהביה מאד. ויעש לה היכל זהב ארכו עשרה אמה, ורוחבו שש
אמה, וגובהו חמש עשרה אמה ויחפה את קירות ההיכל ההוא מאבן יקרה. ולא היה בו
חלון כי האבן יקרה מאירה בלילה כביום.

Esther 8:8.   "אל תכתבי מה שנעשה אין להשיב."[124]
" . . . may no man reverse."

Job 4:2   "ועצור מי יוכל."[125]
" . . . but who can withhold himself from speaking?"

Ezekial 17:63   "ולא יהיה לך עוד פתחון פה."[126]
" . . . and never open thy mouth any more. . ."
See also Ezekial 29:21.

Psalms 137:7   "וערו ערו עד היסוד."[127]
"Raise, it, raise it, even to the foundation thereof."

"Do not tell me to be silent," said the woman, "for I cannot refrain from telling of this. I have become defiled, for I have never been touched by any man but my husband; so how could you tell me to keep silent and not tell." The woman put her hand upon her head and went home wailing.

"What happened to you?" her husband asked. She told him all that had happened, but he could not reproach her nor do anything to her, for he himself had permitted her to go to the temple of Atzilin.

Then her husband went to the king and told him what Matan had done to his wife and that his maid had killed him. The king asked Alexander: "What should my judgment be?"

Alexander answered: "You could not do anything to Matan for he has been killed and his sentence has already been decided. However, if this had happened in my kingdom, I would have destroyed the temple of Atzilin, since it has become defiled and it would not be proper to pray in it."

The king ordered the temple of Atzilin destroyed to its foundation and the slain Matan burnt.

Then Alexander said: "If I have pleased you, send for that woman so I may see her beauty."

The king sent for her and she came. When Alexander saw her beauty he was astounded and it was wondrous in his eyes, and he said to the king: "Give her to me as a wife."

"God forbid if you take a woman away from her husband while he is still alive, for the land will be filled with abomination."

King Alexander said: "If you will not give her to me as a wife, know that great battles will be waged in your kingdom."

He replied: "Do as you wish but I will not give you this woman, for my entire kingdom is honored by her and if she should depart it will leave a tremendous impression."

When Alexander saw that the king refused to give the woman to him he prepared his weapons and fought against him. Alexander had the upper hand, and he easily destroyed many of his opponents' warriors. The king was captured alive and Alexander ordered him bound with iron chains. Then Alexander forcibly took that woman and loved her greatly. He erected a temple of gold for her measuring eleven cubits long, six cubits wide and fifteen cubits high. He studded its walls with precious stones. It did not have a window, for the precious stones shone

ורצם המולך **מתומח וזת חזושח** ויתקע חוז'ע' על' או בע אפני בו ז/' וימשכוהו סוסים הרבה. ואין האשה הזאת* מה מתוכה של היכל כי כל מאכלה נתון בתוכה. ותהרי האשה מאלכסנדרוס ותלד בן. וישמח המלך מאד ויקרא שם הנער אלכסנדר. ויעש משתה גדול לכל שריו ועבדיו[128] וישם כתר מלכות בראש האשה ההיא וימליכיה.[129]

f. 273[a] וישמחו כל עם חילו עם המלך כי/המלך שמחם בדברים טובים ובמתנות גדולות. ויהי אחרי זאת וימת אלכסנ' בן המלך בן תשעה חדשים. וגם בופסל, סוס המלך, מת באותו היום.

״ויבך המלך בכי גדול ויצו לקבור את בנו ואת בוספול סוסו קבר אצלו. ויצו לבנות עליהם בנין גדול ונחמד למראה. וינחם המלך את אשתו ויבא אליה ותהר לו. ויהי בעת לדתה[130] ויבק המלך וכל חילו בכי גדול* ותמת את האשה ההיא ויקרע המלך בגדיו ויספוק כף אל כף וימרט את ראשו ויפול לארץ. ויבאו כל שריו לנחמו וימאן להתנחם.[131] וילכו שריו ממנו ויניחו את המלך בדד. ויקח המלך חבל אחד לתלות עצמו מרוב צער וירגישו שריו וימהרו וירוצו אליו ויקחו ממנו את החבל ויוכיחו את המלך ויאמרו לו: ״האתה תעצור במלוכה וכי פסו נשים בעולם אשר בקשת להמית את עצמך על אודות אשה אחת. וידברו אליו דברים הרבה ויאמרו אל המלך: ״אם טוב בעיניך נשלח שלוחים וספרים בכל מדינת המלך ויבקשו בתולות או בעולות יפות מראה ויפות תואר,[132] והיה הנערה אשר ייטב בעיני המלך ימליכנה.[133] וייטב הדבר בעיני המלך וישלח מלאכים אל מדינות מלכותו, וימצאו בתולה אחת בארץ אפריקיא ויביאו אותה אל המלך. ותיטב הנערה בעיני המלך ויאהביה כי היא היתה יפת תואר מאד מאד וישם המלך כתר מלכות בראשה וימליכיה.

ויהי אחרי זאת ויסע המלך עם כל מחנהו ויבא ביער גדול וירוצו לפני החיל חיות משונות בעלי חמש קרנים וישחיתו רבים מן החיל. ויבא אלכסנדרוס ויאמר אל עמו: ״קחו לכם אש וגופרית וזפת והדליקו עצי היער. אולי יעשה השם כרוב רחמיו ויושיעינו מן החיות הרעות האלה.״ וימהרו ויעשו כן וידליקו עצי היער, וינוסו החיות וינצל המלך וכל חילו מהם.

---

* זה is missing; מה is senseless in this position.

Esther 1:3.   ״עשה משתה לכל שריו ועבדיו.״ [128]

"...he made a feast unto all his princes..."

Esther 2:17.   ״וישם מלכות בראשה וימליכה תחת ושתי.״ [129]

".. so that he set the royal crown upon her head and made her queen instead of Vashti."

Genesis 38:27   ״ויהי בעת לדתה.״ [130]

"And it came to pass when she travailed..."

* The sentence should read: ויהי בעת לדתה ותמת את האשה ההיא ויבך המלך וכל חילו בכי

גדול ויקרע המלך את בגדיו...״

Genesis 37:35   ״ויקמו כל בניו וכל בנותיו לנחמו וימאן להתנחם.״ [131]

"And all his sons and all his daughters rose up to comfort him; but he refused to be comforted."

Esther 2:2   ״יבקשו למלך נערות בתולות טובות מראה.״ [132]

"Let there be sought for the king young virgins fair to look on..."

Esther 2:4   ״והנערה אשר תיטב בעיני המלך תמלוך תחת ושתי.״ [133]

"...and let the maiden that pleaseth the king be queen instead of Vashti."

at midnight as in the daytime. The king placed the woman in it and mounted the temple on four iron wheels drawn by many horses. The woman did not move from the temple because all her food was brought to her. The woman conceived by Alexander and gave birth to a son. The king rejoiced greatly and named the boy Alexander. He made a great feast for all his princes and servants and placed a crown upon the woman's head and made her queen. The king's army rejoiced with him / because the king presented them with costly gifts.

f. 273ª

The king's son, Alexander, died at the age of nine months. On the same day his horse, Busifal, also died. The king wept bitterly and ordered his son buried and his horse, Busifal, buried near him. He ordered a large, beautiful mausoleum erected over them. The king consoled his wife and came to her and she conceived. However, she died in childbirth. The king rent his garments, wrung his hands, tore at his head and fell to the ground. All his princes condoled with him, but the king refused to be comforted. So they left him alone. From deep grief the king tried to hang himself, but his ministers noticed, and quickly ran to him and took the rope away from him.

They reproved the king saying: "Are you going to put an end to the kingdom? Did you try to take your life because of one woman as if there were no other women left in the world?" They continued speaking: "If you wish, we will send messengers with books[46] throughout your land to seek beautiful maidens or women. Let the king crown the maiden who pleases him most."

This counsel pleased the king and so he sent messengers to all his provinces. They found a maiden in the land of Afrikian and brought her to the king. The maiden pleased the king and he loved her for she was very beautiful. He placed the crown on her head and made her his queen.

Then the king and his entire army set forth and came to a large forest where strange five-horned beasts fell upon them, killing many. Seeing this, Alexander told his men: "Take fire, brimstone, and tar and set the forest on fire. Perhaps the Almighty, in his great mercy, will save us from these wild beasts." They quickly set the trees on fire, the beasts fled, and the king and his men were saved.

---

46 This is reminiscent of the ancient story told in the Book of Esther where messengers were sent far and wide to find a wife for the king.

The manuscript uses the word *books* but the meaning is that messengers or scribes representing the king went out to find the woman.

ויסעו משם ויבואו אל **ארץ** חושך וייצאו ויוציאו **יזח** בהר גדול **ונשוגה ונחמד למראה.**[134]
ויצמא המלך וכל חילו למים וייראו לשתות את מי הנהר ויצו המלך ויחפרו בורות
סביבות הנהר[135] וימצאו שם מים רבים וישת המלך ובעמו. ויאמר המלך אל כל עמו:
"אם טוב בעיניכם נחנה שם על המים כי אני מריח בהם שמועילים הם," ויאמרו
לעשות כן ויחנו שם עשרה ימים. ויהי ביום העשירי ויתפוש צייד המלך עופות
ויחנקם וירחצם במי הנהר ההוא. וכאשר נתנם במים לרוחצה ויחיו ויפרחו להם.
ראה עבד המלך כן מיהר ושתה מן הנהר ההוא וילך ויגד למלך את כל אשר קרהו.
ויאמר לו המלך: "בברור הם מי גן עדן כי כל השותה מהם יחיה לעולם. לך מהרה
והבא לי מן הנהר ואשתה גם אני." וימהר העבד ויקח ספל אחד בידו להביא לו
מימי הנהר ולא מצא שם מים וילך ויגד למלך: לא מצאתי את מי המעיין כי האלהים
העלים ממני." ויחר אף המלך ויקח חרבו ויחתוך את ראש עבדו. **וירץ** העבד בלא
ראש ויאמר מנחם הסופר: "כה אמרו חכמינו שעדיין הוא בים בלא ראש והוא הופך
הספינות שבים וכשבא להפוך הספינות אם יאמרו בני הספינות: "ברח ברח אדוניך
אלכסנדרוס בא!" מיד הוא בורח והספינות ניצולים."

Genesis 2:9

[134] "ונחמד למראה."

"...that is pleasant to the sight..."

Exodus 7:24

[135] "ויחפרו כל המצרים סביבות היאור."

"And all the Egyptians digged about the river..."

They set forth from there arriving at the land of Ofrat[46] where they found a large, unusual river, pleasant to behold. The king and his army were thirsty, but were afraid to drink its waters. The king ordered wells dug in the vicinity of the river and much water was found, and the king and his men drank. The king said: "If it pleases you, we will camp here by the waters, for by their fragrance I know they are beneficial." They agreed to do so, and camped there for ten days. On the tenth day, the king's hunter caught some birds, wrung their necks and washed them in the waters of the river. As he dipped them in and washed them in waters of the river, they returned to life and flew away.[47] Seeing this, the king's servant quickly drank from that river and went to the king to tell him all that had happened. "Obviously, these are the waters of the Garden of Eden," said the king. "Whoever drinks from them shall live forever. Go quickly and fetch me some and I, too, shall drink." The servant hastened, cup in hand, to bring some of those waters to him, but he could not find them. He returned and told the king: "I could not find the waters of the river for the Lord has hidden them from me." The king grew angry, drew his sword, and beheaded his servant. Then the headless servant ran away[48] and Menachem, the secretary, related: "Our sages say that he is still headless in the sea where he overturns ships. When he comes to overturn ships, he is forced to flee if the passengers call out: 'Flee, flee! Your master Alexander is coming.' In this way the ships are saved."

[46] Ofrat or Oferet, meaning land of copper in Hebrew. A form of the name, "Prat," is noted in Genesis 2:14 in the name of the river Euphrates, connected with the story of the four rivers emanating from the Garden of Eden. Hence, Ofrat, is the name used by the writer of the tale to refer to a place near Eden.

[47] P. Meyer, *Alexandre le Grand*, op. cit., II, 175, cites a similar incident in the French *Roman d'Alexandre*.

Note Appendix B, for folklore themes in MS. Bodl. Heb. d. 11, fol. 265–278. They are listed according to the method of Stith Thompson, *Motif-Index of Folk Literature*, 2nd. ed. (Bloomington, Ind.: 1955–1958). See also D. Noy (Neuman)., *Motif-Index to the Talmudic—Midrashic Literature* (Ann Arbor, Mich.: 1954), Microfilm Service, Publication No. 8792.

L. Ginzberg, *Legends*, V, 92 (also II, 314), points to a cycle of legends about the rivers of paradise, which belong to the stream of life. He notes the quotation "living waters," in Enoch 17:4 and in Revelations 22:17.

[48] This is similar to the tale told of King Solomon who retains his power over the djinns after his death by making them believe he was still alive. See J. E. Hanauer, *Folklore of the Holy Land*, op. cit., pp. 49–50.

ויזמר ו**זלכסגדדרוס.** "חבי?זו ל' ?או? פטל' צל'גמ'?י ו'ב'?או לו וישבע **המלך** עליו אשר
לא ישוב עד יבא אל מקום אשר אין דרך לנסות/ימין ושמאל[136] ולא ימצא עוד דרך
דרך לעבור."

f.237^b

ויסע המלך עם כל מחנהו ויעבור את הנהר ויבא לפני שער אחד גבוה כשלשים אמה.
ויתמה המלך על גבוה השער ההוא והנה קול אליו: "זה הוא השומר את שער האלהים
אשר צדיקים בו." וישא המלך את עיניו וירא אותיות חקוקות על השער ויקרא אל
מנחם הסופר ויקרא את המכתב והנה כתוב עליו: "שאו שערים ראשיכם והנשאו
פתחי עולם[137]".

וילך המלך משם ויעבור בין ההרים עם כל חילו ששה חדשים, כלו ההרים ולא נמצא
עוד הרים זולתי מישור. ועל המישור שער יפה וגבוה מאד מאד שלא שלטה עין
לראות עד סוף גובהו והנה כתוב על השער אותיות יפות גדולות מאד. ויקרא מנחם
את האותיות והנה כתוב על השער: "זה השער לה' צדיקים יבואו בו.[138]" ויפרש
מנחם את האותיות אל המלך ויאמר המלך: "בברור זה שער גן עדן." ויצעק המלך
ויאמר: "מי זה אשר על השער הזה?" והנה קול אליו בא: "וזה הוא שער גן עדן
וערל וזכר אשר לא ימול[139] לא יבא הנה."

Numbers 22:26
"אשר אין דרך לנטות ימין ושמאל." [136]
" . . . where there was no way to turn either to the right hand or to the left."

Psalms 24:7
"שאו שערים ראשיכם והנשאו פתחי עולם." [137]
"Lift up your heads, O ye gates; and be ye lifted up, ye everlasting doors . . ."

Psalms 118:20
"זה השער לה' צדיקים יבואו בו." [138]
"This is the gate of the Lord , into which the righteous shall enter."

Genesis 17:14
[139]
"And the uncircumcised male child whose flesh of his foreskin is not circumcised . . ."

Alexander said: "Bring me the statue of my image," and it was brought to him. The king swore by it that he would not return until he reached a place where there was nor road/to turn right nor left nor a place to pass through.

The king and his entire camp journeyed across the river and came upon a gate[49] thirty cubits high. The king was astonished at the height of that gate. A voice called: "I am the keeper of the gate of the Lord through which the righteous enter."[50]

Lifting his eyes, the king saw letters engraved upon the gate. He summoned Menachem, the secretary, who read the inscription as follows: "Lift up your heads, O ye gates; and be ye lifted up, ye everlasting doors."[51]

From there, the king and his entire army traveled for six months across the mountains. Having crossed the mountains, they emerged upon a plain where stood a beautiful, high gate and no human eye could see its top. On it were inscribed large, beautiful letters. Menachem read the letters engraved on the gate: "This is the gate of the Lord through which the righteous shall enter." Menachem exp'ained this to the king who said: "Apparently, this is the gate of the Garden of Eden."[52] Then he cried out: "Who is upon this gate?" A voice called back: "This is the

---

[49] The Latin prose work of Alexander's journey to the Earthly Paradise is *Iter ad Paradisum*, ed. Julius Zacher (Königsberg: 1859) and A. Hilka, in L. P. G. Peckham, and M. S. La Du, *Prise de Defur* and the *Voyage au Paradise Terrestre* (Princeton University Press, 1935: *Elliot Monographs*, 35), pp. xli–xlviii. This Latin work dates between 1100–1175 and is thought to be the work of a Jew since five of the fourteen manuscripts are ascribed to "Salamon didascalus Judaeorum." See G. Cary, op. cit. p. 19.

The history of the journey to paradise in Arabic sagas is the subject of a study by F. Spiegel, *Die Alexandersage bei den Orientalen*, (Leipzig: 1851).

[50] "This is the gate of the Lord, the righteous shall enter into it." (Psalm 118:20). This is repeated in the next paragraph of the romance.

[51] "Lift up your heads, O ye gates, and be ye lifted up, ye everlasting doors, and the King of Glory shall come in" (Psalm 24:7).

See a parallel Solomonic legend in the Introduction to this study. A similar tale is told about St. Basilicus. The doors of the church which had closed upon the heretics swung wide open as soon as he recited Psalm 24:7. L. Ginzberg, *Jewish Folklore*, op. cit., p. 9.

[52] The episode of the Garden of Eden in the Babylonian Talmud, *Tamid*, p. 32a–b. For the Garden of Eden foundations of the *Iter ad Paradisum* and *Roman d'Alexandre* see the Introduction to this study, footnote 56.

ויהי כלילה ההוא וימל **זא**לכסנדרוס את בשר עורלתו ויבא ויראם וירפאהו מיד
בעשבים המעולים ולא נודע הדבר אל מחניהו כי המלך צוה על הרופאים לבלתי יגידו
דבר. ויהי ממחרת ויצעק המלך אל שומרי השער: "תנו לי מכס ואלך לדרכי!" ויוציאו
ויתנו לו ארגז אחד ובתוכו כעין חתיכת בשר עין. ויושט המלך את ידו להגביהו מן
הארץ ולא היה יכול ויצעק להם לאמר: "מה זה שנתתם לי?!" ויענו ויאמרו לו: "זה
הוא עין אחד." ויאמר המלך: "מה אני צריך ממנו!" ויאמרו לו: "זה לך האות שעיניך
לא תשבע עושר וגם לא תמלא עיניך להיות משוטט בכל הארצות." ויאמר המלך:
"מה אוכל לעשות שאוכל להרימו מן הארץ?" ויאמרו אליו: "שים עפר על העין
ותשלוט בו כרצונך, וזה לך האות שעיניך לא תשבע עושר עד שובך אל האדמה
אשר לוקחת משם." ויעש המלך כך וישם עפר על העין וישלוט בו וירם אותו מן
הארץ ויתן אותו אל בית גנזיו עם כל שכיות החמדה אשר לו[140] למען יהיה לו אות
וזכרון את מכסו מגן עדן.

Isaiah 2:16

"... and upon all pleasant pictures."

[140] "ועל כל שכיות החמדה."

84

gate of the Garden of Eden and no heathen or uncircumcised male may enter."

That night Alexander was circumcised and his physicians came and immediately healed him with beneficial herbs. Nothing of this was known in the camp for the king ordered his physicians to keep silent. The next day, the king cried out to the keepers of the gate:

"Give me a tribute and I will go on my way."

He was given a box in which there was something like a piece of eye-flesh. The king stretched out his hand to lift it from the ground, but was unable to, and he cried out to them:

"What have you given me?"

They said: "An eye."[53]

"What use is it to me?" asked the king.

They said: "This is a sign that your eyes will never be satisfied with riches. Moreover, you will not be satisfied roaming over the entire world!"

The king said: "How can I lift it from the ground?"

"Place some earth upon the eye and you will be able to control it as you wish. Let this be a sign to you. Your eyes will not be satisfied with riches until you return to the earth from which you were taken."[54]

---

[53] This legend is found in various forms in the literature of many peoples. As a symbol of human greed, the eyeball sometimes appears, instead, in the form of a skull. See the following: W. Hertz, *Gesammelte Abhandlungen* (Stuttgart-Berlin, 1905), pp. 73ff., in which he notes that in the Ethiopian version, the stone is that which Father Abraham brought out of paradise. G. Cary, *The Medieval Alexander*, op. cit., pp. 150–151, and pp. 299–301, especially n. 61 gives a list of references to this story in medieval books of Exempla.

For a full discussion of Alexander legends in Arabic literature see: F. Spiegeal, *Die Alexandersage bei den Orientalen*, op. cit.; R. Basset, *Mille et un Contes* (Paris: 1926), III, 137–147; V. C. Chauvin, *Bibliographie des ouvrages arabes ou rélatifs aux Arabes* (Liège, 1892–1922); I Friedlaender, *Die Chadhirlegende und der Alexander-roman*, op. cit.

The Wonderstone as a stone or as an eye is thought to be derived from a primitive form of the tale and the primitive interpretation of the stone as a condemnation of Alexander's cupidity. See A. H. Krappe, "The Indian Provenance of a Medieval Exemplum," *Traditio*, II (1944), 499–502.

Note the theme of the "search" in the legend associated with King Arthur and the Holy Grail as influenced by the Alexander legends — as pointed out by M. Gaster, "The Legend of the Grail," op. cit. and by Wm. Matthews, *The Tragedy of Arthur*, op. cit.

[54] Proverbs 27:20. "Hell and destruction are never full; so the eyes of man are never satisfied."

ויהי אחרי כן ויאמר המלך: "איננו שוה לי[141] כל אשר עשיתי ." ויאמר אל גבוריו:
"הביאו לי ארבעה נשרים גדולים וחזקים." ויביאו אל המלך, ויאמר המלך להרעיב
אותם ימים שלשה. ויהי ביום השלישי ויקח המלך דף אחד ויאמר לגיבוריו לקשור
אותן עליו ויעשו לו כן כאשר ציום. ויאמר המלך: "קחו ארבעה קונדיסין ותקעו
בדף בארבע הקצוות של דף." ויעשו כן. ויאמר המלך: "קשרו ארבע חתיכות בשר
על ארבע הקונדיסין," ויעשו כן. ויאמר המלך: "קחו ארבע הנשרים וקשרו את
רגליהם בארבע הקצוות." ויעשו כן. והנשרים היו רעבים מאד ויראו את הבשר קשור
מעליהם וישאו את כנפיהם ויעופו אחרי הבשר כי היו סבורים לאכול את הבשר ולא
יכלו. וישאו את כנפיהם ויעופו עד אשר הגיעו אל העננים. ומרוב חום העננים כמעט
מת המלך, וימהר ויהפוך את היתדות אשר בהם תקוע הבשר ויהפכם למטה. והנשרי'
ראו את הנשרים* למטה וירדו גם המה אחרי הבשר עד אשר ירדו לארץ. ויאמר המלך:

f. 274a "בהיותי בין השמים ובין הארץ ראיתי את כל העולם באמצע/המים והנה נראה
אלי כל יישוב העולם כמו כוס על ים אוקיינוס."

ויאמר המלך אל כל חכמיו: "עשו לי זכוכית לבנה כי לא דיי לי שהייתי למעלה
מכל העולם כי ראיתי אשר מעל לארץ, ועדתה ארדה נא ואראה[142] אשר מתחת
לארץ."

---

[141] "איני שוה לי."

Esther 5:13
" . . . yet all this availeth me nothing . . . "

* Should read הבשר (meat).

[142] "ארדה נא ואראה."

Genesis 18:21
"I will go down now and see . . . "

The king did as he had been advised and placed earth upon the eye. Then he was able to control it and he lifted it from the ground and placed it in his treasury together with all his precious possessions so that he would have a sign and a remembrance of the tribute he received from the Garden of Eden.

After this, the king said: "Whatever I have done so far has no value to me." He turned to his warriors and said: "Bring me four large, strong eagles,"[55] and they were brought to him. He ordered them starved for three days. On the third day, the king took a board and told his warriors to tie eagles to it, and they did as he commanded. The king said: "Take four poles and affix them to the board at the four corners." And they did so. Then the king said: "Take the four eagles and tie them by their legs to the four corners," and they did so. The eagles were very hungry and when they saw the meat tied above them they spread their wings and flew after it, expecting to eat it but were unable to. They continued to fly until they reached the clouds. The heat was so intense there that the king nearly died. So he quickly turned the poles on which the meat was attached and reversed them downwards. When the eagles saw the meat beneath them they descended, following the meat until they came to the ground. The king said: "When I was between the skies and the ground I saw the entire world / in the midst of the waters, and the world and its entire population seemed to me like a cup on the ocean."[56]

f. 274a

The king said to all his wise men: "Make me white glass. I am not satisfied being above the world and seeing everything above land. Now I would like to descend and see what is beneath the ground."[57] His

---

[55] In classical mythology the bird is referred to as a gryphon, and is known by this name in all Alexander romances in English.

[56] In Hebraic literature the tale is found in: Jerusalem Talmud, *Avodah Zarah*, III, 1, 42c; *Midrash Rabbah* (Soncino ed.), VI, *Numbers Rabbah* XIII, 14, pp. 526–531; *Pirke Rabbi Eliezer*, XI, 28b–29a; *Yalkut Shimoni*, 1 Kg. 18, sec. 211, p. 758; H. M. Hurwitz ha-Levi, *Midrash Aseret Melakim*, *Bait Eked ha-Agadot* (Frankfurt, a.M.: 1881), pp. 44–45; J. D. Eisenstein, *Ozar Midrashim* (New York: 1915), II, 465. All these sources contain different versions of the legend, but differ little in basic narrative details. See also: M. Gaster, *The Exampla of the Rabbis*, op. cit., no. V. Alexander and his celestial journey in art is discussed by G. Millet, "L'Ascension d'Alexandre *Syria*, IV (1923), 85–155 and R. S. Loomis, "Alexander the Great's Celestial Journey," *Burlington Magazine*, XXXII (1918), 177–185.

[57] In Talmudic literature, this legend is found in *Midrash Tehillim*, Ps. 93, 5 and *Yalkut Shimoni*, Ps. 93, sec. 848.

ויעשו לו וו(?)מ(?)ו וכ(?)ל(?)ד(?) ל(?)בנו, וישב המלך בתוכה ויקח אצלו תרנגול **אחד ואבן** יקרה
המאירה לו. ויאמר אל חכמיו: "הורידוני בים והמתינו לי שנה תמימה ואם לא
אשוב אליכם לאחר שנה תמימה שובו לכם לאהליכם"143 ויעשו לו חכמיו ויורידו
אותו אל הים. ויצח* הזכוכית מים ועד ים וירד עד עמקי תהום וירא כל אשר
בתוך הים מקטן ועד גדול. וכראות המלך בים ככל רצונו ויקח את התרנגול ויחנוק אותו
ויצא ממנו דם. והים הגדול אינו סובל כל דם, ויקא המלך אל היבשה מקץ שלה
חדשים וישלך אותו תוך עם אחד אשר לא ידע ולא הכיר לשונם. ודמות העם ההיא
אנשים ונשים רחבים כמאתים בין פניהם ובתוך מצחם עין אחת להם ורגליהם רחבים
מאד. ויראו את המלך ותהי אימתו עליהם וישתחו לו אפים ארצה.
ויברח מן הארץ ההיא וילך ויחפש את חילו תשעה חדשים שלימים ותאכל אותו
החורף ביום והקרח בלילה.144 ומקץ שלשה חדשים לטילטולו פגע בו אריה אחד ביער.
וירא אלכסנדרוס את האריה וירא מפניו ויברח מפניו. וירץ האריה אחריו ויתפשהו
בבגדו וירבץ בפניו. ויקם אלכסנדרוס וישב על האריה וירכב עליו. והאריה הביאו
בעל כרחו במערה אחת וימצא שם זקן אחד וישאל לו לשלום. ויאמר לו: "האתה זה
אדוני אלכסנדרוס?" ויבהל המלך מאד ויאמר לו: "מי הגיד לך שמי אלכסנדרס?"
ויען הזקן ויאמר לו: "כי ראיתי אותך בבאך לירושלים להשחיתה." ויאמר לו:
"מאיזה עם אתה ומי אתה ומה שמך?" ויאמ' לו הזקן: "למה זה תשאל לשמי?145 כי
לא אגיד לך וגם לא אגיד לך מאיזה עם אני, אך תשבע לי שלא תעשה שום רע
ליהודים אני אביא אותך אל חילותיך."

Deuteronomy 5:27   143 "שובו לכם לאהליכם."
"Get you into your tents again."

* Should read: ויצף ●

Genesis 31:40   144 "הייתי ביום אכלני חרב וקרח בלילה."
"Thus I was; in the day the drought consumed me, and the frost by night . . ."
See also Jeremiah 36:30.

Genesis 32:30   145 "למה זה תשאל לשמי."
"Wherefore is it that thou dost ask after my name?"

wise men made him a white glass and the king sat in it. He took along a hen and a precious stone that shone for him. Then he told his wise men: "Lower me into the water and wait for me a full year. If I do not return after a year, you may go home." His wise men did this for him and lowered him into the water. The glass floated from sea to sea and descended to the depths of the sea and he saw everything in the sea, large and small. When the king had observed all that he wished to observe he took the hen and strangled it and blood issued from it.[58] Since the great sea did not tolerate blood it vomited the king upon dry land after three months. He was thrown into the midst of a people whom he did not recognize and whose language he did not speak. Their faces were two cubits wide and they had a single eye in their forehead and their legs were very broad. When they saw the king they were terrified and prostrated themselves before him.

He fled from that land and for nine whole months searched for his army. He was bitten by winter [cold] during the day and by ice at night. After wandering about for three months he was met by a lion in a forest and fled in terror. The lion pursued him, seized him by his garments, and crouched before him. Alexander stood up, mounted the lion and rode him.[59] Against Alexander's wishes, the lion brought him to a cave, where he found an old man.

"Are you my lord Alexander?" the old man asked.

"Who told you my name is Alexander?" said the king, startled.

"I saw you when you came to destroy Jerusalem," said the old man.

The king said: "From what people are you? Who are you? What is your name?"

The old man said: "Why do you ask my name? I will not tell you nor will I tell you who my people are, but if you swear that you will do no harm to the Jews, I will lead you back to your armies."

---

[58] This version is also found in the eleventh-century German work *Annolied* which records Alexander's wonderful adventures including the Celestial Journey and this account of his descent into the sea. This account stresses Alexander as the master of great deeds. See *Deutsche Chroniken*, I (Hanover, 1895). The Latin literary source is found in A. Hilka, *Der Altfranzösische Prosa-Alexanderroman nebst dem lateinischen Original der Historia de Preliis*, Recension $_I$ 2 (Halle: 1920). Note Cary, op. cit., p. 341.

[59] M. Gaster in "An Old Hebrew Romance of Alexander," op. cit., p. 824 notes in this a parallel to the legend of Macarius as well as to other legends of saints.

וישמח המלך מאד ויאמר:"אנכי אשבע."¹⁴⁶ וישבע המלך אל הזקן. ויקח הזקן את
המלך ויוליכו בחדר אחד אשר במערה ויצא משם סוס אחד יפה. ויאמר אל המלך:
"רכוב אתה ואני אלך." וירכב המלך וילך הזקן עמו ששה חדשים ויביא אותו אל
תוך מחניהו. ויראו את מלכם וישמחו ויתקעו בשופרות¹⁴⁷ ותבקע הארץ לקולם. ויספר
המלך לכל עמו את אשר קרהו ויצו על מנחם הסופר לכתוב את אשר קרהו.
ויאמר המלך: "אנה הזקן אשר תביאני אליכם?" ויחפשו אחריו ולא נמצא. ויצר
למלך מאד¹⁴⁸ ויצו רכוב אחריו בכל מקומות ויעשו כן כדבר המלך ויחפשו אחריו
ולא מצאוהו.

ויסע המלך עם כל מחניהו ויבאו ארץ כלבינא וכל אנשיה נובחים ככלבים וחלשים
מאד ומליאי שער מכף רגלם ועד קדקדם. והמה נוצים* כאמה וחצי.
ואינם זורעים ואינם קוצרים ואין להם שום מאכל זולתי אגוזים ואין להם שום
מלבוש זולתי עלי אגוזים. ויאמר המלך להביא לפניו¹⁴⁹ אחד מהם וינבח ככלב כנגדו.
ויביאהו המלך לפני המלכה אשר הובאה מארץ אפריקיא ותרא המלכה את האיש
ההוא ותבהל מאד ויופי פניה נשתנו ונהפכו לירקון. ותתעלף האשה ותפול לאחוריה.
וירא המלך ויצעק ויכה כף אל כף וימרט ראשו. וירץ אחד מן הרופאים/ויבא עשב
וישם בפי המלכה, ותקם המלכה ותעמוד על רגליה וישמח המלך וכל שריו.

f. 274

Genesis 21:24   ¹⁴⁶ "אנכי אשבע."
"I will swear . . ."

Judges 7:19   ¹⁴⁷ "ויתקעו בשופרות."
" . . . and they blew the trumpets . . ."

Genesis 32:8   ¹⁴⁸ "ויירא יעקב מאד ויצר לו."
"And Jacob was greatly afraid and distressed . . ."

Esther 1:17   ¹⁴⁹ "המלך אחשורוש אמר להביא לפניו את ושתי."
"The King Ahasuerus commanded Vashti the queen to be brought in before him . . ."

Should read גוצים (short)*.

90

The king rejoiced greatly and said: "I do swear," and he swore to the old man. Then the old man led the king into a room of the cave from which emerged a beautiful horse. He said to the king: "You ride and I will walk." For six months the king rode and the old man walked with him until he arrived at his camp. When the army saw their king they rejoiced greatly and blew horns and the earth quaked from the sound. Then the king told his men what had befallen him and ordered Menachem, the secretary, to record what had happened to him. "Where is the old man who brought me to you?" the king asked. They searched everywhere for him but he was nowhere to be found. The king was greatly saddened and he ordered the horsemen to ride everywhere and search for him. They did as the king ordered, but could not find him.

The king and his army traveled until they arrived at the land of Kalbinah,[60] where all the inhabitants barked like dogs. They were very weak and were hairy from the soles of their feet to the tips of their heads. They were dwarfs, about one and a half cubits high. They neither sowed nor reaped nor ate anything but nuts nor wore anything but the leaves of the nut trees. The king ordered one of them, who barked like a dog, to be brought before him. The king then took him to the queen, who had been brought from Afrikia. When the queen saw that man, she became terrified and her beautiful face turned green. She fell back in a faint. When the king saw this he cried out, wrung his hands and tore his hair. One of his physicians / brought some herbs and placed them in the queen's mouth. The queen rose to her feet, and the king and all his princes rejoiced.

f. 274ᵇ

The king left that land and crossed the sea in large ships. They spent fifty-two days on the water. One night the king looked up and saw a

---

[60] Kalbinah possibly refers to Albani or Albania in Asia, on the western side of the Caspian, a fierce warlike group, a Scythian tribe. Wm. Smith, *Dictionary of Biography, Mythology and Geography*, p. 41.

O. Zingerle, *Die Quellen zum Alexander des Rudolf von Ems, Germanistische Abhandlungen* IV (Breslau: 1885), p. 62 mentions the people of Albani as fighting battles assisted by dogs.

In Hebrew the word for dog is *kelev*. Half-man half-dog figures, or men called Kynocephalus, or men who have dog voices are found in many Alexander stories. See P. Meyer, *Alexandre le Grand*, I, 183; L. Ginzberg, *Legends*, IV, 275 notes that there is a legend told that in the days of King Hezekiah, the throne was occupied by one whose face had changed into that of a dog.

ויצא המלך מן הארץ ההיא ויעבור את הים בספינות גדולות ויהיו על הים ועושים
ושנים יום. ויהי בלילה אחת וישא המלך את עיניו וירא והנה דג גדול עולה מן הים.
ועיניו כשתי אבוקות גדולות. וימשוך המלך את קשתו ויורה את הדג ויפרפר את הדג
ויטבע שלש ספינות מחיל המלך. וייצר למלך מאד כי נטבעו מחיילותיו ויבך בכי גדול.
ותבוא רוח סערה על המלך ויולך את ספינותיו בים המלך וימותו רבים מן העם עד
כי הים הסריח. ויצעק אלכסנדרו׳ אל האלהים בחזקה ובכל לב ויבא האלהים רוח
סערה אל הים ויטל את כל ספינות המלך אל היבשה אל ארץ אלפריק היא הארץ
הטובה ושמינה. ויחן המלך בארץ ההיא שלשה חדשים. וירא המלך את שומן הפירות
ויעבר קול בכל חילו לאמר: "תזהרו ואל תאכלו את הפירות הארץ הזאת כי שמנים
הם יותר מדי ומסוכנים לאכול.". ויהיו מהם רבים אשר לא שמעו אל דברי המלך
ויאכלו מפרי הארץ וימותו מהם כשלשת אלפים.

ויאמר המלך לכל עמו: "הכינו כלי מלחמתיכם וצאו מן הארץ הזאת פן יהיה לכם
למכשול ולפוקה.". ויכינו כלי מלחמתם ויצאו מן הארץ ההיא ויבאו ארץ תוגירה.
ויצא מלך תוגירה לקראת אלכסנדרוס בחיל כבד וביד חזקה ויערוך אתו מלחמה.
וילחמו יחד שלשה ימים ויפלו חללים רבים מאלה ומאלה ותגבר יד אלכסנדרוס
וינס מלך תוגירה ויתחבא בתוך המערה אחת ויוגד לאלכסנדרוס לאמר כי נתחבא
מלך תוגירה במערה ויצו אלכסנדרוס ויביאו עצים גדולים על פי המערה וידליקו
אותם. ויבא העשן בתוך המערה וימת מלך ורבים מגיבוריו עמו והנשארים נסו.[150]
וירדוף אלכסנדרוס אחריהם וירדפם ויכם עד בלתי השאיר לו שריד[151] זולתי מתי
מספר אשר תפש אותם אלכסנדרוס ויחמול עליהם וישלחם וילכו מאתו בשלום.

Genesis 14:10   "והנשארים הרה נסו." [150]
"... and they that remained fled to the mountains."

Deuteronomy 3:3   "ונכהו עד בלתי השאיר לו שריד." [151]
"... and we smote him until none was left to him remaining."

large fish rising from the sea. Its eyes were like two large torches.[61] The king drew his bow and shot it. Writhing about, it sank three ships carrying the king's army. The king was deeply saddened that some of his soldiers had drowned and wept bitterly. A storm came and drove his ships to the Dead Sea, where many of his people died, causing a stench in the sea. Alexander cried out to God with heart-rending cries, whereupon God sent a tempest upon the sea driving all the king's ships to the shore of Alfriq,[62] a prosperous and fertile land. For three months the king camped in that country. Seeing the plumpness of the fruits he issued an order to his army: "Beware! Do not eat the fruits of this land, for they are too plump and are dangerous to eat." Many did not heed the king's words and ate the fruit of the land and some 3,000 died.

The king said to his men: "Prepare your weapons and depart from this land lest it become a hindrance and a stumbling block to you." They prepared their weapons and left that country and came to the land of Togira.[63] The king of Togira advanced with a mighty army and made war against Alexander. They fought each other for three days, and many fell dead on both sides; but Alexander was the mightier. The king of Togira escaped and hid in a cave. When Alexander was informed of the king of Togira's hiding place, Alexander ordered that large trees be brought to the entrance of the cave and set them on fire. The smoke entered the cave, killing the king and many of his warriors with him. The remaining warriors escaped. Alexander pusued them and struck them until none were left except a few who were caught by Alexander. He took pity on them and sent them from him in peace.

The king set forth from this country and crossed the water on rafts and went toward the land of Yovila.[64] There it was the custom for the

---

[61] A parallel story about fish with two eyes like moons or torches is found in the Babylonian Talmud, *Baba Batra*, p. 74 a–b. A reference to the eyes of Leviathan appearing like mirrors is found in Job 41:10.

[62] Since Africa was mentioned before, it is difficult to locate Alfriq. It is possible that this is a copyist's error, thus explaining the addition of a letter to Afriq.

[63] This name is close in sound to Turkia or Turkey.

[64] This name is similar to Havilah mentioned in Genesis 2:11. In Genesis the reference is to the special quality of this land, i.e., containing gold and this is not mentioned by the writer of this manuscript. Furthermore, the reference in Genesis is mentioned in connection with one of the rivers, Pishon, which emanates from the Garden of Eden, and encompasses the land of Havilah.

ויסע משם המלך ויעבור את המים ברפסודות וילך אל ארץ **יובילה. ושם מנהג הנשים**
שלובשות מכנסיים והאנשים אין להם. וכשתלד אשה ושוכבת תחת היריעה שני חדשים
אז היא יוצאת מן היריעה ובעלה נכנס תחת היריעה ושוכב במקומה ארבעה חדשים.
ויגידו למלך ויתמה מאד וישלח אל מלך יובילה לומר: "לך ונראה פנים אל פנים
אני ואתה יחד." וישובו המלאכים אל אלכסנדרוס לאמר: "כה אמר עבדך מלך יו־
בילה: "הן היום עשרים ותשעה יום ששכבתי תחת היריעה כי אשתי ילדה בן ועדיין
לא מלאו ימי לצאת מן היריעה עד לאחר ג׳ חדשים. והיה כי ימלאו ימי אבוא
אליך." ויהי כשמע אלכסנדרוס את דברי מלך יובילה וישחק מאד בעיניו וילעג על
דבריו ויהי כמצחק בעיניו ויאמר אל כל עמו: "הכינו עצמכם ובואו עמי לראות את
מלך יובילה אשר ילד בן והנה הוא שוכב תחת היריעה." וילך המלך עם כל גיבוריו
ויבאו אל מלך יובילה והנה הוא שוכב תחת היריעה והמלכה משמשת לפניו במאכל
ובמשתה ובכל מיני תפנוקים. וירא המלך וישחק מאד ויאמר אל מלך יובילה: "ובעוד
f. 275ª זה הזמן אשר אתה שוכב תחת היריעה מי הוא מלך תחתיך/ומי ישפוט עמך, ומי
יושב על כסא מלכותך?" ויען המלך ויאמר לו: "כל ארבעה חדשים האילו שאני
שוכב תחת היריעה הכלב המובחר שלי יושב על כסאי והמליץ יושב אצלו והעם
באים לשפוט לפניו." ויתמה המלך ויאמר לו: "וכי נכון הדבר לעשות כן להושיב
כלב על כסא המלוכה?" ויאמר לו: "הלא כבוד המלוכה הוא שהמלך כל חזק ומושל
במלוכה שהוא מושיב כלב במלכותו ועמו באים לשפוט לפניו." ויאמר המלך: "אם
נא מצאתי חן בעיניך הראיני נא ¹⁵² את הכלב היושב על כסא המלוכה." ויאמר לו:
"איני רשאי לצאת מן היריעה עד אשר ימלאו לי ארבעה חדשים שלימים כי אם
הייתי יוצא מן היריעה קודם הזמן היו ממליכים אחר תחתי והיו דוחפים אותי מן
המלוכה." ויאמר לו המלך: "הגידה נא לי. אותם ששה חדשים שבינך ובין אשתך
מה המה באתה אליה באותו הזמן כדרך כל הארץ או פירשתה הימנה כל אותם חדשים?"

Exodus 33:3   "ועתה אם נא מצאת חן בעיניך הודיעני נא את דרכיך.".¹⁵²

"Now, therefore, I pray thee, if I have found grace in thy sight, show me now thy way . . ."

women to wear trousers, but not for the men. Whenever a woman gave birth she remained in the tent for two months. Then she left the tent and her husband entered and lay in her place for four months.[65] When the king was told about it he was greatly astonished and he sent messengers to the king of Yovila: "Let us meet face to face, you and I together." The messengers returned to Alexander with the message: "Your servant, the king of Yovila, says: 'Twenty-nine days have elapsed since I lay down in the tent after my wife bore a son. My time has not yet come to leave the tent. After three months have elapsed, I will leave. When the time is fulfilled, I will come to you.'" When Alexander heard the words of the king of Yovila, he laughed them to scorn and said to his men:

"Prepare yourselves, and come with me to see the king of Yovila who bore a son and is lying in his tent."

The king and all his warriors went to the king of Yovila and found him lying in the tent, the queen serving him food and drinks and all kinds of delicacies. At this, the king laughed and said to the king of Yovila:

"Who rules for you while you are lying here / and who judges your people and who sits on your throne?" ^{f. 275a}

"For the four months that I lie here," said the king "my pet dog sits on my throne with an interpreter beside him. The people come before him to be judged."

The king was amazed and said: "Is it right to do this — to place a dog on the throne?"

"It is to our credit," said the king, "that the king's rule is so firm that he can set a dog upon his throne and his people come to be judged by it."

The king said: "If I have found favor in your eyes, please show me the dog that sits on your throne."

"I am not permitted to leave the tent until four full months have elapsed," he said. "Were I to leave the tent before that time, the people would crown another in my stead and drive me from the kingdom."

The king said: "Please tell me, is it customary for you to come to your wife during these six months or have you refrained from coming to her during that time?"

[65] Couvade is a practice among some primitive peoples by which, at the birth of a child, the father takes to bed and performs other acts natural rather to the mother.

ויען ויאמר לו: בזה נודע כח המלכות כי כל איש ואשה הבאים יחד כל אותן ששה
חדשים גבות עיניהם נופלות כולם. ושלוחי המלך יוצאים בכל יום ויום ומחפשים
ומסתכלים. אם איש ואשה באו יחד כדרך כל הארץ גבות עיניהם מוכיחות עליהם.
מיד תופסים את שניהם ומביאים אותם אל המלך ושורפים את שניהם. ואת עורפים*
שולחים בכל מדינות המלך. אבל המלך לאחר שני חדשים יבא אל אשתו פעם
אחת בשבוע ולא יותר וביום שמוליכים אותו ישב** על זה שלא יוסיף על פעם אחת
בשבוע." ויאמר לו המלך: "ככלות אותן ששה חדשים מה עושה המלך?" ויען ויאמר
לו: "כי חק ומשפט שמתכנסין ובאין כל עמי הארץ ומביאין למלך איש לפי עושרו. זה
מביא סוס וזה בהמה וזה מביא כבש וזה מביא חמור כל אחד לפי עושרו. והמלך
עושה להם משתה גדול שלשה ימים ואחר כך הולכים איש לביתו." ויאמר לו אלכסנ־
דרוס: "מיום שיצאתי מארץ מצרים ועברתי בכל המקומות לא ראיתי מנהג משונה
כזה."

ויסע המלך משם וילכו במדבר תשעה ימים וישאו עיניהם ויראו והנה עשן גדול
ומשונה עולה עד לב השמים ואש מתלקחת בתוך העשן. ויאמר המלך: "לכו מאה
מכם וראו את המראה הגדול הזה." וילכו מאה מן הגבורים ויעלו אל ראש ההר
גבוה מאד ולא יכלו לגשת אל מקום העשן ואש מתלקחת מפני חמימות האש. וישמעו
קול נהי ונהיה כקול בני אדם: "ווי ווי."

וירדו הגבורים מן ההר ויגידו למלך ויאמר להם: "מהרו ועלו על ראש ההר ושאלו
מה קול ההמון הגדול הזה." כה אמרו וצעקו פעמים ושלש ואין קול ואין עונה להם;
אך לאחר שעה גדולה נדמה להם כדמות אריה ולו ידים ורגלים כבני אדם ויאמר אל
הגבורים: "למה זה עליתם?" ויענו ויאמרו לו: "המלך אלכסנדרוס שלחנו לחקור
מה קול ההמון הגדול הזה."

         Should read: אפרת   .*
         Should read: ישבע   **

He said, "Therein lies the strength of the kingdom. Whenever a husband and wife come together during these six months, their eyebrows fall out. Each day, the king's messengers go and search. If a husband and wife come together and have intercourse, their eyebrows will incriminate them. Both are arrested at once and brought before the king and burned to death and their ashes sent to all the king's provinces. After two months,[66] however, the king may come to his wife once a week but no more and he takes an oath to this effect on the day of his coronation."

"What does he do at the end of six months?" asked the king.

He answered: "This is the law and the custom: All the people assemble with gifts for the king, each according to his means; one brings a horse, another cattle, another a sheep and another a donkey, each one according to his wealth. The king prepares a banquet for them which lasts for three days after which they all return to their homes."

Alexander said: "From the day I left Egypt and passed through many lands I have never witnessed such a strange custom."

The king journeyed from there and traveled in the desert nine days. They looked up and beheld a strange, soaring smoke ascending to the heart of the heavens[67] and there was a fire flaming in the midst of the smoke. The king said: "Let 100 of you go and observe this great sight." So 100 of the warriors climbed to the top of the mountain. The mountain was very high and they were not able to reach the place from which the smoke and the flame emanated because the fire was so hot. They heard sounds of lamentations which resembled human voices crying: "Woe, Woe!" The warriors descended the mountain and told the king who said: "Hurry! Ascend to the top of the mountain and ask what that great noise is." Thus they did and cried out two or three times, but no sound resounded. After some time a semblance of a lion appeared before them,[68] with hands and feet like those of a human.

It said to the warriors: "Why did you climb up here?"

"King Alexander sent us to investigate the cause of this great noise," they said.

---

[66] Meaning: "After two months have elapsed during the six month period...."

[67] Exodus 24:15–17 relates Moses' ascent of Mount Sinai while a cloud covered the mountain. The Presence of the Lord appeared as a consuming fire on the top of the mountain.

[68] The meeting of a lion and a man is found in Daniel 6:17–21.

ויען לוטו ויאמו : לא אגיד לנפש דבר עד בא המלך אלי ואגיד לו את שאילתו
אשר ישאל מאתי.״ וירדו הגיבורים ויגידו למלך את כל הקורות אותם. ויאמר
המלך לעלות אל ראש ההר ויאמרו לו עבדיו: ״אם נא מצאנו חן בעיניך אל
יעלה על לבבך לעלות על ראש ההר כי אינו נראה לנו טוב ללכת יחידי ולדבר אל
אותו אריה.״/ויען המלך ויאמר להם: ״אם אתם חפצים בי אל תאמרו כך כי אין
כבוד מלכות להתפחד משום דבר, ועתה הזהרו אם אעכב יותר משלש שעות על
ההר מהרו ועלו אלי אל ההר.״ וירע הדבר מאד בעיני כל הגיבורים. ויעל המלך
אל ראש ההר ויבא אליו האריה ויחזק בו וישליכהו ארצה בשערותיו. ויקח זפת
וישלך/על המלך. ויצעק המלך קול גדול. וישמעו גיבוריו ויבהלו וימהרו ויעלו אל
ראש ההר וימצאו את המלך לא חי ולא מת. וישאו אותו גיבוריו וירדו מן ההר. ויראו
כל עמו אשר נעשה למלך וישאו את קולם ויבכו בכי גדול. ויבואו כל רופאי המלך
ויעשו כל חכמתם ולא הואיל מאומה. ובראותם כן, רבתה הבכיה והאנחה. וישבו
על המלך תשעה ימים. והמלך לא פתח את עיניו ולא דיבר דבר כל אותם תשעה
ימים. ויהי בלילה העשירית והנה נחש בא אל מחנה המלך ובא בפיו עשב גדול ורחב.
ויראו העם ויבקשו להרוג את* ויהי בהם זקן אחד ושמו אפיליייס ויאמר אלי** ״שמרו
בנפשכם שלא תהרגו את הנחש אך תניחו אותו ללכת אל מקום אשר יחפץ. וישעו
אליו ויניחו ללכת. וילכו אחריו הזקנים והחכמים לראות מה יעשה באותו עשב.
וילך הנחש אל מיטת המלך וישם העשב על המלך ויפתח את עיניו ויזורר עד שלשה
פעמים ויקם ויעמד על רגליו. וישמחו כל עמו ויריעו תרועה גדולה ותבקע הארץ

---

*   הנחש does not appear in this manuscript.

** העם is missing in this manuscript.

f. 275^b

It answered them: "I will not tell you anything until the king comes to me and I will tell him the answers to the questions he will ask me."

The warriors descended and told the king all that had happened to them. The king said he would climb to the top of the mountain, but his servants said: "If we have found favor in your eyes, do not plan to cllmb the mountain for it does not seem advisable to us that you go alone to talk to that lion."

The king answered saying: "If you are truly solicitous of my welfare, do not tell me this for it is not honorable for royalty to fear anything. Now, take heed, if I am detained for more than three hours on the mountain, hasten and climb to me."

This greatly displeased the warriors. When the king ascended to the top of the mountain, the lion approached him, seized him by his hair and threw him to the ground. Then he took tar and threw it / on the   f. 275ᵇ king, who screamed. The warriors heard this, were greatly alarmed and quickly climbed the mountain, and found the king neither alive nor dead. His warriors carried him down the mountain. When the people saw what had happened to the king they raised their voices and wept bitterly. All the king's physicians came and applied their skills, but with no success. When they saw this the weeping and wailing increased. For nine days they sat with the king, but he did not open his eyes nor utter a word. On the night of the tenth day, a snake suddenly appeared in the king's camp, carrying in its mouth a large, broad herb. When the people saw it they sought to kill it.

Among them was an old man, Affilus, who said to them: "Beware! Do not kill the snake but allow it to go wherever it chooses."

They listened to him and allowed it to proceed. The sages and the wise men followed it to see what it would do with the herb. The snake came to the king's bed and placed the herb on the king. He opened his eyes at once, sneezed three times, and arose and stood upon his feet. The people rejoiced greatly and sounded a loud trumpet call[69] so that the earth quaked at the sound. The king prepared a large banquet for all

[69] It was traditional for Jews to sound the trumpet announcing good news, heralding the celebration of the new month, proclaiming freedom throughout the land; the announcement of the forerunner of the Messiah is to be preceded by the sound of the trumpet.

לקולם. ויעש המלך משתה גדול לכל שריו ועבדיו ויחלק להם מתנות גדולות לכל
איש ואיש כפי הראוי לו. וישאלו הגבורי' והחכמים אל המלך: "מה נעשה בך על
ראש ההר?" ויגד להם את כל אשר קרהו. ויאמרו לו: "הלא העד העדנו בך[153] פעמים
ושלש ולא שמעת בקולינו."

ויהי אחרי הדברים האלה ויבא מכתב מארץ מצרים אל המלך לאמר: "כה אמרו
אנשי מצרי': עד מתי יהיה זה להם למוקש ולמכשול ולפוקה אשר יצאת מן הארץ
וכל עובר ושב שורק עלינו ומתגרים בנו כל מלכי מזרח ומערב.
ואנו כיתומים ואין אב[154] וכאלמנות חיים ואין לנו מנהל מכל סביבותינו ואנחנו לא
נדע מה נעשה. ועתה אתם תשוב לארץ מצרים מוטב; ואם לאו ידוע תדע כי נמליך
עלינו מלך אשר יצא יצא לפנינו ויניח לנו מכל אויבינו, כי לא נוכל לסבול עוד עול
טורח מלכיות המש' המתעברים בנו. ויקרא המלך את המכתב וייעץ אל הזקנים
ואל החכמים מה להשיב. וייעצו לו לשוב אל לארץ מצרים ויאמר להם המלך: "גם
בזאת אינני שומע לשוב ארץ מצרים כי כבר נשבעתי שלא לשוב עד אשר לא אמצא
יישוב עוד ומקום לעבור אם כל חילי או עד אשר אכבוש ממלכות ועממים תחת
כפות רגליי." ויאמר לו חכמיו: "ומה תעשה לאנשי מצרים אם יקימו עליהם מלך
חדש?" ויקרא המלך אל טיכוסה, בן אחותו, ויבא אל המלך. ויקח המלך כתר מלכותו
וישים על ראש טיכוסה וימלך אותו על ארץ מצרים עד ישוב המלך. וישלח אותו
המלך עם עשרה גבורים כי אמר: "לא טוב הדבר להרבות לו סוסים פן יבולע לעמי
הארץ ויתפשהו בדרך."
ויצו המלך על טיכוסה לאמר: "בבאך לשלום אל ארץ מצרים עשה דין ומשפט בכל
אשר יורה אותך אמי ואל תעבור את פיה ובקטן ובגדול תשמע. ואל תגור מפני איש
וכל איש אשר ימרה את פיך תכתוב באגרת על בואי לשלום."

ויצא טיכוסה מאת המלך וילך בהחבא בסוסים ובחמורים כאשר הולכים הסוחרים
ברוכליהם לחזר מעיר לעיר. ויהיו בדרך שנתים ויבואו אל ארץ מצרים ויוציאו
אם חותם המלך ואת כתרו. ויכירוהו וימליכו עם מצרים את טיכוסה עליהם.

Jeremiah 11:7   [153] "כי העד העדתי באבותיכם."
"For I earnestly protested unto your fathers . . ."
See also Genesis 43:3.

Lamentations 5:3   [154] "יתומים היינו ואין אב."
"We are become orphans and fatherless . . ."

his princes[70] and servants and distributed costly gifts to each and every one according to his merit.

The warriors and wise men asked the king: "What happened to you on top of the mountain?" and he told them all that had happened. They said: "Although we warned you several times, you did not heed us."

After this, a letter came to the king from the land of Egypt stating: "Thus say the people of Egypt: How much longer will we continue to be a prey to the kings to the east and west of us? Since you left the country every passer-by scoffs at us. We are as orphans without a father and as widows living without guidance and we do not know what to do. Now, then, if you return to Egypt, it will be to our good but if you do not, know that we shall appoint a king to lead us and bring peace to our land. No longer can we endure the yoke of oppression from the kings who wrong us."

The king read the letter and then took counsel with the sages and wise men as to what his answer should be. They advised him to return to Egypt, but the king said: "In this matter, too, I will not heed you and return to Egypt. I swore I would not return until I found no other region or place to pass through with my army and until I subdued kingdoms and nations before me."

"What will you do to the people of Egypt if they appoint a new king?" his wise men asked. The king summoned his nephew Tikosa,[71] and crowned him king of Egypt until he would return. He dispatched him together with ten warriors to Egypt saying: "It is not wise to give him many horses lest they be destroyed by the people of the land and he be captured on the way." The king commanded Tikosa saying: "When you arrve safely in Egypt, do justice as my mother advises you and do not ignore her words. Attend to her in trivial and important matters. Do not fear any man and inscribe the names of those who disobey you upon a scroll until I return safely."

Tikosa departed from the king and traveled secretly accompanied by horses and donkeys in the manner of merchants who traveled from city to city. After journeying for two years they arrived in Egypt. They

---

[70] The Hebrew word used here meant *princes* or *nobles* in medieval times. Its meaning is akin to guides or mentors. See "sar" in *Milon Ha-Lashon Ha Ivrit Ha-Yishanah, v'Ha-Chadashah*, ed. E. ben-Yehudah (New York-London, 1960), VIII, 7609.

[71] Similar to this name is the city Tibus, Thebes. It also may be similar to Tybots, the name of one of the officers of Darius.

ויומר אלכסנדרוס ציווה את כל חילו לאמר: "הכינו כלי מלחמתכם ועשו מרכבות מרובות." ויעשו כדבר המלך, ויעשו מאה ותשעים מרכבות ברזל על כל המרכבות אשר היה למלך בתחילה, ויקח המלך את דגלו בידו וילך בראש העם ויצאו/אחריו

f.276ᵃ

ויבואו על נחל אחד רחב מאד. וימצאו בנחל דגים ובאזניהם כעין נזמי זהב. ויקחו מהם ויבשלום ויאכלום וימותו רבים מחייולותיו. ויצר למלך מאד ויאמר אל העם לאמר: "וכי לא היה לכם לאכול דבר זולתי דגים האלו?" ועוד הדבר בפי המלך מתווכח עם חילו והנה עלה מן הנחל אדם אחד משונה בכל דבר וזה דמות האדם. ראשו כראש נשר ולו אזנים ארוכים כעין החמור וידיו כידי אדם ורגליו כרגלי אריה ולו זנב כזנב הסוס. ויצו המלך לתופשו. וישמע האיש ויקח מאבני הנחל ויזרוק כנגד הגיבורים ולא יכלו לתופשו. המלך הלך לתופשו וירא האיש את המלך וישתחו אפיו ארצה ויפול לפני רגליו. ויאמר לו המלך: "למה השלכת כנגד גיבורי וכנגדי לא זרקת?" ויען ויאמר אליו: "כי ראיתי מלאך האלהים עומד לימינך וידעתי כי מלך אתה ואחלוק כבוד למלכות למען תרחם עלי ועל בניי." ויען המלך ויאמר לו: "וכי יש לך בנים, ואנה הם?" ויאמר האיש: "אותם דגים שאכלו אנשיך הם היו בניי." ויאמר לו המלך: "אם בניך אכולים מה אוכל לעשות?" ויאמר לו האיש: "לא תעשה לי מאומה אך תצוה להחזיר לי הנזמים אשר היו באזני הדגים ואתה תראה מה אעשה." ויצו המלך ויעבירו קול בכל חילו להביא את הנזמים לפניו אשר לקחו מן הדגים, ויביאו כולם אל המלך.

ויאמר המלך אל האיש: "קח לך הנזמים." ויקחם וישליכם למעלה למעלה עד תשע פעמים, וכשהשליכם עשירית קפץ האיש לתוך הים ויהי שם שעה גדולה. והמלך וכל חילו עומדים על שפת הנחל לראות מה יהיה אחרית הדבר.

brought out the king's seal and crown. The Egyptian people recognized them and crowned Tikosa king.

King Alexander commanded his army: "Prepare your weapons and build many chariots." They did as the king commanded and built 190 chariots, in addition to the chariots which they already had. The king advanced with the banner borne aloft at the head of his army. / They f. 276ᵃ followed him and came to a very wide river. In the river they found fish with golden rings in their ears. They caught a few, cooked and ate them. Many of his army died.

The king grieved greatly and said: "Was there nothing else to eat but these fish?"

As he was reprimanding his warriors, a strange-looking man arose from the river. His head was like an eagle's, his ears were long like a donkey's, his hand like a man's, and his feet like a lion's, and he had a tail like a horse. The king ordered his men to seize him. Hearing this, the man took stones from the river and cast them at the warriors; thus, they were not able to seize him. The king tried to seize him. When the man saw the king he bowed low before him, prostrating himself at his feet.

The king said: "Why did you cast stones against my warriors but not against me?"

"I knew you were a king, because I saw the angel of God standing at your right. Therefore, I showed honor to your majesty so that you would have mercy on me and my sons."

The king answered saying: "Do you have sons? Where are they?"

The man said: "The fish your men ate were my sons."[72]

"If your sons have been eaten," the king said, "What can I do for you?"

The man said: "You can do nothing for me, only command your army to return the golden rings found in the ears of those fish, and you will witness what I will do."

So the king commanded, and an order was sent throughout the army to bring him the rings taken from the fish. They were all brought to the king whereupon he said to the man: "Take the rings." He took them, thrust them upward nine times and, on the tenth, the man jumped into the sea where he stayed a long time. The king and all his army stood at

---

[72] A similarity is noted to the Ichtiofags found in the French romance, *Otifal*. See P. Meyer, *Alexandre le Grand*, op. cit., II, 173.

ולאחר שעה גדולה עלה האיש מן הנחל ותעל גם אשתו אחריו ותלקט כל הקשקשים
אשר העבירו מן הדגים, ותקחם ותעבירם אל הנחל. ותקח עשב אחד ותשם על
הקשקשים ותשלך אל הנחל ולא נודע למלך וגיבוריו מה נעשה בקשקשים האילו
וגם האשה ובעלה חזרו אל הנחל ולא נראו עוד.

ויסע המלך משם ויעבור את ארץ קלילא ולא ראה שם כי אם אשה בעלי
זקן ובעלי קומה ולהם שער שחור ושיניהם דקות. ולא ידע המלך וכל עמו להבין
לשונם.

ויאמר המלך: "מה אריב עם עם אשר לא ידעתי לשונם." ויצא המלך מן הארץ
ההיא וירדפו אחריו אנשי קלילא. ויבט המלך וירא והנה חיל גדול נוסע אחריו ויהפוך
להלחם עמהם ויהרגו אנשי קלילא מחיל אלכסנדרוס כשלשים אלף איש. ויאמר
אלכסנדרוס: "הכזאת גמול אנשי קלילא אשר גמלו לי רעה תחת טובה, אשר יצאתי
מארצם והנחתים שקטים ושליווים על שמרם?" וישבע המלך שלא יצא מן הארץ
עד אשר ישחית ארץ קלילא. ויהי ביום השני ויאמר המלך: "הכינו כלי המלחמה
ואנקום נקמת עמי מאנשי קלילא." ויכינו כלי מלחמתם ויצורו על עיונה עיר מלוכה
של אנשי קלילא. ויהיו שם ימים חמשה ונלחמים תמיד עם אנשי קל* העיר. ויהי ביום
השישי ויקם המלך בחמתו וישפך סוללה על העיר ויהרוס את החומה ותפול לארץ.
ויראו אנשי עיונה כי נפלה החומה וימהרו ויבנו חומה חדשה בלילה ההוא. ויהי אור
הבוקר ויבא אלכסנדרוס לפני העיר וירא החומה החדשה ותהפך רינתו לקינה ושמחתו
לאבל. וישפך סוללה פעם שניה ותפול החומה.

*   .קלילא :Should read אַ

the edge of the river watching to see what the outcome of this would be. After a while, the man arose from the river, his wife following him. She gathered all the scales that had fallen from the fish. She took them, and she brought them to the river; then she took a certain herb, placed it on the scales and threw them into the river. The king and his warriors did not know what had happened to the scales. The woman and her husband returned to the river and were never seen again.

From there, the king traveled and passed through the land of Qualila,[73] where he did not see any women, only tall bearded men with black hair and small teeth. Neither the king nor his men could understand their language.

The king said: "Why quarrel with a nation whose language I do not understand?"

The king departed from that country, but the people of Qualila pursued him. When the king saw a large army pursuing him, he turned back to fight them. The men of Qualila killed some 30,000 of Alexander's army.

"Is this my reward from the men of Qualila?" Alexander said. "They repaid me with harm for the favor I did them by departing from their land and leaving them in peace and quiet."

Then the king swore that he would not leave the land of Qualila until he had destroyed it. On the second day, the king said: "Prepare your weapons and I will take vengeance upon the men of Qualila for the death of my men."

They prepared their weapons and laid seige to Ayuna, the capital of Qualila. They fought there for five days. On the sixth day the king arose, and filled with rage he poured earth forming an embankment against the city destroying the wall, which then fell to the ground. When the men of Ayuna saw that the wall had toppled, they quickly erected a new wall that night. At dawn, Alexander came before the city. Confronted by a new wall, his exaltation turned to lamentation and his joy to sorrow.

[73] M. Steinschneider, "Zur Alexandersage," *Hebräische Bibliographie*, XLIX (Berlin: 1863–1869), IX, 52 notes that the region "Quilla" is Abdera. Now a Greek city of ruins on the Thracian coast east of the mouth of the Nesus, it was colonized in 656 B.C. and again in 543 B.C. In the fable, Hercules founded it on the spot where his favorite, Abderus, was torn to pieces by the horses of Diomedes. It was the birthplace of Protagoras, Democritus, and other men of genius; however, Abderites were proverbially stupid. *The Encyclopedia Americana* (New York: 1957 edition), I, 29.

וייבא המלך וגיבוריו בתוך העיר ויהרגו כל אנשי עיונה מקטן ועד גדול. ויקחו את
שלל העיר וביזה ויחלקו ביניהם בגורל. ויהי המה חולקים את השלל וישאו עיניהם/
ויראו והנה חיל גדול לרוב בא עליהם. ויבואו אל החיל והנה כולם כל אנשי עיונה. ויגידו למלך: "הנה נשי
אנשי עיונה באות." ויאמר להם: "הלא לא ראיתי אשה בכל ארץ קלילא, ועתה אתם
אומרים נשי אנשי עיונה באות?" ויאמרו אל המלך: "גם אנחנו לא ראינו אשה בכל
הארץ הזאת זולתי עתה, ועתה הגד נא לנו מה נעשה אם נלחום נלחם בם או
לאו?" ויאמר להם המלך: "וכי עלה על רוחכם להלחום עם הנשים?" ויאמרו
אל המלך: "אם יבואו עלינו להלחום בנו מה נראה בעיניך לעשות אם נשב
לפניהם ויהרגונו?" ויאמר להם המלך: "אל תלחמו בהם תחילה עד אשר תראו אם
יתחילו במלחמה או לאו." ויעמדו החיל ויבואו נשים על האנשים[155] ויכו בהם מכה
רבה. והאנשים התחזקו וילחמו בהם שמונה ימים עד אשר תשש כחם. וירא המלך את
תשות כח גיבוריו ויצעק בקול גדל: "שמעוני אחיי ורעיי אנשי מוקדונייא! איה
איפה גבורתכם אשר כבשתם כמה ארצות וכמה ורבים ותגדיל שמכם בכל העולם?
ועתה מה תוכלו להשיב לכל עובר ושב אם ינצחו אתכם נשים? על כן, חזקו ויהיו
לאנשים והלחמו מלחמתם!" וישמעו האנשים את קול המלך ויקנאו ויוסיפו להלחם
עם הנשים ויכו בהם מכה גדולה מאד עד בלתי השאיר להם שריד[156] זולתי זקינה
אחת אשר תפשוה חיה. ולא יכלו להורגה כי מצאו בצוארה עור מלא כשפים. ויצו
המלך לחתוך את העור מעל צוארה. ויחתכו אותו וימצאו בעור תשעה גרעיני פיל-
פלין, ותשעה ראשי שומין, ותשעה חלוקי אבנים, ותשעה ראשי נחשים ותשעה
ראשי דגים הנקראים פליפלן בלשון ישמעאל, ובלשון מוקדונייא, צמילייא. ויצו
המלך להשליך את הכל באש. ויהי כהשליכם באש ותצעק האשה בקול גדול ותשא
את קולה ותבך. ויאמר לה המלך: "ומה לך כי תבכי וכי תצעקי?" ותדבר האשה לשון

Exodus 35:22   "ויבואו הנשים על האנשים."[155]
"And they came, both men and women."

Numbers 21:35   "ויכו אותו ואת בניו ואת כל עמו. עד בלתי השאיר לו שריד."[156]
"So they smote him and his sons, and all his people, until there was none left him
alive. . ."

He erected an embankment upon the wall for the second time, and it fell. The king and his warriors entered the city and killed all the men of Ayuna, from the smallest to the biggest. They pillaged the city, and divided the spoils among themselves by lots. As they were dividing the booty they looked up / and saw a huge army approaching. Alarmed, f. 267b they arose to prepare their weapons. They met the army, which consisted entirely of the wives of the men of Ayuna.

When they told the king that the wives of the men of Ayuna were approaching, he said to them: "Why, I have not seen a woman in all of Qualila and now you tell me that the wives of these men are coming."

They said: "We, too, have not seen a woman in the entire land until now. Tell us what to do. Should we wage war against them, or not?"

"Did it occur to you to fight women?" the king said.

They said: "If they should descend upon us and fight us, what would you think it proper for us to do? If we do nothing they will slaughter us."

"Do not begin the fight until you see whether they do," he said.

The army stood still and the women descended upon the men and inflicted heavy blows upon them. The men gathered their courage and fought against them for eight days until their strength waned. When the king saw his men weakening, he cried in a loud voice: "O, hear me, my brothers and friends, the people of Macedonia! Where is the strength that conquered many lands and people and exalted your name throughout the world? What answer could you give to passers-by if women subdued you? Therefore, take courage! Be men and fight your battle!"

When the men heard the king's voice they assembled and zealously fought the women, inflicting heavy blows upon them until none remained except one old woman whom they captured alive. They were unable to kill her because of a leather pouch filled with magic amulets which they found about her neck. When they cut it off they found in it nine grains of pepper, nine stalks of garlic, nine chips of stone, nine heads of snakes, and nine heads of fish known as Feliflan in the language of Ishmael, and Semelya, in the language of Macedonia. The king ordered it all cast into the fire. When they threw it into the fire, the woman screamed loudly and wept.

"Why are you weeping and screaming?" asked the king, but the woman spoke in a strange language and no one in the army understood her. "What shall we do with her?" the king said.

107

אשר לא יבינו כל חוויל. ויאמר המלך: "ומה נעשה לזאת?" ויאמרו[157] ויאמרו לו עבדיו: "אם טוב בעיניך נאסור אותה בכבלי ברזל." וישימו לפניה לאכל ותאכל האשה מאכל חמשים אנשים, — ויתנו לה לשתות ותשת שתייה מרובה מאד. ויהי ככלותה לאכול ולשתות ותתחזק האשה ותתפוש בכבלי הברזל ותשבור אותם כפשתי העץ. ותקח את הכבליים ותך בהם מאה ושמונים איש. ותרץ כאשר ירוץ האיילה אחרי מאהביה וירוצו הגיבורים אחריה ולא יכלו לרדוף אותה ולהשיגה. ויאמר המלך: "אסרו הרכב ורדפו אחריה!" ויאסרו הרכב וירדפו אחריה עד הנחל ולא השיגוה. ותבא הזקינה אל הנחל ותשלך עצמה ולא ידעו הגיבורים מה נעשה בה. וישובו אל המלך ויגידו לו את אשר עשתה הזקינה ויצו המלך לחפש אחריה כל הנחל ההוא. ויחפשו ימים שמנה ולא מצאו. ויצו המלך ויחפשו את כל בגדי הנשים אשר הרג וימצאו תחת בגדיהם שני ראשי נחשי' ויצו המלך וישרפום ויקחו שלל רב מאד ויחלקו האנשים והגיבורים ביניהם.

ויסע משם המלך ויבא ארץ אמרישא והארץ ההיא יבשה וצמח אין בה. וכל האנשים שמינים מאד ושער ראשם לבן כשלג/ושער הנשים אדום כדם. ואינם אוכלים כי אם אגוזים קטנים הגדילים באילנות בתוך המים.
והאגוזים ההמה מתוקים כדבש ושחורים כזפת ונימסים בתוך המעיים.

f. 277ᵃ

ויהי אחרי זאת ויסע המלך עם כל חילו ויבואו ארץ לפיש והארץ ההיא מליאה בריכות מים ושמינה מאד מאד, ולא יכלו לבא בארץ כי אם בספינות, ויעש המלך כשלש מאות ספינות גדולות ויעבור את ארץ לפיש. ויהי כעוברם במים והנה רוח גדולה וחזקה מאד השליכה המלך עם כל ספינותיו מעבר לנהרי כוש, היא הארץ הסמוכה לעשרת השבטים.

II Chronicles 20:12   [157] "ואנחנו לא נדע מה נעשה."
"...neither know we what we do."

His servants replied: "If it pleases you, let us bind her with iron chains." They put food before her and the woman ate enough for fifty men. They offered her drink and she drank a huge quantity. When she had finished eating and drinking she was strengthened and seized the iron chains, breaking them as if they were threads of flax. She struck one hundred and eighty men with the chains. She was pursued by the warriors, but she ran quickly as a doe after its lovers and they could not overtake her. The king said: "Harness the chariots and pursue her." They did so and pursued her to the river, but could not overtake her. She came to the river, threw herself in and the warriors did not know what happened to her. They searched for eight days and did not find her. The king ordered that the clothes of all the women be searched. Beneath them they found the heads of two snakes which the king ordered burned. They captured a large booty, and the people and the warriors divided it among themselves.

The king journeyed from there and arrived at Amrisa,[74] an arid land in which nothing grew. All the men were very obese and their hair was as white as snow. / The women's hair was as red as blood. They ate   f. 277ª nothing but small nuts which grew on trees in the midst of the water. Those nuts were sweet as honey and black as pitch, and they melted in the intestines.

Afterwards, the king and his army traveled and came to the land of Lapish,[75] a fertile land filled with lakes. They could not pass through the land except by boats, so the king built some 300 large boats and crossed the land of Lapish. As they crossed the waters, a strong wind drove the king and all his boats across the rivers of Kush,[76] a land neighboring the Ten Tribes.[77] The king came as far as the river encircling

---

[74] In MS. Modena Liii this place is written as Abumrisa which could be a combination of two Palestinian cities, Abu M'risa and Lachish. However, the writer is not referring to Palestinian cities; according to the story in the manuscript, Alexander left Palestine some time earlier.

    In India, however, there is a city Amritsar, closest in sound to the city in the manuscript.

[75] MS. Modena Liii has Lachish for the name of the land.

[76] Possibly related to the Paropamisus mountains through which Alexander marched in 329 B. C. before arriving at Bactria. These mountains are known in Hindu as Koosh. Wm. Smith, *Dictionary of Biography, Mythology and Geography*, op. cit., pp. 48–51.

[77] The Ten Tribes of Israel constituted the northern kingdom in the Biblical period and were taken into captivity by the Assyrians in 721–715 B. C. Eldad Ha-Dani

ויבוא המלך עד חצות הונובב עשו ה והשבטים ולא יכול לעבור אליהם מאבנים גדולים
מתהפכים ומתנודדים בו כל ימות החול עד ערב שבת סמוך לחשיכה. ויחן שם המל׳
עד יום הששי עד כל חיילותיו עד חשכה וינוחו האבנים ולא יתנודדו. ויבא המלך
ויעבור עם כל חילו את מעבר המים ויחן שם על המים עד אשר ידע איך יפול הדבר.
וישלח המלך מלאכים אל עם הארץ לאמר לחקר ולידע איזה עם המה. ויגידו להם:
"אנחנו יהודים עם יי׳ אשר מארצו יצאנו בימי סנחריב מלך אשור." וישובו המלאכים
ויגידו למלך וישמח המלך מאד וישלח את מנחם הסופר לבוא אל היהודים ולשאול מהם
אם יעבור עם כל חילו דרך ארצם. ויהי כבוא מנחם הסופר אל היהודים וידבר
אליהם לשון עברי ויאמר אליו: "יהודי אתה?" ויאמר להם: "כן". ויהי בשומעם כי
הוא יהודי ויחר אפם מאד ויאמר לו: "ואיך לא יראת את אלהי אבותיך ותעש הרע
בעיני ה׳ ותחלל את יום השבת. דע כי בן מות אתה!" ויען מנחם ויאמר להם: "אל
יחר אפכם בי כי אימת מלכות עלי והוצרכתי לעבו׳ המים ביום השבת, שאם לא

the Ten Tribes,[78] but they could not cross over to them because large stones were turning and whirling in it during weekdays, until the Sabbath eve at twilight. The king camped there with his entire army until the sixth day at twilight when the stones did not whirl. Then the king and his army crossed the water and camped there until they saw what would develop. He dispatched messengers to investigate what people inhabited that land.

They were told: "We are Jews, God's people, who left His land in the days of Sennacherib, King of Assyria."

The messengers returned and told this to Alexander, who rejoiced. He sent Menachem, the secretary, to go to the Jews to request their permission to pass through their country with his entire army. When Menachem, the secretary, came to them and spoke to them in the Hebrew tongue, they asked him:

"Are you Jewish?"

"Yes " he said.

When they heard that he was a Jew, they grew angry and told him: "Had you no fear of the God of your fathers when you did evil in the eyes of God by desecrating the Sabbath? Know you are doomed!"

Menachem said: "I beg you, do not be angry with me, for I feared the crown and was compelled to cross the water on the Sabbath. Had

(ninth century) reported them apparently in the mountains of Africa. Historically, some members of the Ten Tribes remained in Palestine.

In Jewish legendary, there is a description of the Ten Tribes living far away, behind the Mountains of Darkness, by the river Sambatyon. The opposite peoples, the unclean people of Gog and Magog, are locked in forceably. They continually try to break the wall in order to escape and annihilate the world.

See A. R. Anderson, *Alexander's Gate, Gog and Magog and the Enclosed Nations* op. cit., pp. 62ff., who points out that during the Middle Ages the Ten Tribes were equated or fused with Gog and Magog by theologians and secular writers.

[78] The lost Ten Tribes were supposed to have lived near the river Sambatyon, a mythical river resting on the Sabbath day. The name is found in Josephus, *The Jewish War*, op. cit., VII, chap. 5, para. 1; the Babylonian Talmud, *Sanhedrin*, p. 65b, and in the *Jerusalem Talmud, Sanhedrin*, chap. 10. The historical basis may be a river in Syria called by a name similar to the word Sabbath. Josephus knew of the mythical river, the waters of which ran dry for six days at a time; Pliny, however, came closer to the Talmudic view, saying that it was dry only on the Sabbath. The ninth-century traveler, Eldad Ha-Dani related that this river carried sand and rubble rather than water, but with such a force that it could crush a mountain. On its other side lived the children of Moses. *The Jewish Encyclopedia*, X (1912), 681–683.

כן חַיִּיתִי לְבְנִי וְנְסְתַכַּנְתִּי בְחיות רעות זאת ענִני׳ ותורח זוּגוּרַח, ׳רק חשמר לך ושמור
נפשך מאד׳158 ואף חכמינו אמרו: ׳אשר יעשה אותם וחי בהם, ולא שימות בהם׳
ויאמרו לו: ״שקר דברת, כי לא נסתכנת בחיות רעות, כי אין חיה רעה בכל הארץ,
כי בנינו ובנותינו הולכים כמה מהלך ימים עם צאנינו ובקרינו לרעות בשדה ואינם
ניזוקין לא ביום ולא בלילה. ועתה צא מן הארץ כי בן מות אתה כי חיללת שבתות ה׳
ללכת יותר מאלפים.״* וַיְהִי כשמוע מנחם הסופר ויתעצב אל לבו.159

ויבוא אל המלך. ויאמ׳ לו המלך: ״מדוע פניך רעים היום?״ ויספר לו מנחם את
כל הדברים האלה. וישמע המלך ויבהל מאד ויוסף עוד המלך שלוח שרים
רבים ונכבדים מאלה ויבואו אל היהודים ולא רצו להשיב להם דבר עד אשר ימולו
בשר ערלתם, וישיבו למלך זה הדבר. ויאמר המלך: ״אם דבר זה מעכבכם הרי אני
נימול.״ וילך המלך אל היהודי׳ וימצאם חונים בתוך אהליהם והאוהלים צבועים
בכל מיני צבע. ויבא אל אהל אחד והנה זקן אחד יושב וספרו בידו. וישאל לו המלך
לשלום, ולא ענה אותו דבר. ויאמר המלך: אני נימול כמוך ואני מלך בן מלך.״
וכשמוע הזקן כן עמד כנגדו ודיבר עמו והושיבו באהלו ויכבדהו מאד. ויאמר לו
המלך: ״מה זה שאני רואה שאינכם מתקבצים יחד להלחם כנגדי? הלא ידעתם הלא
שמעתם וראיתם שיש לי חיל גדול לרוב מאד כחול אשר על שפת הים/מדוע לא
יראתם ממני?״ ויען הזקן ויאמר אל המלך: ״וכמה יש מכל חייליך?״

Deuteronomy 4:9   158 ״רק השמר לך ושמור נפשך מאד.״
"Only take heed to thyself and keep thy soul diligently . . ."

* MS Modena LIII reads אמא after מאלפים.

Genesis 6:6   159 ״ויתעצב אל לבו.״
" . . . and it grieved him at his heart."

I not, I would have remained alone and in danger of the wild beasts, for the Law says: 'Take care and guard your soul.' Even our sages have said: 'Man should perform God's commandments and live by them and not die through them.' "

"You have uttered a lie," they said "for you were not in danger of wild beasts. Our sons and daughters are accustomed to lead our flocks and cattle to graze in the fields which are several days' walk from here and they are unharmed during the day and night. Now, leave this land for you are doomed, since you have desecrated the Sabbath day of the Lord by walking in excess of 2,000 cubits."[79]

When he heard this, he was deeply saddened. He came before the king, who asked him: "Why do you appear so sad today?" Menachem related all that had happened. Upon hearing this, the king was frightened and he continued to send many princes to the Jews, each more exalted than the previous, but the Jews refused to answer them unless they would become circumcised.

The messengers related this to the king, who answered: "If it is this that restrains them, then I am circumcised."

The king went to the Jews and found them dwelling in tents dyed in many colors. Entering one tent, he found an old man sitting with his book in his hand. The king greeted him with "Peace,"[80] but he did not reply.

The king said: "I am circumcised just as you are and I am a king, son of a king." Hearing this, the old man arose, spoke with him and showed him great honor by seating him in his tent.

"Why don't you gather together to fight me? Surely you have known, heard of, and seen my huge army, as numerous as the sands of the sea-shore/and why are you not afraid of me?"   f. 277[b]

The old man answered the king saying: "How many are there in your entire army?"

---

[79] See Babylonian Talmud, *Sota*, p. 27, *Shabbat*, pp. 69, 153, which comment on the law in the Torah which forbids a man to walk beyond twelve miles. The Talmud extends this prohibition to 2000 cubits. The punishment for going beyond this limit is a whiplash but not death. Either the writer did not know the law or he exaggerated for purposes of his story.

[80] The Hebrew word "Shalom" is used in several ways: "Peace be to you," "Hello," "Goodbye."

ויאמר לו המלך: "איני יודע מטעו וויל". ויאמו לו הזקן: "אין [100] אנו יודעים נמען
שהרי נתקיים בנו: "ורדפו מכם חמשה מאה, ומאה מכם רבבה ירדופו ונפלו אויביכם
לפניהם לחרב". [161] ויאמר לו המלך: "מה מעשיכם שאתה מתפרנסים?" ויאמר הזקן:
"ממנו יש עשרה שבטים וחמשה שבטים ממנו יוצאים למלחמה על עם אשר סביבותינו
פעם אחת לעשר שנים לצד דרום ובוזזים ושוללים כל אשר להם. וממנו מתפרנסים
אנחנו. ולסוף עשר שנים, יוצאים חמשה שבטים שבטים האחרים והולכי' צפון ובוזזים ושוללים
כל אשר להם וממנו אנו מתפרנסים כל עשר שנים. ובסוף עשר שנים השווים
חוזרים חלילה השבטים הראשונים ויוצאים לצד מזרח. ואחריהם חמשה השבטים
השניים יוצאים לצד מערב ובוזזים ושוללים. כך עושים וחוזרים חלילה לעולם."
ויאמר לו המלך: "וכי זה מידה טובה ומידת חסידות שאתם גוזלים את האומות?"
אמר לו הזקן: "מיום שניתנה תורה לישר' לא רצו אומות העולם לקבל את התורה.
התיר הבורא את ממונם לישראל שנ': "ראה ויתר גוים". [162] ויאמר המלך: "ומה מעשי-
כם כל ימות החול?" ויאמר לו הזקן: "אין אנו עושים כל ימות החול כי אם עוסקים
בתורה יומם ולילה, וביום השבת אנו מתענגים בכל מיני מאכל ומשתה עד חצי
היום, ומחצי היום ואילך אנו עוסקים בתורה ודורשים אנו מעניין שבת." ויאמר
המלך אל הזקן: "אם נא מצאתי חן בעיניך דבר נא באזני העם [163] לתת לי רשות לעבור
דרך ארצם." ויאמר למלך: "אנכי אעשה כדבריך!" [164] ויתקע הזקן בשופר ויקבצו
אליו עם רב כחול אשר על שפת הים. ויבואו אל הזקן וידבר הזקן את דברי המלך
ויענוהו דבר ויאמ': "לא נוכל לעשות את הדבר הזה לתת לערלים ולטמאים דרך
לעבור בינינו." וישמע המלך ויתעצב אל לבו ויהי שם עוד היום השבת השנית
ויעבור את המים עם כל חילו.

Should read: אין. [160]

[161] "ירדפו מכם חמשה מאה מאה מכם רבבה ירדפו יופלו אויביכם לפניהם לחרב."
Leviticus 25:8
"And five of you shall chase a hundred, and an hundred of you shall put ten thousand
to flight, and your enemies shall fall before you by the sword."

[162] "ראה ויתר גויים."
Habakkuk 3:6
" . . . he beheld and drove asunder the nations . . . "

[163] "דבר נא באזני העם."
Exodus 11:2
"Speak now in the ears of the people . . . "

[164] "אנכי אעשה כדבריך."
Genesis 47:30
" . . . I will do as thou has said."

"I do not know how many soldiers I have," said the king, and the old man retorted:

"We do not fear you for we have realized this, saying: 'Five of you will pursue one hundred, and one hundred of you will chase ten thousand, and your enemies will fall before you by the sword.' "

The king said: "How do you maintain yourselves?"

The old man said: "We are Ten Tribes. Five tribes go to war once in ten years against the surrounding nations to the south. They pillage and take booty. From this we maintain ourselves. At the end of ten years, the procedure is repeated; the first five tribes go to the east and afterwards, the other five tribes go to the west capturing booty. This is repeated continually."

"Is this the goodness and righteousness you practice, robbing nations?" the king said.

The old man said: "Since the time the Torah was given to Israel, the nations of the world did not want to accept it. Therefore, the Almighty permitted Israel to take their riches, as it is said: 'He beheld and drove asunder the nations.' "[81]

The king asked: "What do you do during the week?"

The old man said: "We do nothing but occupy ourselves with the study of the Torah day and night and, on the Sabbath, we delight in all kinds of food and drink until midday and from noon on we busy ourselves with the study of the Torah and deliberations on topics befitting the Sabbath."

The king said to the old man: "If I have pleased you, convince the people to permit us to traverse their land."

"I shall do as you have asked," the old man said, and he blew a horn, and a multitude as numerous as the sands of the seashore gathered before him. They came to the old man and he told them the king's words.

They replied: "We cannot do this, to allow the uncircumcised and unclean to pass among us."

The king heard this and was saddened. He remained there until the second Sabbath, when he crossed the water with his entire army.

They prepared themselves for the trip to the land of Sinoria[82] for the

81 Habakkuk 3:6

82 Possibly Syria or Sidon=Tyre. Alexander did pass through Tyre in 332 B.C. Sidon was one of the most powerful of the ancient cities of Phoenicia, and was the

115

ויכינו פעמם ללכת ארץ צינוריא כי שמע המלך וכל העם אשר שם יורד המן. וילכו
במדבר שבעים וחמשה יום ויעברו את הנהר ויבואו ארץ צידון וימצאו שם הרים
גבוהים מאד ועל ההרים כעין שלג לבן. ויעל המלך וגיבוריו אל ראש ההר וימצאו
שם כעין מן. וישם המלך בפיו ויקא את מאכלו מרוב מתיקות המן. ויהי בעוד המלך
בראש ההר ויבוא אליו אדם אחד ארוך כשתים עשרה אמה, ויאמר אל המלך: "מה
לך כי נבהלת מן המן הזה?" ויאמר לו המלך: "כי נחליתי מרוב מתיקות המן." ויאמר
לו הזקן: "הלא אצל המן נח עשב אחד והוא מר מאד והיה לך לערב עם המן ולא
היית ניזוק." ויעש המלך כן, ויתן בפיו ותהי בפיו מר כדבש למתוק. וילקט המלך
וגיבוריו מן המן ומן העשב ויביאו אל החיל ויאכלו ויותירו כי היה מתוק מאד ולא
יכלו לאכל אותו. ויתן המלך וכל מחניהו בארץ דיצניא ימים שלשים כי נדמה בעיניו
הארץ בריאה.

ויהי בלילה ההוא וישא המלך את עיניו והנה שני כוכבים נלחמים זה עם זה וינצח
האחד את חברו ויפילו לארץ, ותרעש הארץ רעש גדול. וכראות המלך כן נבהל מאד
ויקרא לכל חכמיו חכמי המזלות ויגד להם את אשר ראה. וישמעו חכמי המזלות את
דברי המלך /ויספו* אל כף ויבכו בכי גדול. ויאמר להם: "מה לכם כי נבהלתם?"   f. 278ᵃ
ויענו ויאמר לו: "אדוני המלך הרגשנו בזה כי בא קיצך, כי אין אדם רואה מלחמת
כוכבים זולתי המלך ובסוף ימיו."

* כף (clapped) is missing.

king and all his men heard that manna[83] fell there. For seventy-five days they marched through the desert and crossed the river. They came to the land of Sidon and there found very high mountains. On the tops of the mountains there was something that looked like white snow. The king and his warriors climbed to the top of a mountain and there found something similar to manna. The king tasted it and vomited it because it was so sweet.

While the king was on top of the mountain, a tall man, some twelve cubits high, approached him saying: "What is the matter? Did the manna disagree with you?"

The king said: "I became ill from the excessive sweetness of the manna."

"Next to the manna," said the old man, is found an herb that is extremely bitter. You should have mixed the herb with the manna and you would not have become ill."

The king did this and the taste in his mouth became bitter. The king and his warriors gathered some manna and some herbs and brought them to the army and they ate it. Some remained since it was too sweet and they could not eat it all. Sidonia appeared to be a healthy land so the king and his army camped there for thirty days.

One night, the king lifted his eyes and noticed two stars fighting one another.[84] One conquered the other and they fell to the earth. The land trembled. The king grew frightened and summoned all his wise men and astrologers and told them what he had seen. When the astrologers heard the king's words / they clasped their hands and wept bitterly. f. 278ª

The king said: "Why have you become so frightened?"

They said: "Our lord king, we see in this that your end is coming for no man can see fighting stars except the king himself and only at the end of his days."

chief seat of maritime power of Phoenicia. The city was burned in 351 B. C. but rebuilt later. Wm. Smith, *Dictionary of Biography, Mythology and Geography*, op. cit., p. 873.

[83] Food eaten by the Israelites in the desert (Exodus 16:4–35). It was found on the ground every morning except on the Sabbath (a double portion was collected on Fridays), and as much as could be eaten was collected by the people. In form, it was thin and rough, white in color, and tasted like honey cake.

[84] This legend is also mentioned in connection with the birth of Abraham and the fall of Nimrod. Cf. L. Ginzberg, *Legends*, I, 186, n. 7.

וישמע המלך ויבך בכי גדול ויאמר: "ה' הוא הטוב בעיניו יעשה."[165]
ויהי אחרי הדברים האלה ויכעס המלך על אפיק שר המשקים. ויקח אפיק את כוס
המות ויתן בכוס המלך ובמאכלו. וישב המלך לאכול ולשתות ויבא הסם המות במעיו
וירגז וישתנה דמותו ומראיתו והיה לו כאב וצירים במעיו כחבלי יולדה. ויקרא
ויאמר: הביאו לי נוצה אחת ואשימה בגרוני אולי אקיא ואנצל." וימהר אפיק ויקח
נוצה אחת וישם אותה בסם ויתן אותה אל המלך וישם בפיו.

וכאשר הרבה בנוצה רבתה כאבו וצערו. וירא המלך כי בא קיצו ויקרא לכל חכמיו
ולכל גיבוריו ויאמר להם: "שמעוני עמי! אתם ידעתם את כל התלאה אשר מצאתנו
בדרך[166] ועתה חזקו ואמצו ויהיו לבני חיל כי כבשתם עם רב כחול אשר על שפת
הים[167] והנה עליכם נשאת כל עמים כי הכבשנום לעבדים תחת כפות רגלינו. ועתה
הנני הולך כדרך כל הארץ[168] ואתם עשו חסד ואמת[169] עם אמי והחזיקו את הממלכה
בידה. והעבירו את הממלכה בטיכוסה בן אחותי ואת כתר המלוכה תנו לאמי". ויקרא
המלך אל טומלייא ואל צביט ואל פוליסיים ואל אגמני ראשי חיילותיו. ויבואו אל המלך
ויאמרו לו: "מה אדוני מצוה?" ויאמר להם המלך: "אתם עשיתם חסד ואמת עמדי,
ותעזבו אב ואם ותלכו עמי ארץ רחוקה וזה כמה ימים ושנים אשר יצאתם מארצכם ולא
ראיתם את נחלתכם. ועתה תחלקו את המלכות ביניכם והחזיקו את הממלכה ביד אמי.
ואל תעיזו כנגדה ואל תמרו את פיה כי אשת חיל היא. וביום מותי קחו עצמי ושאו
ארץ מצרים וקברו אותם בקברות המלכים וספדו עלי שבעים יום. וכל שכיות חמדתי
אשר אצרתי, זהב ואבן יקרה, תחלקו לשנים, החלק האחד תנו לאמי, והחלק השני

I Samuel 3:18   "ה' הוא הטוב בעיניו."[165]
"It is the Lord: Let Him do what seemeth him good."

Exodus 18:8   "את כל התלאה אשר מצאתם בדרך."[166]
" . . . and all the travail that had come upon him by the way . . ."

Genesis 22:17   "כחול אשר על שפת הים."[167]
" . . . and as the sand which is upon the seashore."

I Kings 2:2   "אנכי הולך בדרך כל הארץ."[168]
"I go the way of all the earth . . ."

Genesis 47:29   "ועשית עמדי חסד ואמת."[169]
" . . . deal kindly and truly with me."

When the king heard this he wept bitterly and said: "Let the Lord do what is just in His eyes."

After these events, the king grew angry at Afiq, the cup-bearer. Afiq took some poison and placed it in the king's glass and in his food.[85] As the king ate and drank, the poison entered his stomach, and he trembled and his appearance changed. The pain in his intestines resembled labor pains. He cried out: "Bring me a feather to place in my throat. Perhaps I can vomit and be saved." Afiq hastened and took a feather and dipped it into poison and handed it to the king, who placed it in his mouth. As he continued to manipulate the feather, his pain and suffering increased. He realized that his end was approaching and he summoned all his wise men and warriors and said to them:

"O, hear me, my people. You know all the troubles and tribulations we have encountered on our journeys. Now take courage and be men of valor! You have conquered people as numerous as the sands on the seashore and you have incurred the enmity of all the nations we have subdued and made our servants. Now I am dying and I implore you to act kindly and honorably to my mother and place the kingdom in her hands. Transfer the kingdom from my nephew Tikosa and give the crown to my mother."

The king summoned Tomalia, Sabil, Polysium, and Agmani, chiefs of his army.[86] They came to him and said: "What does our lord command us?"

The king said: "You have always acted justly and kindly to me. You left your father and mother and came with me to distant lands. Many days and years have elapsed since you lef your country and have seen your inheritance. Divide the kingdom among yourselves and strengthen the government in the hands of my mother. Do not defy her or rebel against her word for she is a valiant woman. When I die, take my remains and carry them to the land of Egypt and bury them in the sepulcher of the kings and mourn over me for seventy days. Divide my treasures — gold and precious stones — into two parts. Give one part to my mother. The second part place in the temple of Digonia, god of Egypt; and the remaining silver which I have accumulated divide among

---

[85] See Genesis 40, the tale of the attempted poisoning of Pharoh.

[86] Tomalia should read Talmai; Sabil should read Selucedes; Polysium should read Phillipus; Agmani should read Omani, in order for the names to be historically accurate.

תנו בהיכל דיגוניא, אלוה מצרים, ושאר הכסף אשר אצרתי, תחלקו ביניכם." ויהי ככלותו לצות ויאסוף רגליו אל המטה וימת[170] בתחלואים רעים כי הסם שיבר כל עצמותיו.

ויבכו עליו חיילותיו שבעים יום. ויעברו ימי בכיתו[171] ויקחו את גוף אלכסנדרוס ויחתכוהו חתיכות ויבשלו אותם. וילקטו העצמות ויתנום בעור צבי להוליכם ארץ מצרים. ויערכו כלי מלחמתם וישובו ארצה מצרים ויבואו מוקדונייא אל אמר מקץ שלש שנים למיתת אלכסנדרוס. ויביאו אל המלכה גלופטריאה כל שכיות החמדה ואבן יקרה ויימליכוה ויתנו עליה כתר מלכות. ותמלוך חמש עשרה שנים בכל תאות לבה.

ואת טולמייא ואת צביל ואת פוליסיים ואת אגמני השליטה על כל הממלכה ותעש המלכה משפט וצדקה. ואת עצמות אלכסנ' לא קברה המלכה כי נתנה באוצרותיה ואמרה: ביום מותי יקברו עצמותי בני בקברי."

ותמת המלכה בת שמונים ותשע שנים ויקברו אותה בקברות המלכים ואת עצמות אלכסנדרוס נתנו בקברה. ואת הממלכה ניתנה לארבעה השרים וישפטו את עם הארץ כל ימי חייהם ויעשו משפט וצדקה בארץ. ואת כל שכיות החמדה אשר אצר המלך אלכסנדרוס בהיכל דיגונייא לקחו משם ובנו היכל גדול אשר לא נעשה כמוהו בכל ארץ מצרים מיום היוסדה.[172]

"נשלם הספר של אלכסנדרוס מוקדון אשר מלך בבית שני"

---

[170] Genesis 49:33   "ויאסוף רגליו אל המטה ויגוע."
"He gathered up his feet into the bed and yielded up the ghost."

[171] Genesis 50:4   "ויעברו ימי בכיתו."
"And when the days of mourning were past . . . "

[172] Exodus 9:18   "אשר לא היה כמוהו במצרים למן – היום הוסדה ועד עתה."
" . . . such as hath not been in Egypt since the foundation thereof even until now."

* The queen's name is given variously as Golofira and Galopatria in the manuscript.

yourselves." When he concluded his testament he pulled his feet together into his bed and died in great pain, for the poison had crushed his bones.

For seventy days his armies mourned him. At the end of this time, they took Alexander's corpse and cut it up into many pieces and boiled them. They collected the bones and placed them in deerskin to carry, them to Egypt. They prepared their weapons and returned to Egypt. Three years after the death of Alexander they came to his mother in Macedonia. They brought all the precious possessions and precious stones to Queen Galopatria* and they crowned her queen. She ruled as she wished for fifteen years. She appointed Talmai, Sabil, Polusium and Agmani as provincial rulers and the queen reigned with justice and righteousness. She did not bury the remains of Alexander but placed them in her treasury saying: "On the day of my death, bury the remains of my son in my grave."

At the age of eighty-nine years the queen died and was buried in the sepulchre of the kings, and the remains of Alexander were placed in her grave. The kingdom was given to the four princes, who ruled the people in justice and righteousness all their lives. They removed from the temple of Digonia all the precious possessions that Alexander had placed therein and they erected an immense temple such as had never been built in Egypt since the days of its founding.

This concludes the Book of Alexander of Macedon who reigned in the days of the Second Temple.

---

* The queen's name is given variously as Golofira and Galopatria in the manuscript.

APPENDICES

A. Glossary of Hebrew Terms

Aggadah or *Haggadah* consists of stories, sayings of the wise, and moral instructions; it is distinguished from the Halachah, which is composed of the customs, usages, interpretations forming the Law which the Jew observes in his daily activities.

Apocrypha and Pseudepigrapha: These constitute fourteen Hebrew and Greek texts written during the period of the Second Temple and for some time after its destruction (516 B. C.–135 A. D.). Though resembling the canonical books in style and materials, they were not admitted as part of the sacred Scriptures (i. e., they were not included in the canon) because they were composed after the era that the rabbis permitted books to be included into the biblical canon, or because they were written in Greek. The term "Apocrypha" is normally applied only to the non-Biblical books incorporated into the Septuagint which were canonized by the Catholic church. The non-canonical works are called Pseudepigrapha.

Cabbalah (Hebrew "tradition") is the mystical religious stream in Judaism. In the twelfth century, the term Cabbalah was adopted by mystics to denote the alleged continuity of their mystical "tradition" from early times.

Haftorah (Heb. "conclusion"): This term is applied to the selection from the Prophets read in the synagogue immediately after the reading of the Torah on the Sabbath and on festivals.

Megillat Ta'anit (Hebrew, "Scroll of the Fast"): An Aramaic text compiled before 70 A. D. which lists by month, those days which commemorate miracles and joyous events, and in which it is forbidden to fast. It had been used as a source for Jewish holidays during the Hellenistic and Roman periods.

Midrashic Literature consists of rabbinical interpretations and commentaries on the Old Testament from the first century A. D. to the tenth century A. D. Some scholars extend this date to the fourteenth century. This literature can be divided into works connected with books of the Bible and works whose subject matter is taken from the readings for festivals. Of the Biblical collections *Midrash Rabbah* is the best known. This contains expositions of the texts of the Five Books of Moses and also of the Five Scrolls (Song of Songs, Ruth, Lamentations, Ecclesiastes and Esther). For example, the Midrash to the Book of Numbers is known as *Numbers Rabbah*. The group of Midrashim linked with festivals and special Sabbaths are known as *Pesiktot*. The *Pesikta d'Rav Kahana* is one such collection. *Pirke d'Rabbi Eliezer* and *Yalkut Shimoni* are others.

Pirke d'Rabbi Eliezer: This Midrash, dated variously from the third to the eighth century A. D., is a collection of commentaries on Genesis and the first chapters of Exodus.

Sambatyon: This is a legendary river whose turbulent waters are active six days a week and rest on the Sabbath. In time, tales circulated that the Ten Lost Tribes lived near the Sambatyon. Josephus mentions this legend in the *Jewish Wars*, Book 7, Chapter 5, para. 1. Babylonian Talmud, *Sanhedrin*, p. 65b and Jerusalem Talmud, *Sanhedrin*, Chapter 10 also note the Sambatyon. Ginzberg (*Legends of the Jews*, VI, p. 407, n. 56) notes that Pliny, *Historia Naturalis*, 31.2, agrees with the Rabbis that this river rests on the Sabbath.

Talmud (Hebrew, "teaching"): This name is applied to each of two great compilations, the Babylonian Talmud and the Palestinian (Jerusalem) Talmud. Here are collected the Jewish civil and religious law, and the related rabbinic commentaries and records of decisions made by scholars and jurists during several centuries after 200 A. D. The Babylonian Talmud (better known, and studied more, than the Jerusalem Talmud) was compiled about 500 A. D. and the Jerusalem Talmud about the end of the fourth century A. D.

Targumim (*Targum*, Aramaic, "Interpreter"): The *Targum* is the Aramaic translation of the Bible. All Targumim are written in a somewhat artificial Aramaic, partly Biblical Aramaic and the Hebrew language spoken in Palestine.

Ten Tribes: After the fall of the northern kingdom of Israel, (586 B. C.) the Israelites were carried away by the king of Assyria. Popular fancy locates the Ten Lost Tribes in different countries. One reference places these tribes near the legendary river Sambatyon.

Yalkut Shimoni: This is a Midrashic commentary on books of the Bible, and was compiled in the thirteenth century by Simeon ha-Darshan, presumably of Frankfurt am Main.

B. Motif-Index of Folklore Themes in Ms. Bodl. Heb. d. 11

Folklore themes in the Bodleian manuscript are categorized here according to the method of Stith Thompson's *Motif-Index** by the motif number and title appearing in the *Motif-Index*. These appear in italics. To those motifs which are not listed by Stith Thompson, I have given appropriate numbers which appear in parenthesis and are followed by a description. Themes that are listed in the *Motif-Index* but do not mention this Alexander romance are recorded under the appropriate number and title, but I have placed two asterisks before my reference to the Alexander romance in the Bodleian manuscript.

A1101.2.1 *Trees Speak in the Golden Age*

(A1101.1.2)   Trees speak to Alexander and tell him how long he will rule and whether he will return to his native land.

B25.1 *Man with Dog's Head*

(B25.1.3)   People bark like dogs in the land called Kalbinah, one of the lands Alexander visits.

B240.9 *Dog as King of Animals*

(B240.9.1)   Dog as ruler of men when the king is confined because his wife has given birth. See T583.1.0.2.

B512 *Medicine Shown by Animal*

It heals another animal with a medicine and thus shows the man the remedy. Sometimes the medicine resuscitates the dead. (The animal who heals is frequently the serpent.)

* Stith Thompsn, *Motif-Index of Folklore*, 2nd. ed., 7 vols. (Bloomongton, Indiana: 1955–1958).

(B512.1)   Serpent appears with herb in mouth and this is used to cure the king. Wise men urge people not to kill serpent.

B776.5.2 *Blood of Lion Venomous*

(B776.5.2.1) Vomit of a lion in the form of pitch, apparently kills the king.

C631.1 *Tabu: Journeying on the Sabbath*

** Menachem, the secretary of Alexander and a Jew, is admonished by the Jews for crossing the river on the Sabbath.

D692 *City's Inhabitants Turned into Fish*

(D692.1)   Children transformed into fish.

(D1262.1.1) Magic stone makes dwarf invisible.

D1274.1 *Magic Conjuring Bag Filled with Nail Parings, Human Hair, Feet of Toads, and the Like*

** Magic bag of old woman contains nine stalks of garlic, nine grains of pepper, nine chips of stone, nine heads of serpents, and nine heads of fishes.

D1346.10 *Magic Water (Sprinkled) Gives Immortality*

** Servant of the king, having drunk of the life-giving waters, remains immortal even after head is cut off.

D1361.11 *Magic Herb Renders Invisible*

(D1361.11.1) Magic stone of dwarf renders him invisible.

D1645 *Self-Luminous Objects*

(D1645.1.1) Stone provides light to Alexander as he descends into the sea.

127

D1665.4 *Manna Tastes Bitter to Gentiles*

(D1665.4.1)   Alexander tastes manna and it is too sweet for him.

D1889.7 *Rejuvenation by Being Reborn. Man in Fish Form Eaten and Reborn*

(See D692.1) Children transformed into fish, fish eaten and earrings found as remnants.

D2126 *Magic Underwater Journey*

** Alexander's descent into the sea to see all that there is therein.

E1 *Person comes to Life*

** Alexander and the queen come to life by means of herbs. See D1505.1.1.

E80 *Water of Life*: *Resuscitation by Water*

** Dead birds come to life and fly away after being dipped into water (of life).

E149 *Means of Resuscitation — Miscellaneous*

(E149.4)   Resuscitation by black horn of ram filled with glowing coals placed on Alexander's neck.

E783 *Vital Head*: *Retains Life After Being Cut Off*

** Faithless servant, headless, goes to sea and remains there, alive, unable to be killed because he drank of the water of life.

F110.1 *Wonder Voyages*

** Alexander's ascent to heaven by means of four eagles and his descent into sea in a glass cage.

Γ112 *Journey to Land of Women*

      ** Alexander visits the land of women and learns wise counsel from them; upon another occasion he fights with the wives of the men whom he has slaughtered.

F157.1 *Journey to Other World in Crystal (Glass) Boat*

  (F157.2)   Journey into sea in a glass cage.

F167.5 *Headless People in Other World*

  (F167.5.1)   Headless person in sea, frightened by the utterances of Alexander's name, refrains from harming travelers.

F451 *Dwarf*

F451.3 *Characteristics of Dwarf*

  (F451.3.3.9)   Dwarf made invisible by magic stone.

F451.5.1.8 *Dwarf Serves King Sleeping on Mountain*

  (451.5.1.8.1)   Dwarf aids King to detect those men who were not loyal to the king, by means of the dwarf's stone which renders him invisible.

F511 *Person Unusual as to His Head*

  (F511.0.9.4)   Alexander meets person with eagle's head.

F511.2.2 *Person with Ass's Ears*

      ** Alexander meets such a creature.

F541 *Remarkable Eyes*

F541.6.1 *One Eye Brown, the Other Blue*

  (F541.6.1.1)   One eye resembling a cat's, one eye a lion's, one looks up and the other down.

F566.2 *Land Where Women Live Separately From Men. Cohabit with
Water Monsters*

(F566.3) Land where women live separately from men, cross
the river to the men in order to become pregnant.

F817 *Extraordinary Grass*

(F817.5) Herbs and grass serve as remedies.

F931 *Extraordinary Occurrence Connected with Sea*

(F931.3.2) Sea vomits up blood of hen killed by Alexander
during his descent into the sea.

F932 *Extraordinary Occurrences Connected with Rivers*

(F932.6.4) River vomits up blood.

F962.2 *Extraordinary Behavior of Stars*

(F962.2.6.1) Fighting stars portend death of Alexander.

F989.17 *Marvelously Swift Horse*

(989.17.1) Alexander owns such a marvelous horse.

F1041.1 *Extraordinary Death*

(F1041.1.11.5) Men die from stench of frog.

(F1041.1.11.6) Dogs die after eating fish given to Alexander by a
people he visits.

H1257 *Quest for Location of Paradise*

** Alexander seeks paradise after seeing that the waters
revive the dead birds.

H1321 *Quest for Marvelous Water*

H1321.1 *Quest for Water of Life (Which will Resuscitate)*

** Alexander seeks water which resuscitated dead birds.

H1596.3 *Women to Appear Naked in "Beauty Contest"*

    (H1596.4)   20,000 women appear before Alexander with one breast bared.

K2248 *Treacherous Minister*

    (K2249.4.2)   Alexander's prince seeks to poison him.

L400 *Pride Brought Low*

L410.1 *Proud King Humbled*: *Realizes that Pomp, Possessions, Power, Are All of Short Duration*

    (L410.1.1)   Alexander is given a piece of eye-flesh and learns from this symbol that his appetite will never be satiated until he dies.

    or: (L425.1)   Alexander is shown how death takes all, (in the symbol of the eye-flesh).

L414.1 *King Vainly Attempts to Measure the Height of the Sky and Depth of the Sea*

    ** Alexander seeks to learn the secret of the heavens and sea.

M302.7 *Prophecy Through Dreams*

    (M302.7.1)   Alexander sees vision of angel who warns him not to destroy the city of Jerusalem.

M312 *Prophecy of Future Greatness of Youth*

    ** Maidservant prophesies that Alexander will become a great ruler.

V570 *Guardian of Treasure*

    (N595.1)   Guardian of king's treasure refuses to tell Alexander where the treasure is hidden if the king punishes him for violating a woman.

P481   *Astrologer*

(P481.1)   Astrologers tell King Philip of Alexander's future greatness.

Q241   *Adultery Punished*

(Q242.5)   Alexander advises another king to punish the adultery of a priest by destroying the entire temple.

T551.4.1   *Child Born Beautiful on One Side, Hairy on Other*

** Alexander born hairy from sole of feet to navel.

T583.1   *Couvade — Father Goes into Confinement at Time of Childbirth*

T583.1.0.2   *Couvade Imposed on Man During Wife's Menstruation*

(T583.1.0.3)   Husband is restricted from approaching his wife for six months after childbirth; king cannot rule his kingdom during that time and a dog rules in his stead.

V82   *Circumcision*

** Alexander is circumcised in order to enter gates of Paradise.

V235   *Mortal Visited by Angel*

** Alexander is visited by an angel who tells him that it is he, the angel of God, who guides Alexander into battle and makes him victorious.

C. Stemma

I. THE PSEUDO-CALLISTHENES TRADITION

The following brief survey is a summary of Professor Magoun's and George Cary's conclusions.*

a. Pseudo-Callisthenes, c. 200 B. C.–300 A. D. was composed by an Alexandrian; it is the source of numerous translations. The four major recensions are called: $\alpha \beta \gamma \delta$; the latter three are dependent upon the earliest, the α recension.

1. The α recension is represented by Paris, Bib. Nat. MS. Fonds Grec. 1711. It was translated by Julius Valerius, *Res Gestae Alexandri Macedonis*, c. 320 A. D. and became the source of many of the versions of the Alexander romance known in the Middle Ages.

2. The β recension, a revision of the α recension, is the source for the majority of Greek manuscripts of the *Pseudo-Callisthenes* tradition.

3. The γ recension is represented by Muller's MS. C (Paris, Bib. Nat. MS. Suppl. Grec. 113). This recension was expanded by a Jew from a β type manuscript. Its principal interest to this study lies in one of its derivatives, the Hebrew romance, Bodl. Heb. d. 11 which is the subject of this study. The manuscript is concerned principally with the marvelous elements in Alexander's life.

4. A δ recension can be postulated only from its apparent ultimate (lost) source, a Syriac and an Ethiopic version, and the (lost) Greek manuscript translated into Latin by Archpresbyter Leo of Naples in the tenth century. This translation is called *Historia de Preliis* and was one of the most important sources for medieval knowledge of Alexander.

b. Medieval Derivatives of Pseudo-Callisthenes

1. As we have indicated, *Res Gestae Alexandri Macedonis* by Julius Valerius, the earliest Latin translation of *Pseudo-Callisthenes*

was translated (c. 320 A. D.) from a a type manuscript of the Greek text. It is best known by its abridged version, the Zacher Epitome (c. ninth century) which was the principal source for Thomas of Kent, author of *Roman de Toute Chevalerie*, as well as for chroniclers of the Middle Ages.

2. *Alberic*. The earliest vernacular Alexander book, extant only in a fragment, was written in the early twelfth century by Alberic, a native of Pisançon near Romans in southern Dauphiné. The principal sources of Alberic's work were Julius Valerius and the I^2 *Historia de Preliis*. Alberic's work was rewritten in part in 1165 to form the *Decasyllabic Alexander*.

3. *Alexander* of Pfaffe Lamprecht. The earliest German Alexander poem, the *Alexander* of Pfaffe Lamprecht continues the incomplete Alberic poem. It exists in three manuscripts: Vorau MS. (c. 1155), the Strassberg MS. (c. 1187) and the Basel Alexander (final revision c. thirteenth century).

4. *Decasyllabic Alexandre* and *Roman d'Alexandre*. The *Decasyllabic Alexandre* (c. 1165–1175) is based upon Julius Valerius and I^1 of the *Historia de Preliis*. It was one of the earliest components and foundation of the great French *Roman d'Alexandre*.

A redaction, based on the above versions was made after 1177 by Alexandre de Bernai, also called Alexandre de Paris, and subsequently divided into four "branches" corresponding to the original independent sections of the text. The *Roman d'Alexandre*, where Alexandre is pictured as a courtly prince, became very popular, giving rise to various other poems which were finally interpolated into it. These are:

1. a) *Venjance Alexander* (c. 1181) by Jean le Nevelon.

b) *Vengement A* (before 1191) by Gui de Cambrai.

2. *Prise de Defur* (c.1250) by Picard containing a version of the Wonderstone story.

3. The *Voyage au Paradise Terrestre* (an altered French version of *Iter ad Paradisum*, c. thirteenth century).

4. *Voeux de Paon* by Jacques de Longuyon (c. 1312) is famous for its introduction of the figures of the Nine Worthies. This romance appears as an episode in two Scottish Alexander books, the *Buik of Alexander* and the *Buik of King Alexander*.

5. *L'Histoire d'Alexandre* by Jean Wauquelin (before 1448) is a prose life of Alexander. Wauquelin's sources are *Roman d'Alexandre* (including *Prise de Defur*, *Voeux de Paon*, and *Venjance Alexandre*).

6. *Scottish Alexander Books*

a) The *Buik of Alexander* is a fifteenth-century Scottish poem known from an edition appearing in 1580.

b) *The Buik of King Alexander* written by Sir Gilbert Hay (c. 1456) includes a life of Alexander and *Fuerre de Gadres* and *Voeux de Paon*.

7. *Derivatives of 'Zacher Epitome'*

a) *Roman de Toute Chevalerie* (c. second half of the twelfth century) by Thomas of Kent, an Anglo-Norman verse romance extant in Cambridge MS. Trinity College, 0.9.34. It is derived from the *Zacher Epitome* of Julius Valerius and was the principal source of the Middle English *Kyng Alisaunder*.

b) *Kyng Alisaunder* (before 1330) based on *Roman de Toute Chevalerie* is an adaptation of the work by Thomas of Kent.

8. *Historia de Preliis*

This work (c. 950 A. D.), a Latin translation of *Pseudo-Callisthenes* by Archpresbyter Leo of Naples, is from the Greek manuscript of the δ recension of *Pseudo-Callisthenes*. This version does not exist, but the text closest to the original has survived in the Bamberg Manuscript (E.iii.14). Interpolations of the *Historia de Preliis* are known as I^1, I^2, and I^3.

c. Interpolated Recensions of the 'Historia de Preliis' and Their Derivatives

1. *The I^1 recension*: This recension is thought to date earlier than Alberic's poem (c. 1110) in which this recension was used for the first time. The editor of Leo's edition of the *Historia de Preliis* improved the style of the book and added new material. This recension was used as a source by Alberic, Lamprecht, and Jacques de Vitry.

2. *The I^2 recension*: This recension, a revision of the I^1 recension, is of uncertain date, despite attempts to establish an eleventh century date. It was used from the twelfth to the fifteenth century.

a) *The Old French Prose Alexander Romance* is the most important and successful of the medieval vernacular prose renditions of the Alexander tale. Written between 1206 and about 1290 it probably was translated by an unknown writer of northeastern France.

135

b) *English Fragments*

1. *Alexander A* (c. 1600). This fragmentary Middle English alliterative poem (Bodl. Library MS. Greaves 60) is derived from the I^2 recension of the *Historia de Preliis*.

2. *Alexander B* (c. fifteenth century). This fragment (MS. Bodl. 265) tells of Alexander's meeting with the Gymnosophists and his correspondence with Dindimus.

c) *Hebrew Derivatives of I^2 'Historia de Preliis'*

1. *Anon. A.*, a translation of the eleventh or twelfth century is attributed to the translator Samuel ben Jehuda ibn Tibbon.

2. *Anon. B.* Both *A.* and *B.* may descend from the *Historia de Preliis* through a lost Arabic version.

3. *Chronicle of Yossipon* (c. tenth century) contains an account of Alexander. These three works date from the eleventh or twelfth century and were probably written in southern Italy or Sicily.

3. *The I^3 recension* (before 1150): This recension appears to have been derived independently of I^2, from the I^1 recension. Most of its interpolations appear to have been derived from Oriental sources and are of a moralizing nature. It is supposed that its redactor was probably a Jew.

About 1150 it underwent a revision in England and this second edition is called the I^{3a} recension and is the source of the *Wars of Alexander* and the *Thornton Alexander*.

a) The *Thornton Alexander* is an abridged English prose translation of the I^{3a} *Historia de Preliis* (first half of the fifteenth century).

b) The *Wars of Alexander* is a translation of a I^{3a} manuscript of *Historia de Preliis*. This work (c. first half of the fifteenth century) is extant in two manuscripts: MS. Bodl. Ashmole 44, and MS. Trinity College, Dublin, D.4.12.

c) The *Dublin Fragment* is incorporated into the Dublin manuscript of the *Wars*. It is a fragment of a Middle English version of the popular medieval work: *Dicts and Sayings of the Philosophers*.

II. MEDIEVAL HEBREW ALEXANDER ROMANCES

Medieval Hebrew versions of Alexander's history further attest its popularity among the Jews. Except for the version under study, all the extant Hebrew manuscripts are based on the *Pseudo-Callisthenes* or the I^2 recensions of the *Historia de Preliis*. There are five manuscripts in the latter category and though they are not relevant to our study deserve mention:

1) MS. Cod. Heb. 671.5, Bibliothèque Nationale, Paris.

2) MS. 145, Jews' College, London.

These two manuscripts are similar to each other in content and order of events and follow the I^2 recension of the *Historia de Preliis*.

3) MS. Cod. Heb. 1087, Bibliotica I. B. de Rossi, Parma, apparently is based primarily on recension β of *Pseudo-Callisthenes*.

4) MS. Cod. Heb. 750.3, Bibliothèque Nationale, Paris, is a translation based on recensions I^1 and I^2 of the *Historia de Preliis*.

5) An Alexander romance is also found in *Yosippon* (c. tenth century), a popular medieval history of the Jewish people dealing with the period of the Second Commonwealth.

6. Three manuscripts, similar in content and differing greatly from the other medieval Alexander romances noted above are:

a) MS. Bodl. Heb. d. 11, the subject of this study;

b) MS. Modena L111, Estense Library, Modena, Italy;

c) MS. Damascus. present whereabouts unknown.

BIBLIOGRAPHY

LIST OF WORKS CITED

The principal modern editions of ancient and medieval works are listed under their author, or in the case of anonymous works under the titles.

Alexander and Dindimus, ed. W. W. Skeat. EETSES 31. London: 1878.

Alexander A and Alexander B, ed. F. P. Magoun, Jr., in *The Gests of King Alexander of Macedon*. Cambridge, Mass.: 1929.

Alphabet of Tales, ed., M. M. Banks, EETSOS, 126, 127. London: 1904–1905.

Anderson, A. R., "The Arabic History of Dulcarnaim and the Ethiopian History of Alexander," *Speculum* VI (1931), 434–445.

———, *Alexander's Gate, Gog and Magog and the Inclosed Nations*. Cambridge, Mass.: 1932.

———, "Alexander's Horns," *Amer. Phil. Assn. Tr.* LVIII (1927), 100–122.

The Apocrypha and Pseudepigrapha of the Old Testament in English, ed. R. H. Charles. 2 vols. Oxford: 1913.

Ausfeld, A., *Der Griechische Alexanderroman*. Leipzig: 1907.

Basset, Ren, *Mille et Un Contes, Récits et Légendes Arabes*. 3 vols. Paris: 1926.

Berzunza, J., *A Tentative Classification of Books, Pamphlets, and Pictures Concerning Alexander the Great and the Alexander Romances*. Privately printed, 1939.

Budge, E. W., ed., *The Life and Exploits of Alexander the Great*. 2 vols. Cambridge: 1896.

Cary, G., *The Medieval Alexander*. Cambridge: 1958.

(*The*) *Catalogue of the Hebrew Manuscripts in the Bodleian Library and in the College Libraries of Oxford*, compiled by A. Cowley and A. Neubauer. 2 vols. Oxford: 1896–1903.

Chaucer, G., *The Poetical Works of Chaucer*, ed. F. N. Robinson. Cambridge, Mass.: 1933.

Chauvin, V., *Bibliographie des ouvrages arabes ou rélatifs aux Arabes*. 12 vols. Liège: 1892–1922.

Donath, L. *Die Alexandersage in Talmud und Midrasch*. Fulda: 1873.

(*The*) *Encyclopedia Americana*. 30 vols., 1957 edition.

(*Ha-*) *Encyclopedia Ha-Ivrit*. 18 vols., Jerusalem: 1949–1965.

Five Megilloth, ed. A. Cohen. London: Soncino Press, 1952.

138

TALES OF ALEXANDER THE MACEDONIAN

Friedlaender, I., *Die Chadhirlegende und der Alexanderroman.* Leipzig. 1913.

Gaster, M., "An Old Hebrew Romance of Alexander," *JRAS* (1897), 485–549; *Studies and Texts*, II. London: 1925.

———, trans., *The Chronicles of Jerahmeel. Oriental Translation Fund, New Series* IV. London: 1899. (KTAV Reprint 1972. Prolegomenon by Haim Schwartzbaum.

———, *The Exempla of the Rabbis.* London-Leipzig: 1924.

———, *Ilchester Lectures on Greeko-Slavonic Literature and its Relation to Folklore of Europe during the Middle Ages.* London: 1887.

———, "The Legend of the Grail," *Studies and Texts*, II (London: 1925), 879–901.

Geiger, A., *Judaism and Islam*, trans., F. M. Young. Madras: 1898.(Reprint 1970: KTAV).

Ginzberg, L. *Jewish Folklore: East and West.* Cambridge, Mass.: 1936.

———, *The Legends of the Jews.* 7 vols. Philadelphia: 1911–1938.

Goitein, S. D., *Jews and Arabs: Their Contacts Through the Ages.* New York: 1955.

Golagros and Gawane, in *Scottish Alliterative Poems in Rhyming Stanzas*, ed., F. J. Amours. STS, 27, 38. Edinburgh: 1881–1897.

Gower, J., *The Works of John Gower*, ed., G. C. Macaulay. 4 vols. Oxford: 1899–1902.

Grossman, R., *Compendious Hebrew-English Dictionary.* Tel Aviv: 1946.

Guillaume, A., "The Influence of Judaism on Islam," *The Legacy of Israel*, ed., E. R. Bevan and C. Singer. Oxford: 1927.

Gur, Y., *Milon Ivri.* Tel Aviv: 1946.

Haight, E. H., *The Life of Alexander of Macedon by Pseudo-Callisthenes.* New York: 1955.

Halkin, A. S., "Judeo-Arabic Literature," *The Jews: Their History, Culture and Religion*, ed. L. Finkelstein. 2 vols., New York: 1960.

Hanauer, J. E., *Folklore of the Holy Land.* London: 1935.

Harkavy, A. Y., "Neizdannaya Versiya romana obū Alexandrê," *Akedemiya nauk. Otdeleniye russkovo yazyka i slovesnosti. Sbornik:* LIII (1892), 65–155.

———, transl., *The Twenty-four Books of the Old Testament.*, 2 vols. New York: 1916.

Hasluck, F. W., *Letters on Religion and Folklore.* London: 1926.

Hermann, A., *The Taymouth Castle Manuscript of Sir Gilbert Hay's Buik of King Alexander the Conqueror. Wissenschaftliche Beilage zum Jahresbericht der 12. Stadtischen Realschule zu Berlin.* Berlin: 1900.

Hertz, W., *Gesammelte Abhandlungen.* Stuttgart: 1905.

Hilka, A., *Der altfranzosische Prosa-Alexanderroman nebst dem lateinischen Original der Historia de Preliis.* Halle: 1920.

Jacobs, J., *Jewish Contributions to Civilization.* Philadelphia: 1920.

(The) Jewish Encyclopedia. 12 vols., New York: 1901–1912. Reprint 1965: KTAV.

Josephus, F. *The Jewish Antiquities.* Loeb ed., trans. H. St. J. Thackeray and R. Marcus. London: 1930–1943.

———, *The Jewish War.* Loeb ed., trans. H. St. J. Thackeray. London: 1927.

————, *Collected Works*. Loeb ed., trans. H. St. J. Thackeray and R. Marcus., 8 vols. London: 1926–1963.

Katsh, A. I. "Li-She'elat Hashpa'at ha-Talmud al ha-Koran," *Hatikufah*, XXXIV–XXXV (1950), 834–838.

————, *Judaism in Islam*. New York: 1954.

Kazis, I., *The Book of Gests of Alexander of Macedon*. Cambridge, Mass.: 1962.

Krappe, A. H. ,"The Indian Provenance of a Medieval Exemplum," *Traditio*, II (1944), 499–502.

Kyng Alisaunder, ed. H. Weber in *Metrical Romances*. 3 vols., Edinburgh: 1810.

————, ed. G. V. Smithers. EETSOS 227,237. London: 1952–1957.

Lascelles, M., "Alexander and the Éarthly Paradise in Medieval Writing," *Medium Aevum*, V (1936), 31–47, 74–104, 173–188.

Levi, I., "La Dispute entre les Egyptiens et les Juifs devant Alexandre," *REJ*, LXIII (1912), 210–215.

————, "Sefer Alexandrus Mokdon," *Festschrift zum achzigsten Geburtstage Moritz Steinschneiders* (Leipzig: 1896), 142–163.

————, "La Légende d'Alexandre dans le Talmud et le Midrasch," *REJ*, VII (1883), 78–93.

————, "La Légende d'Alexandre dans le Talmud," *REJ*, II (1881), 273–300.

Loomis, R. S., "Alexander the Great's Celestial Journey," *Burlington Magazine*, XXXII (1918), 177–185.

Lydgate, J., *Fall of Princes*, ed. H. Bergen. EETSES 121–124, 4 vols. London: 1924–1927.

————, *The Minor Poems of John Lydgate*, ed. H. N. MacCracken. EETSES 107,192. London: 1910–1934.

Magoun, F. P., Jr., *The Gests of King Alexander of Macedon*. Cambridge, Mass.: 1929.

Mandeville's Travels, ed. P. Hamelius. EETSOS 153,154, London: 1919–1923.

Matthews, Wm., *The Tragedy of Arthur*. Berkeley: 1960.

Megilloth Ta'anith. Warsaw: 1874.

Meissner, A. L., "Bildliche Darstellungen der Alexandersage in Kirchen des Mittelalters," *Archiv. für das Studium der neuren Sprachen*, LXVIII (1882), 177–90.

Meyer, P., *Alexandre le Grand dans la Littérature Française du Moyen Age*. 2 vols., Paris: 1886.

————, "Etude sur les Manuscrits du Roman d'Alexandre," *Romania*, XI (1882), 213–332.

Midrash Aseret Melachim, ed. H. M. Hurwitz ha-Levi, in *Bait Eked ha-Agadot*. Frankfurt am Main: 1881.

Midrash Rabbah, Warsaw: 1877–90; English translation, Soncino Press. 10 vols., London: 1939.

Midrash Tanhuma, ed. S. Buber. Vienna: 1885.

Midrash Tehillim, ed. S. Buber. Vilna: 1891.

The Midrash on Psalms, trans. W. G. Braude. 2 vols., New Haven: 1959.

Millet, G., "L'Ascension d'Alexandre," *Syria*, IV (1923), 85–133.

Milon Ha-Lashon Ha-Ivrit Ha-Yishanah, V'Ha-Chadashah (Hebrew Dictionary), ed. E. ben-Yehudah. 8 vols., New York-London: 1960.

Neubauer, A., *La Géographie du Talmud*. Paris: 1868.

———, "Jerahmeel Ben Shlomoh," *JQR*, XI (1897), 364–386.

Noy, D. (Neumann), *Motif-Index to the Talmudic and Midrashic Literature*. Ann Arbor, Mich.: 1954. Microfilm Service, Publication No. 8792.

Ozar Midrashim, ed. J. D. Eisenstein. 2 vols., New York: 1915.

Pesikta d'Rab Kahana, ed. S. Buber. Lyck: 1868.

Pfister, F., *Der Alexanderroman des Archpresbyters Leo. Sammlung. mittelalt. Texte*, VI. Heidelberg: 1912.

———, *Kleine Texte zum Alexanderroman. Sammlung. vulgaerlateinischer Texte*, IV. Heidelberg: 1910.

Pirke Rabbi Eliezer. New York: 1946.

Plutarch, *Parallel Lives*. Loeb ed., trans. B. Perrin. 11 vols., London: 1914–1926.

Polychronicon, trans. R. Higden, ed. J. R. Lumby. *Rolls Series*, IV. London: 1865–1886.

Pseudo-Callisthenes, ed. C. Muller. Paris: 1846.

———, ed. J. Zacher. Halle: 1867.

Rabinowitz, L., *Jewish Merchant Adventurers: A Study of the Radanites*. London: 1948.

Rapoport, S., *Erech Millin*. Warsaw: 1914.

The Medieval French "Roman d'Alexandre." Elliott Monographs 36–40. Princeton University Press, 1937–1949.

Ross, D. J. A., *Alexander Historiatus, A Guide to Medieval Illustrated Alexander Literature*. London: 1963.

Rossi, A. de, *Meor Eynayim*. Warsaw: 1899.

Smith Wm., *A Classical Dictionary of Greek and Roman Biography, Mythology and Geography*. London: 1848.

———, *A Dictionary of Greek and Roman Biography and Mythology*. 3 vols., London: 1844.

Spiegel, F., *Die Alexandersage bei den Orientalen*. Leipzig: 1851.

Standard Jewish Encyclopedia, ed. C. Roth. New York: 1959.

Steinschneider, M., "Zur Alexandersage," *Hebräische Bibliographie*, XLIX (Berlin: 1869), 13–19.

Strack, H. L., *Introduction to the Talmud and Midrash*. Philadelphia: 1945.

Talmud Bavli (Babylonian). 20 vols., Vilna: 1883–1892; English trans., *Babylonian Talmud*. Soncino Press, 35 vols., London: 1935–52. Reprinted in 18 vols., 1961.

Talmud Yerushalmi (Jerusalem). 6 vols., Vilna: 1911–1917.

Tarn, W. W., *Alexander the Great*. 2 vols., Cambridge: 1948.

Tcherikover, V., *Hellenistic Civilization and the Jews*. Philadelphia: 1959.

Thompson, S., *Motif-Index of Folk Literature*, 2nd. ed. 7 vols., Bloomington, Indiana: 1955–1958.

(*The*) *Torah. A New Translation of the Holy Scriptures according to the Masoretic Text.* Philadelphia: 1962.

Tur-Sinai, N. H., *The Language and the Book*. 3 vols., Jerusalem: 1948–1955.

(*The*) *Universal Jewish Encyclopedia*, 10 vols. New York: 1939–1943. Reprint 1968: KTAV.

Wallach, L. "Alexander the Great and the Indian Gymnosophists in Hebrew Tradition," *Proceedings of the American Academy for Jewish Research*, XI (1941), 47–83.

The Wars of Alexander, ed. W. W. Skeat, EETSES, 47. London: 1886.

Wells, J. E., *A Manual of the Writings in Middle English*, with nine supplements. New Haven: 1916–1951; 2-volume edition edited by J. Burke Severs, with additional material to 1500. Hamden, Conn.: 1967 and 1970.

Wunsche, A. "Die Alexandersage nach jüdischen Quellen," *Die Grenzenboten*, XXXIII (1879), 269–280.

Yalkut Shimoni, ed. Lewin-Epstein. Jerusalem: 1952.

Yosippon, eds. D. Günzburg and A. Kahana. Berditschev: 1896–1913.

Zacher, J., *Alexander Magni Iter ad Paradisum*. Königsberg: 1859.

Zingerle, O., *Die Quellen zum Alexander des Rudolf von Ems. Germanistische Abhandlungen* IV. Breslau: 1885.

ADDENDUM

THE BABYLONIAN TALMUD, general editor, I. Epstein. 35 vols.
(London: Soncino Press, 1935–1952): 18 vols. (1961).**

English Translations in Order of Publication

SEDER NEZIKIN II, trans. Maurice Simon (1935).
    Baba Batra (Heb. ed., p. 53b), pp. 218–220; see p. 218.
        (Heb. ed., p. 74 a–b), pp. 292–298; see p. 294.

SEDER NEZIKIN III, trans. Jacob Shachter (1935).
    Sanhedrin (Heb. ed., p. 20b), pp. 108–111. see p. 110.
        (Heb. ed., p. 65b), pp. 445–446.

SEDER NASHIM III, trans. A. Cohen (1936).
    Sota (Heb. ed., p. 27a), pp. 132–134.

SEDER NASHIM IV, trans. Maurice Simon (1936).
    Gittin (Heb. ed., p. 6b), p. 20.

SEDER MO'ED I, trans. H. Freedman (1938).
    Shabbat (Heb. ed., p. 30a), pp. 132–133.
        (Heb. ed., p. 69), pp. 328–331; see p. 330.
        (Heb. ed., p. 153a), pp. 780–782.

SEDER MO'ED III, trans. Leo Jung (1938).
    Yoma (Heb. ed., p. 69a), p. 325.

SEDER MOED IV, trans. Maurice Simon (1938).
    Megillah (Heb. ed., p. 18b), pp. 113–115.

SEDER KODASHIM I, trans. Eli Cashdan (1948).
    Menachot (Heb. ed., p. 32b), p. 205.

SEDER KODASHIM III, trans. Maurice Simon (1948).
    Tamid (Heb. ed., p. 31b), pp. 24–26.
        (Heb. ed., p. 32a), pp. 26–28.
        (Heb. ed., p. 32b), pp. 28–29.

**   The above pagination in the Soncino edition is to the 1961 edition. Dates in parenthesis refer to first printings.